THE GREAT RIFT

DARYL N. PATTERSON

CABIN
BOOKS

CABIN BOOKS
PARADISE, CA.

Published by Cabin Books
Paradise, California 95969

Printed in the United States of America

Additional copies of this book may be obtained from Cabin Books

EAN-13   978-0-9646761-3-8

Library of Congress Catalog Card Number: 2013916869

First Printing: April, 2014

Second Printing: November, 2016

Third Printing: September, 2020

To My Family,
May Life Always be an Adventure

MORE THAN LEGEND
IS THE FIRST BOOK IN THIS SERIES

INDIAN SKY
IS THE SECOND BOOK IN THIS SERIES

THE GREAT RIFT
IS THE THIRD BOOK IN THIS SERIES

ALL OF THESE ARE AVAILABLE FROM CABIN BOOKS

TABLE OF CONTENTS

THE

GREAT

RIFT

1

A HINT OF RED IN THE MORNING

May 2, 1998
Camino Cavern, Sierra Nevada

Bryan gazed up at the loud thundering sound of a descending helicopter as it drowned out the surrounding sound of generators, men, and equipment in motion around him. More supplies and personnel were arriving daily. The western side of the caldera located on the Relief Range was now a bee-hive of activity. Snowdrifts were melting quickly in the spring thaw.

He dreaded all of this, but knew it had to pass. His quest to find answers concerning his great-great-grandfather had driven him to this place. The Federal Government also has had a keen interest in this matter for many years. But an interesting realization came to him out of his Washington D.C. research. Namely, that the U.S. Government had a clandestine involvement in the outcome of the famous battle at the Alamo. An agreement was more or less struck with them. The understanding was that he would not go public with these so-called 'suspicions.' Bryan knew it was true. He had seen the proof.

To buy his silence, Bryan was given a paid position as a consultant having access to all levels of the Project—the Camino

Cavern Archeological Site. However, there were some parts of the Cavern that were completely off limits except for himself and those that had selected clearance, some of which were very secretive as to their identity. The archeology team itself was only allowed access to the 'Empire of the Sun' room and not beyond.

Evening was coming on fast, sending shadows across the caldera engulfing the camp. Lights surrounding the heliport were activated. Walking toward the cave entrance, Bryan noticed that the lights surrounding "the cage" were now coming on line. Armed guards were checking personnel as they came out of the cavern. A steel and wire fabric cage along with a welded steel gate created a formidable barrier restricting access to the discovery site.

Bryan could feel cool air exiting from the cave; reminding him that some 16 months before, he had been rescued out of this cave. Tammy had been with the rescuers when they went into the cave searching for him.

He reflected on how the crew had been impressed by her determination to find him. One crewman commented, "She sure must think you're something special." Although, since then he felt she hadn't shown him the same strong feelings as she had in the past. What with her language studies and various classes she was taking to get her Bachelor's Degree, it seemed they had slowly drawn apart. Additionally, with everything he was involved in, here at the Cavern and other assignments, running around eastern California and Nevada that in itself was not making things any easier. Any wedding plans were on hold until these things settled down.

A voice over a loudspeaker announced that the final transport of the day would be leaving in five minutes. Walking back to the heliport he boarded the aircraft. A last call for passengers was given, but no one else came. Powering up they were soon ascending above the snow covered cliffs of the caldera. Swiftly they crossed over Emigrant Meadow and Leavitt Lake descending into the canyons below.

Bryan thought ahead to the short drive from the Marine Corps' Mountain Warfare Training Base at Pickel Meadows, to his motel room in Bridgeport. The office that he worked out of was actually up in Reno. He looked down at his badge which designated him as an Associate Archeologist. He laughed to himself. How was it that he was now an archeologist and not in forest management? Governmental authority has its privileges, right or wrong.

After another three minutes they had landed at the Marine Camp. Security was tight getting in and out of this place. His government pickup truck was parked in an adjacent lot just outside the base's secured perimeter.

The sun was setting in the western sky as Bryan drove across the expansive meadows north of the town of Bridgeport, which was also at one time called 'Big Meadows' because of its extensive fertile and open grazing land. Bridgeport was a small town, about six hundred in population, and the county seat for Mono County. Sitting on the edge of a high desert at 6,463 foot elevation it is not uncommon to reach -20° below zero during winter.

Pulling into a café parking lot, his pager went off. He had become a regular at the small café, brightly lit with red and blue neon signs in the windows. Finding a comfortable booth that looked out at the street, Bryan checked the numbers on his pager. In the corner of his eye he could see a waitress approaching. The first number was from Tammy, and the second was probably from Josh.

Bryan looked up to see a smiling face. "Bryan, it's good to see you again tonight. Did your day go well?"

"It was a good day," he answered. "But it's getting kind of lonely out here on this assignment."

"Well, you can always stop and see me," she offered.

"Sorry I'm already engaged," informed Bryan.

"Oh," she realized. "How nice for you," was her curt response. "It seems like all the good ones are already taken. So, what would you like to drink? " she asked dejectedly.

3

Bryan eyed what was on the chalk board next to the order and pick-up counter. "Some hot chocolate sounds good along with tonight's special; that should do it."

"Your loss," she commented writing on her order pad and then abruptly walking away.

Bryan smirked to himself, thinking how Tammy better hurry; things out here on the frontier are getting rough. He glanced northerly along the hills toward *'Whispering Valley,'* and connected briefly with the memory of *'Indian Sky'* which had led him to the Captain's hideaway.

Back at the motel, Bryan first took a shower and then tried calling Tammy, but there was no answer at the apartment that she still shared with Rachel. Sitting there in an overstuffed chair he paused to reflect on the last time he had seen her. It was some two weeks before, back at Columbia. She acted like she didn't have any time for him, and maybe she really didn't.

Dialing up the old 209 area code, he tried Josh next. He was still living at home until he could get a place of his own. Josh picked up and immediately recognized his voice. "Hey old Buddy, what's happening?" he asked.

"Oh, nothing of any real consequence, except, I want everyone back home to know that in a day or two I'll be heading down to Bishop," answered Bryan.

"Sounds like they want you out of the way," commented Josh.

"Yeah," laughed Bryan. "There's not a lot they can do or hide, that I wouldn't find out about. Besides if they did try something our agreement would be dissolved. And I don't think they would like what follows."

"Any word back on the examination of the box, and the DNA samples that were taken?" asked Josh.

"No, but I suspect I'll be hearing about them any day now. Say, how's your Mom doing? And how is your construction business going?" wondered Bryan.

"Mom is doing okay. She is still working nights at the hospital, but I have noticed it has been taking a toll on her. As

4

regards my work, it's booming. I have four lots to grade and one foundation to pour."

"That's great. I'll be up one of these days and I can help you set some forms," replied Bryan.

"Oh, by the way, when can I expect to start on the house for you and Tammy?" Josh queried.

"I really don't know. We haven't finalized the plans yet," answered Bryan.

"Really? Wow, I thought we had the country boy—city girl thing licked."

"Well, you may be able to take the girl out of the city, but it's harder to take the city out of the girl, if you get my drift."

"Guess I better rock the boat a bit," laughed Josh.

"I have to get up early and be in Reno for a staff meeting first thing in the morning," informed Bryan. "So I'll talk to you next week then," he finalized.

And so it was, he was off early in the morning headed north watching the sunrise out of the east. There was a hint of red in the early morning sky. Was there to be stormy days ahead? He really hoped not.

Before long he had crested the hills south of Reno and could see the skyline of the City. Exiting onto South Virginia Avenue, Bryan soon spotted the large government complex off to his right. A variety of different government agencies used this facility. The numerous offices were all inter-connected by long hallways.

Different crews were arriving, some from as far away as the eastern side of the Humboldt Basin. A majority of them were young men and just a handful of women. The combined staff meeting was scheduled for ten that morning; and he was a good fifteen minutes early.

Bryan made his way to the conference room finding a seat on the left side. Only a handful of others were already in the room. He could hear the click of the second hand of the clock on the wall. As different ones came in they seemed to avoid where he sat. The technicians and the assistants really didn't know him or what he did. Some were looking at him and whispering, but he kind of expected it and ignored it.

Soon the room was pretty well filled. He recognized Director Campbell, coming in with two of his assistants. He had been working directly under his direction since he started with them.

Budge Campbell introduced himself and his immediate staff to kick off the meeting. He talked about an ambitious season of projects. On a large blackboard he listed all the major projects and briefly gave an update of each. The Director next announced that there would be some personnel changes on a few of the crews.

One of his assistants was given the floor next to run down through the crew lists. "We are also putting together a new crew, who will be mapping and cataloging petroglyphs in the Chalfant Valley area."

There was a bit of stir in the audience. "I'd like to volunteer for that project," someone spoke up.

"Settle down now, the criteria for this project calls for someone with rock climbing experience, because of the many elevated rock faces. Rick Sanchez will take the lead on this team, and Joe Flynn and Bryan Anderson will round it out."

"Who?" someone asked.

At that Budge Campbell stood up. "Bryan, stand up. Many of you have not met Bryan yet. He's been with us for just a short while, working up at the Camino Cavern Site." Bryan stood up and smiled. "Our work is winding down up there so we're happy to have him help us on this one."

After a few minutes of concluding comments, everyone was dismissed. Most of them would be heading right out, while two of the teams were to reconvene in one of the smaller conference rooms for a strategy session. One of which was Bryan's.

Rick Sanchez came over immediately to introduce himself and seemed initially to be very pleasant. He appeared to be about forty years old, of slender build with sandy hair. Rick gave him rough directions to where their meeting was to be held. At the same time Bryan noticed a young woman with a black ponytail staring his way. She kind of grimaced and walked out.

After a twenty minute break he sought out the small conference room where they were to regroup. Finding it down one of the side hallways he spotted Rick across the room busy digging out some files from a box.

"Bryan, take a seat. Give me a few minutes to get organized here," spoke up Rick acknowledging his presence.

"10-4 boss," replied Bryan.

"Oh, don't call me boss. Think of us as a team. Just plain Rick will do nicely."

"Okay," Bryan readily agreed. Noticing a large map hung on the wall he stepped over to take a closer look.

"That's the general area that we'll be working in," informed Rick without looking up. Bryan noted the indications of petroglyph sites.

Sitting down he pulled out a tablet and made a few notes. Suddenly, there was someone standing next to him. Looking up, it was the young woman with the ponytail that was in the main conference room.

"Hi, I'm Jo," she spoke up introducing herself.

"Nice to meet you," returned Bryan. "I'm Bryan, as you probably already know. When they said Joe, I thought it was another guy."

"No, it's J-O, short for Josephine."

"I see," answered Bryan looking into her dark eyes.

"I'm glad you two have finally met," spoke up Rick. "Take a seat. As Jo is aware we usually run four or five members on the crews, but this time it will be just the three of us. Both of you are experienced climbers and must rely on each other for safety. Our main objective initially is to map known sites as well as find and document unknown glyphs. The idea behind all of this is that hopefully we'll be able to see a pattern to the migration of the early inhabitants of that area."

Bryan thought about Captain Camino and his rock carvings, and all the searching he had done for them.

They next discussed in what order they would visit each of these different sites. Also, how they would investigate any adjacent areas that had potential.

Bryan brought up the issue of equipment they would need. Rick informed him that Jo had already purchased or traded for the necessary equipment. That made him squirm a bit in his seat. Those old feelings concerning a trust issue with the opposite gender were once again trying to resurface.

Their lodging needs had already been pre-arranged for them at the Forest Service barracks at the White Mountain Ranger Station in Bishop. That would be their base of operations.

How meals were handled was up to them. They could purchase groceries and cook for themselves, or use the voucher system to eat out, up to a certain limit. Lunches would be worked out later.

Through the discussion, Bryan noticed how quiet Jo was, and that she never seemed to smile. Before loading up, Rick took him aside. He wanted Bryan to know that Jo was unhappy due to the fact she was transferred from another crew, where she was with her on-again off-again boyfriend. Bryan kind of understood now. He thanked Rick and said he would take that into consideration.

He felt a little uneasy about how this situation was developing. How would Tammy react? Probably not a problem he figured, or at least it shouldn't be. He had bigger fish to fry and more important things to think about.

Rick would meet them at the Ranger Station first thing in the morning. In the meantime they would have to pack up all the extra gear in Bryan's work truck, and head south to Bishop. Jo seemed to be reluctant to go along with this new assignment.

"Jo, are you ready?" asked Bryan coming around the truck.

"I guess," she replied taking a deep breath.

"Come on, I'll buy you dinner tonight. I know just the place," he coaxed trying to loosen things up a bit.

Getting on the way, it wasn't long before they were passing through Carson City, the state capitol. Jo slouched down in her seat and was quiet at first.

"Can I ask you a question?" she suddenly asked.

"By all means," smiled Bryan.

"What's so hush-hush about the Camino Cavern Project?" she wondered. "They never share anything at any of our meetings about it. And I understand there are all kinds of security surrounding it."

"You're right; there is a ton of security up there. A person has to go through all kinds of security checks just to get on an air transport."

"But what's up there?" she demanded straightening up in her seat.

"There's not a lot that I'm allowed to tell you," he replied.

"What can you tell me?"

"Well, let me put it this way. History as we know it here in the West could be rewritten."

"Wow," she commented. "I'm majoring in history. This is so fascinating. I guess this is why I've worked these last two summers on these archeological projects."

"What school are you attending?" asked Bryan.

"UCLA," answered Jo.

"You're from LA then?"

"No, actually I'm from a small place called Apple Valley, north of San Bernardino," she answered.

"I know where that's at. Matter of fact I knew someone who also lived down there and knew Roy Rogers. Apparently, he was a real nice person."

"Yeah, he did have a ranch there," she acknowledged.

Having broken the ice, the remainder of the trip went much better. At the Highway 108 turnoff Bryan indicated the direction of the Marine Base where flights originated for the Camino Cavern site.

"Say, can you smuggle me in next time you go up?" she asked.

"Nope," was his blunt reply. "We'll be at Bridgeport in a few minutes, and we can stop at a small café that I know."

"Sounds good," she replied.

Bryan wondered if that one waitress would be there. What was her name? Katie?

Entering Bridgeport Valley, he thought about the history that connected him to this place, but he wasn't willing to share it with just anyone.

"Here we are," announced Bryan pulling into the parking lot. The café was moderately busy and alive with conversation as they walked in.

"Where do you want to sit?" asked Jo.

"Over by the far window, one of the booths is fine." Walking through, Bryan thought he spotted Katie with her back turned to them. Finding a booth to their liking they slid into the seats on opposite sides facing one another.

"Jo, what's your opinion of Rick since you worked on some of these crews in the past?" asked Bryan.

"I've never worked with him, but from what I hear he's good to work for. He takes things very seriously, but he treats everyone fair," she answered.

Bryan shook his head, acknowledging those thoughts. "Sounds like the three of us should be able to work together," he optimistically commented.

"I think there is potential there," she replied.

At that moment Bryan spied Katie headed over their way. "Here comes Katie, beware," he warned. She began to open her mouth to ask why, but it was too late.

"Nice seeing you, Bryan. Oh, this must be your fiancée," she speculated.

"Katie, this is Jo, and Jo this is Katie," introduced Bryan without answering.

Katie looked at Jo in all her work clothes and then back at Bryan giving him a look that said: "You could have done better for yourself."

"I'm not his fiancée!" protested Jo.

"Oh! Bryan, you dog," Katie responded.

"Ha ha. No, Jo and I have just been assigned to work together," he confessed. Katie dropped her arms and turned away in embarrassment.

"You love to torment women, don't you?" surmised Jo.

"No! Not at all."

"What have I got myself into?" she wondered.

"Possibly the best summer of your life," he answered.

"Ha!"

Katie finally came back and he apologized for his 'oversight.' They still appeared to be ticked off at him.

Before long they were back on the road passing Mono Lake and Lee Vining. He remembered this was a place of hiding and discovery. Bryan silently relived these memories and thought someday how he would write concerning all these things that were interconnected.

A sign indicating that Yosemite was only fourteen miles away provoked the subject of rock climbing. They shared some experiences. Jo had learned from numerous trips to the desert; climbing various formations and peaks. Some were with classes and other times it was more recreational. After hearing about some of Bryan's excursions, she remarked that he must be world class. Bryan didn't really think so. He never considered climbing K-2 or any of the other peaks, only because "it was there."

Before no time it seemed, Mammoth Lakes and Tom's Place was behind them as they descended into Owens Valley and finally into Bishop itself.

The Ranger Station was easy to find on a major side street. The barracks were fairly new and state of the art. Jo was happy to discover there was a women's barracks. Checking in with the barracks manager, each one was assigned a bunk and a locker. It was twilight as Bryan carried his stuff in and put it away. While doing so it gave him a chance to meet some of the others who were stationed there. He learned that some of the crews were already out in some of the remote forestry camps. Before settling in he decided he better leave a message for Tammy and his parents concerning his new location and contact number.

Propping himself up on the bunk to unwind for a moment Bryan thought about Josh's comment about the Government's attempt to distance him from the project site. Could they be up to something? How long could his blackmail knowledge concerning the U.S. Government's involvement at the Alamo hold out for him?

That knowledge and all the gold in the Cavern would no doubt be a great incentive for them to make him go away. That quantity of gold was a resource that had to be carefully managed in the world's economic market. A sudden injection of gold on the market could collapse the world monetary system.

How convenient if he had some tragic accident while out in the boonies, perhaps on a typical rock climb or something. Should he be suspicious of Jo or Rick? He didn't feel that way. But submarines don't announce their presence until it's too late.

And on top of everything else could there be a problem developing over Jo working with him? How was Tammy to react to this new development? Truly, there was a hint of 'red in the morning.'

2

THE CAPTAIN IS MISSING

s promised Rick arrived early, waking up everyone in the barracks as he dragged all his gear in. It certainly didn't make him very popular.

Their first day out was just a reconnaissance mission scouting out the four main areas in the Chalfant Valley, north of Bishop. They were back in the afternoon in time to get organized for their first full day of work. Bryan and Jo sorted out the climbing equipment and personal gear that they would most likely need.

There was even time to run over to the neighborhood market and buy a few groceries to prepare a meal. Bryan volunteered to cook that evening and ended up feeding an additional three. Suddenly he had made himself very popular.

Getting out of doing the dishes and the cleanup he ventured outside in the declining light. There was a slight chill in the air. He thought about Ben Coleman and wondered if he ever did catch up with his landlady to retrieve his belongings. That was over on Sixth Street as he recalled.

He was pretty much out of the picture now. Suffering from a form of post-traumatic stress, Ben was staying with some shirt-tail relatives. Bryan recollected the difficult task it was to go up to Hell's Mountain in that terrible rain storm, find him, and persuade him that it was now safe to come out of hiding. The primitive shelter he had constructed being hidden in the trees had made it very difficult to find him.

Next morning they were off to Fish Slough about 11 miles north of Bishop. This whole area was apparently a decomposing tableland of volcanic tuff, a hardened ash flow on which the native inhabitants left their rock art. This particular area near the confluence of the Owens River was a natural wetland rich in wildlife.

Bryan learned that a pictograph was a painted image on the rock surface, but petroglyphs were incised, carved, or abraded into the rock itself. In addition there was what is called petroforms, made up of patterns and shapes created by placement of large rocks on the ground. Some of these carvings were thought to be thousands of years old.

Photographing and locating each grouping was an integral part of their activity. A set of GPS co-ordinates was observed and recorded for each group. A couple of isolated panels were additionally found by hand-climbing through the rock formations nearby.

As the days passed, after mapping several hundred petroglyphs, many of them became familiar and were recurring themes. Rick told them, that's exactly what the outcome of their work would result in. It was a way to track the movement of the ancient inhabitants of this land. Many of the carvings were shield symbols, maps, and zoomorphs, which were animal shapes. Overall the local petroglyphs were classified as Great Basin Curvilinear, because of all the circles and curved interconnecting lines.

It wasn't long before they had moved on to the Chidago Petroglyph Zone. Here Bryan and Jo had to use their climbing gear to safely access all the sites. The longer they worked together the more comfortable it had become.

"Hey Jo, what do you know?" asked Bryan as he slid down his rope to match Jo's location on the cliff face. She didn't answer, but smiled. "Say, I haven't heard you mention your boyfriend anymore. Is everything okay?" he inquired.

"Yeah, it's probably a good thing," she answered. "Have you talked to Tammy recently?"

"Just the other day, but she's so-o busy with her classes right now," he replied. In the previous days Bryan had shared with Jo a number of things about his relationship with Tammy.

"Well, I'm happy for you two. It seems you guys have the real thing," she commented.

"It's kind of funny, she was always after me to be more romantic, but now she's the one being aloof."

"Oh, just hang in there it'll all work out," encouraged Jo.

"I'm hanging. I'm hanging," joked Bryan.

Two days later after work, Bryan heard an argument ensuing outside the barracks. Taking a look he spotted Jo telling a strange man to "get out of here!" He abruptly left.

"Is everything okay," asked Bryan stepping outside.

"Yes! Everything is fine," she answered visibly upset. She wanted to say something but didn't, and quickly left the scene.

Rick came out with a couple others wondering what had happened. "Boyfriend problems?" he guessed.

"Possibly, I'm not sure," answered Bryan.

Things kind of settled down after that, until Bryan got an unexpected phone call. His presence was requested at a meeting with Federal Authorities the very next day at the Marine Corps Training Base. He wondered what was up. It sounded serious. Everyone else split for home for the weekend and would return on Sunday night. Bryan had plans to visit his parents as well as Tammy if the meeting didn't interfere.

Next morning on the drive up he felt apprehension about this meeting. Perhaps in part due to how far into the Project things had progressed. Soon things would have to be resolved one way or the other. Up to that point he had no legal counsel due to the classified nature of the Camino Project.

Going in through security he noticed a caravan of black sedans arriving at the main gate. Proceeding across to the main building his identity was again checked. It was another fifteen minutes before he was allowed into the conference room. Bryan told himself he would not be intimidated by Big Brother. If everything went totally south, just one phone call to Tammy was all that was necessary to release the historical bombshell to the public. Of course they no doubt had a plan to circumvent that if things did begin to unravel.

"Mr. Anderson, thank you for meeting with us on such short notice," came a booming voice from the front of the room. Bryan recognized James Reinhold, whom he had met in some of the initial negotiations. He was one of the highest ranking officials in the Department of Interior and was known to work under Presidential direction.

"Well, I'm hoping there is some good news," replied Bryan.

"It seems an issue has come up," he answered. After introducing his two associates, Jonathan Rothchild and Nancy Loy, he continued. "We have received the results from the DNA samples taken on the two subjects found in the Cavern." He paused. "The results do not support the conclusion that the male subject is your great-great-grandfather, Maximo Camino."

"You're not feeding me false results are you?" asked Bryan.

"We ran two independent tests and the results were all the same. There is a very low probability that he's related," spoke up Jonathan.

"My Mother's DNA was used as the comparison was it not?"

"It was," Jonathan reaffirmed.

"What's wrong with this picture then?" asked Bryan angrily.

"He's not a relative of yours," reaffirmed Reinhold.

"The female subject has only a sixty percent probability of being a match," also revealed Nancy.

"This is troubling," continued Reinhold. "This leads us to believe that this 'Camino' may only be a historical shadow with no real significance. Or that he ever existed at all."

"What! This doesn't prove that he wasn't there. He did exist and he's real," fired back Bryan.

"No-o, but it doesn't prove your stand on this matter," he firmly replied. Bryan said nothing in reply. "Your help on this project has been invaluable. However, as certain portions of this project wind down we're re-evaluating the need for you and others to have any further access to the site. We'll let you know shortly. And further more, there still is a gag order on the 'assets' and everything will remain classified."

Bryan knew they were resolved to weaken his position, and would endeavor to keep the Captain out of the history books. Secondly, their strategy would be to discredit him if the Alamo issue ever came to the fore. This was like a chess move, his strategy had been checkmated.

"One more thing," added Jonathan standing up. "We have something to return to you." Opening up a cardboard box he pulled out a recognizable object. It was the wooden box that had been extracted from under the ice in the upper room of the Cavern. "We're returning the box and its contents to you. A report should be issued soon on these items. Researchers are still looking into the claims made by these documents. There still may be some historical value to them."

"Please sign this, showing you have received these items back," requested the other assistant.

"Fine," Bryan agreed taking a deep breath.

After the meeting ended, Reinhold and his female assistant left the room. Jonathan delayed his departure offering him the cardboard box to carry the things out.

"Thanks," responded Bryan.

"Take this," he also offered, handing him a business card with all his phone numbers. "If you ever get in a pinch, call me." Putting his finger over his lips he indicated to keep silent about this.

Bryan thanked him again. Perhaps he had an unknown ally, for what reason he did not know. The title on the card showed that he was the Assistant Director of Internal Affairs.

With his security clearance in question he decided to go up to the Mountain while the opportunity still availed itself and visit the scene of the controversy in the Upper Room. In a half hour he was air lifted to the Caldera. The guards at the tunnel entrance allowed him through, and he was able to ride on an electric cart most of the way down.

Additional guards were stationed in the main cavern securing access to the Obelisk and the Upper Room. Bryan knew the guards and indicated he was going up. They took his name down and let him through. "You'll have to tell us someday what's up there," commented one of the guards. Bryan just smiled.

The ice stairwell was all too familiar to him. Limited lighting led the way to the upper ice chamber. A carpet like material had been placed across the ice.

There before him under the ice were the two dark figures separated by about four feet. He had assumed in the past that these were Captain Camino and his wife, White Feather. Taking a deep breath he tried to peer into the ice to get a closer look. But frankly, he really could not make a positive identity on the man or the woman. In the past he just felt it had to be them. This was disturbing!

"Captain! Where are you?" he called out. Was this a ploy, then and now? Had he escaped this existence to pursue another dream elsewhere? The Captain is missing! I don't believe this, he told himself.

Bryan returned to base camp in kind of a daze, not knowing what to do. Carrying the box of items out to his truck, he just sat there. The plan was to head over to Columbia for a visit, but it wasn't in him. He didn't want to face anyone. Since the day was pretty well shot, Bryan decided to head back to Bishop. He needed to think things through. Even the towering cumulus clouds that were building along the crest of the Sierra did not cheer him.

He recalled a small hot spring just out of Bridgeport that he had been meaning to check out. Travertine Hot Spring was basically just a large crack in the earth with a nice pool dammed at one end. Happily no one was there when Bryan drove up. The solitude felt good. It didn't take him long to get into the warm therapeutic waters. A nice view extended out over the whole

Bridgeport Valley. An occasional cloud drifted over. Bryan closed his eyes and imagined he heard Captain Camino laughing at him. Opening his eyes, he looked around adjusting to the light. Had he been chasing a man with broken dreams all this time, never finding his own way? Maybe it was time to quit this whole thing. His clout was about ready to go down the tubes anyway and maybe the temporary position he was given as well.

The respite at Travertine did him good, making him feel more relaxed for the remaining trip back to Bishop. Perhaps this eventuality was a good thing and he needed to move on.

That evening Bryan heard the barracks phone ringing a number of times and ignored it. No one else was apparently around. Finally, he went down and answered it and discovered it was Tammy at the other end.

"Bryan, are you alright? What happened to you?" she asked.

"Sorry I didn't call. The Feds wanted to meet with me today and I guess I'm just bummed out."

"I wish I was there with you. But Bryan, you've set yourself up for a world of hurt by pursuing this."

"I know; I'm just about ready to walk away."

"Bryan, I love you and I'm sorry I've not been there for you. But I think there's light at the end of the tunnel."

"I'll see you next week, I promise," he replied.

After the phone call he realized he need not be so negative. He had Tammy and that was the one ray of sunshine in his life.

The quiet was noticeable Sunday morning. A squirrel could be heard running down the length of the roof.

Remembering the box of items that were returned to him, he decided to bring them in. The ornate wooden box was skillfully decorated with numerous markings. Prominent were two partial sun symbols sitting on two undulating waves facing away from each other. The documents that were found in the box were now in protective sleeves. Attached were English translations of each of the four sheets. Glancing down these, he recalled the legal claims that the Captain had established. There were certain large blocks of land along the Sierra, some west, some east. Much of these now were part of National Forest and Park lands, private properties, and even some towns. Signatures were present, from a Mexican Head of State granting these lands to Camino and his heirs.

There were two other land grants that were quite vague as to their location. References on one indicated a possible match to the Groom Lake site. That made sense to Bryan, but the other land grant was more puzzling. It was further south and was described as "barren desert land."

It wasn't all that long before the weekenders would be returning, reminding him that he better get his laundry caught up and run to the market. Jo arrived just before dark, and Rick finally showed up about ten o'clock.

Soon as Jo got in she came looking for Bryan wondering if everything went well that weekend. Not wanting to talk about it, he vaguely told her about the meeting and how things did not go so well.

The next day they were off to search for a new site north of where they had been working, a place called Spy Rock. It was mid-afternoon and they were about to give up when they found a most significant site. It was by far the richest panel they had yet seen to date. They marveled at the intricacies of the carvings—all interconnected. There was a clear view of all the mountains and the surrounding land, and at night all the vast array of stars would have been visible. This was no doubt Spy Rock.

While photographing this complex petroglyph Jo came up behind Bryan to talk with him. "I'm curious," she began, "why does it seem that you have such an adversarial relationship with the Feds on the Camino Project?"

Putting the camera down and making a face, he hesitated to answer. "You're asking me a complex question that I can't fully answer. But I can tell you that the real reason that I have an inside track at the Cavern is that I was the one who made the discovery, and I know what's there." Bryan turned the camera off. "Besides that, I'm related to Captain Camino."

Jo opened her mouth to ask further.

"Jo—no more questions," he stated. "The issue that I'm having right now is that I could be losing my project clearance at any time."

"They haven't threatened you have they?" she asked.

"Threatened? No, not in a physical sense," he answered.

Her only response was "Hmm."

Jo's heightened interest made him a little suspicious.

3

SECRET OF THE BOX

Spy Rock had proved to be the most exciting discovery made to date. They worked late cataloging the full contents of this site. It was a thirty minute hike back out to the nearest road. Once back at the Ranger Station, they couldn't wait to pour over the photographs encompassing the mystery of Spy Rock. One of the pictures that Jo had taken caught Bryan's eye. It was closely matching one of the designs on the wooden box.

The next day also promised to be exceptional as they headed south toward Lone Pine, to a place made famous in motion pictures, called the Alabama Hills.

Setting at the base of the Sierra Nevada Mountain Range this mini-granitic range seemed to be older than time. Eroded down into rounded forms and arches this amazing range became the natural backdrop of many old westerns and other motion pictures depicting off-planet landscapes.

This area was also well known for recreational rock climbing with established technical climbs such as the Western Wall and the Poodle Wall.

The tip that they received took them to the southern end of this formation. Stepping out of the vehicle, the majestic summit of Mount Whitney towered over them, the highest peak in the continental United States.

The hieroglyphic panel they found was not as impressive as at Spy Rock, but it held some of the same patterns as they had seen before. This panel gave the two climbers an opportunity in the afternoon to do a climb and a rappel down to the upper section of this grouping.

"We'll have to stop meeting like this," she joked.

"That could be very true," he somberly replied. Jo realized what he was inferring and said nothing in return.

Bryan had noticed a number of sun orientated symbols, but the one that Jo photographed at Spy Rock was a complete stand alone, and was unmatched by any of these found here in the Alabama Hills.

That evening no one noticed when Bryan slipped out and went to try his hand at fishing. He was told of a nice place north of town along the Owens River. Bryan drove down along the gravel bars to find a spot among the willows. It was peaceful there along the water. The River that descended from Lake Crowley was renowned for its trout fishing, and was considered an angler's paradise.

Darkness gradually closed in around him as he waited for the last glimmer of sunlight catching only a couple of fish. Bryan stumbled back to the truck, and then tried to figure out how to navigate back through the gravel bars up to the highway.

Morning came, but Rick and Jo noticed Bryan was nowhere to be found. His bed had not even been slept in.

They were at a loss, and didn't know what to do. This wasn't like Bryan. Jo feared the worst.

Rick made calls to the main office and the Highway Patrol. Finding Bryan's emergency contact numbers, Jo called his parents and finally Tammy. Rachel answered and said she would forward the message and took the phone number. Twenty minutes later Tammy called back.

"Hello, is this Jo?" she asked.

"Yes, it is, thanks for calling back."

"What's this about Bryan being missing?"

23

"He wasn't here this morning and his truck is missing," explained Jo.

"Was he there yesterday?" asked Tammy.

"Yes, we worked a full day in the field. He must have went somewhere in the evening and never came back, because his bed was never slept in.

"Oh my, now you really have me worried," replied Tammy.

"I'm worried too. I haven't told this to anyone yet and it has been bothering me for days," stated Jo.

"Is there something between you and Bryan that I should know about?"

"No, not the way you mean. I can tell he really loves you and you have nothing to worry about in that department. But the reason I'm so worried is that several days ago I was approached by a man who wouldn't identify himself. He offered me money, if I would—how did he put it, 'be less than safe,' with Bryan, creating some accidental situation," revealed Jo.

"Really! What did you tell him?"

"I told him to get lost!"

"Wow! This is scary. Has a search been started for him?" queried Tammy.

"Yes, the Highway Patrol and everyone working out of this office are on the watch for him," she answered. "Oh, by the way, Bryan was worried that the Fed's were cutting him off from the Cavern Project," added Jo.

"Yes, I know," replied Tammy taking a deep breath. "I guess I've been too wrapped up in myself to know what's been happening. Did Bryan know about the man who approached you?"

"No, I didn't want that to worry him. In a sense I went into kind of a protective mode."

"Thanks Jo for watching out for him, if it's not too late. You see, he has this notion at times that he is immortal or something. I'll call his parents, and try to get on the way. Thanks for calling," finalized Tammy.

Later in the morning Rick received a phone call that Bryan had been located just ten miles north of town near the Owens River. He had been taken to the local hospital emergency room for x-rays. After relaying the information to Bryan's parents, they headed over to the hospital.

They found him in an emergency room bed sitting up with a sling on his left arm. He appeared to be battered and bruised as well.

"This is one heck of a way to get out of going to work today," stated Rick.

Bryan laughed. "Oh-h, it hurts to laugh," he replied holding his arm.

"What happened?" asked Jo.

"After dinner last night I headed up the Owens River to try a little trout fishing. Coming back just after dark, a deer jumped out of a willow thicket. Then I swerved and hit a rock, which flipped the truck sending me down an embankment."

"Woe," commented Jo.

"Apparently it knocked me out for a while. I was eventually able to get up and crawl out through the passenger door. Then I just waited for dawn," Bryan related.

"What a relief you're okay," commented Jo.

"I think some of your family is on the way," informed Rick.

"Oh, no," fussed Bryan. "I didn't want them upset by this."

"Yes, but they were worried about you," explained Jo.

The doctor soon came in and informed Bryan that he had a minor break in his upper arm, and advised him to stay away from work for a week. Then after that, he was to take up a light duty schedule and report to his regular physician.

Back at the Ranger Station, it wasn't long before Bryan's mother and Tammy arrived, visibly distressed. But they were nevertheless relieved at seeing him. He felt so bad having caused all this commotion.

Tammy and Jo got to meet each other face to face. At first it seemed they were kind of sizing each other up, and afterward enjoyed pleasant conversation, glancing at Bryan occasionally, and continuing their discussion.

It was good to see them again since it had been a few weeks since he visited them last.

Rick suggested that Bryan follow doctor's orders and take the week off. He would notify the office and let them determine what to do. Bryan got an inkling that he may not be back.

The trip back afforded Bryan a chance to catch up on the latest news.

After arriving at the Anderson's in Columbia, Bryan went with Tammy to visit his future mother-in-law.

"Bryan, I'm so glad you're okay. You're going to have to stop scaring us that way," Mrs. Holden greeted them as they came in. "How can I ever expect to have grandkids?"

"I've done a lot of dangerous things in the past, but driving up from the river, who would have known," replied Bryan.

"Bryan has a pretty girl working on his crew that he neglected to tell me about," teased Tammy.

"She was kind of emotionally messed up when she started with us, but since then she's done well," he replied.

"I like Jo," confessed Tammy. "She seems like a person you can trust."

"Bryan, what is going on with the Cavern Project?" asked Tammy's mother who had apparently heard some rumors.

Bryan paused. "There's been a new development. I didn't expect this possibility. I'm probably breaking confidentiality in sharing this, but I really don't care anymore." He paused again. "The Captain is missing."

"What-t?" asked Tammy.

"DNA tests show that the two bodies buried under the ice are definitely not Captain Camino, and probably not White Feather," he further explained.

"Well, what happened to him?" asked Mrs. Holden.

"That's the big question," replied Bryan.

"Uh oh, is this whole thing starting all over again?" questioned Tammy.

26

"There's nothing that leads me to believe that there is anything for me to follow up on," he answered.

The following day Bryan had a chance to spend some time with his father as he went around taking care of chores. Graffiti, their family dog joined them, but lacked the same energy as in years past.

The next day, Josh came by and they went out to one of his job sites. Bryan was able to hold a leveling rod to shoot cuts and fills on a building pad.

On the third day, Bryan began to get bored. He recalled that Tammy wouldn't be back for a couple of days. His thoughts turned toward his great-great-grandfather, and what may have become of him. Was he back to square one or did it make any difference anymore?

The box that had been returned to him from the Cavern bore sun symbols that were different, not matching the symbols of the Empire of the Sun. There were just random shapes and patterns scattered all over the exterior of the box. But was it also on the inside? He couldn't remember. Finding the box with his stuff in the bedroom, he set it on a small table by the window.

Lifting the lid up, Bryan could see that the decorative shapes were also present on the inside. How unusual for someone to do that. It was made of juniper wood as he had been told, which was very resistant to rot and decay. Bryan noticed that some of the small carvings on the inside walls were right down against the bottom or in a corner. The thought came to him that these carvings were done prior to the assembly of the box. Turning the box over and over he examined its construction and noticed it was put together by small pegs. Minor grooves which appeared to serve no purpose ran around many of the wood panels.

It seemed to him that all of this detail had to be more than decorative. There had to be a purpose in it. Did he dare disassemble the box? The Feds were done with it. But no, that wouldn't be right, it was a key item that belonged to the Captain and it should be preserved.

Bryan went out to his pickup that had been stored out behind the barn for the past several months. Instead of just running the engine for twenty minutes he decided to take it out for a spin. With one good arm he thought he could manage an easy drive out on Yankee Hill Road and return by way of Sawmill Flat Road.

While on the drive Bryan kept toying with ideas on how he could get the box apart without damaging it. There was a possibility that since it was wood, what may help was to use a de-humidifier to shrink the wood as well as the pegs. That thought intrigued him.

Once back home he wondered if he could make a home-made de-humidifier. Bryan figured that trying this should not damage the box. If it failed to shrink the wood enough there was no harm done. So he set to work making a small framework wrapped in plastic. The de-humidifier would set inside with the box and the outlet hose would be sealed off with duct tape. Bryan kind of laughed. It reminded him of a school boy's science project.

Bryan decided to do this on the sly and set this up in the far corner of the shop. That evening when no one was around he took the box out and plugged in the de-humidifier. It would run all night. He slipped out periodically to check on it.

By mid-morning of the following day the box seemed to have loosened up. Setting it on a work bench and bracing it in place he was ready to work on it. Using a blunt-nosed punch and a small hammer he tapped on the pegs. It was a slow process. Even the lid separated into two parts, each exhibiting one of the opposing suns riding on waves. Bryan laid out the individual pieces on a towel as they came apart. To facilitate reassembly, he took a few snapshots.

Once the job was complete and everything was apart he wondered if he had made a mistake in doing this. What if a piece breaks when going back together? "That's water under the bridge now," he told himself.

28

Packing up all the pieces, Bryan carried them back to his bedroom and laid them out on the table. Including the two lid pieces there were eight panels, and each one was inscribed on both sides.

Placing the exterior sides of the boards face up, Bryan shuffled them around to see if he could get the shapes to join up, but nothing seemed to match. There was yet the flip side. Turning a couple of the pieces over, Bryan noticed that the grooves were now able to link up.

There were some voices coming from the front of the house. It sounded like Tammy's voice conversing with his mother. He had forgotten she was going to be back that day.

"Where's my future husband?" she called approaching his room.

"Tammy, I'm glad you're back, I'm about to go stir crazy," he replied.

After a long hug she inquired, "How's your arm? Does it still hurt?" Before he could answer Tammy continued. "What is this on the table? What have you done? It looks like the box that came out of the Cavern."

"Yes, it's just fine. I have an idea there's a message in this," Bryan replied.

"You really must be bored," she commented.

Turning over a piece she matched it with one Bryan had already turned over. "Look, a match!" she excitedly pointed out.

"Yes, you're right, the curved lines are connecting up," he realized.

"You're getting me hooked on this thing," Tammy commented as she matched up others pieces as well.

"This could very well be a map!" concluded Bryan.

Ultimately, the eight small boards formed an 8" x 14" rectangle; and with the orientation of shapes they could see it had to be viewed vertically. At the top end was an upward curvilinear sun image.

"See how good a team we make," she stated.

"Yes I do, and that's why I love you so much," he replied.

29

"Every time you tell me that it melts me," confessed Tammy taking a deep breath.

"I believe I've seen this symbol before," recalled Bryan.

"You have?" she asked.

"Yeah, at one of the petroglyph sites," he replied.

"I wonder if the curved lines are representative of ocean waves or the like?" Tammy speculated.

"You mean like, Point Lobos?" questioned Bryan. "Where we found the gold bars in the sea cave? I guess that could always be true, but—"

"The only problem is, it's a moot point now, because you've already been there and done that," she recalled.

"Perhaps, the Cavern is not the Captain's last resting place," pondered Bryan.

"Wow, what a complex picture map," commented Tammy.

"Look here, a route or a trail is designated running down through all these sun symbols," he noticed.

"A bird's face maybe?" pointed out Tammy.

"We have a starting point and an ending point, a sunrise and a sunset so to speak," Bryan understood. "There is the *Empire of the Sun* symbol up here in the left corner and down here in the opposite corner as you mentioned is the head of a bird or hawk, or possibly even a helmet. But what is this ugly distorted face down here that is aimed toward the bird head?" he wondered.

"I don't know, but if this row of peaks is the Sierra crest, then I would say that its location is way out in the desert somewhere," she observed.

"That could very well be. Maybe the Captain's new symbol is depicting heat waves or sand dunes," Bryan added.

"Look at that!" realized Tammy.

"What?" he asked.

"A faint silhouette of the bird head in the background is almost as big as the map itself," she pointed out.

"Wow, there must be some special significance to that particular image," thought Bryan. "And there is another side to this map, too."

"Bryan, I'm going to trust you, that whatever is here you're not going to go crazy, disappear into the wilderness and never be seen again," cautioned Tammy putting her hand on his shoulder.

Bryan smiled. "You better hurry and marry me."

Her answer was, "Yes!"

Flipping the map over they made sure that all the pieces matched back up. Viewing the map vertically, at the top was a sun symbol suspended under a set of curving lines.

"Look here," Bryan traced with his finger. "A continuing trail from the bird head crossing through an area of waving lines to a mountain with a forest at its summit. See these tick marks along the trail?" he noticed. "I wonder if they indicate the number of days travel between points."

"There's another mountain further on, and you finally arrive at the end of the trail at another bird," noticed Tammy. "It is definitely a bird with its wings stretched out and its head facing east with the downward half of the sun being held in its beak."

"Oh, look the bird at the end of the trail is also silhouetted," realized Bryan. "Just like what was done on the other side."

"The mystery of the birds," she phrased.

4

THE PROBLEM IN THE WELL

The other shoe finally dropped when the mail arrived on the following day. A certified letter from the Department of the Interior was stamped confidential. Bryan had indeed lost his access and any authority he had at the Camino Cavern Project. To him this meant they had indeed called his bluff, but it wasn't a bluff. This raised his ire.

"I have proof, and it's time I retrieve it," he told himself.

Additionally, there was no way the Feds were going to find out about this new development and then crush it. Bryan took detailed pictures of Camino's extraordinary map before going through the reverse process to reassemble the box.

Rick called to see how he was doing, and informed him that the office had not sent anyone out to fill in for him. He and Jo were both hoping he would be able to return soon. Bryan said he was really upset with the Government right now and didn't know if he wanted to return. Bryan heard a voice talking in the background. Rick relayed that Jo was missing him and it hasn't been the same since he left. He thanked them for that, and said he would think it over.

He had to go to San Antonio and secure the proof he needed. But there was one problem, the injury to his arm. It would be another two weeks before he could make a viable attempt to reenter the well. Bryan knew he had to just play it cool. He felt he would eventually win, because the truth was on his side.

Bryan made up his mind that he would go back to Bishop and make silent plans for the return trip to the Alamo. He had no intention of telling Tammy and his parents about his plan at this time. On Sunday he said farewell to them promising that he would be extra careful, even while doing so-called light duty.

Bryan had to provide his own transportation to and from Bishop now that he was ousted from the Project. Driving down Bryan thought about the need to set more long term goals. His vision of making a difference had somehow fallen short.

Tammy had shared with him what Jo had told her about the potential danger that he was in. That was no surprise to him. By their actions both Rick and Jo showed themselves to have no part in it. He did not anticipate any problems working with this crew for another two to four weeks.

Activity around the barracks was busy when he arrived. Many were once again returning from their weekend. Bryan noticed Jo closing her car trunk. She must have arrived just ahead of him. Stepping out of his truck she approached.

"Bryan, I'm so glad you're back," Jo excitedly welcomed.

"Thank you," he replied. "I hope you had a nice weekend."

"Not really, I went to a movie and slept in. What did you do with all your time off?" she asked.

"Frankly, I was bored to death," he answered.

"Me too," confessed Jo. "Is Tammy doing well?"

"Yes, she's finishing up some studies in Berkeley and should be back next weekend, I'm hopin'," answered Bryan.

"She must be pretty bright," commented Jo.

"Absolutely, I can hardly keep up with her at times," he replied.

"Okay, you better get your things unpacked," she suggested.

Bryan noticed the change in Jo since they first met. She had become so much more open and talkative.

That week's schedule included a couple of days of reconnaissance to locate additional petroglyph sites. Their primary search was in the Deep Springs area and up toward

33

Westgard Pass, which was a natural route over the mountains into the Great Basin.

Stopping to take a lunch break in Mason Canyon, Bryan shared with Rick and Jo that he had received written confirmation he was now off the Camino Project. Both of his companions were curious about the security surrounding the Project. He felt he no longer had any obligation to keep silent about those matters.

"Are you sure you won't get into trouble?" asked Jo.

"I really don't care anymore," replied Bryan. "They have broken their agreement and I feel no further obligation to them."

"Well, don't put yourself in jeopardy," advised Rick.

"I think I'm already there," he responded. "But I must consider the risk I might be putting you guys in. So let me do this—I can give you just a generic explanation of what is happening up there."

Rick and Jo seemed to be happy with that compromise. Having said that, Bryan went on to explain what kinds of artifacts had been found in the Cavern and their significance. He also shared in a vague way the levels of security that surrounded the Project. The limited information that he shared didn't seem to impress them in any way.

Later that day, Bryan and Jo being well ahead of Rick had hiked further up into the canyon. Coming upon a spring they decided to stop and rest. Dropping their packs they found a place to recline in the shade near the spring.

"Bryan, you mentioned you were related to Captain Camino and somehow that history itself could be rewritten. Who is this Captain Camino?" asked Jo.

"Are you sure you want to hear more? This could draw you into a black hole that you may regret?" he warned.

"There is no one here but us. Tell me about it," she insisted.

Bryan glanced back down the trail. "Maximo Camino was my great-great-grandfather. It took me a number of months to decipher and follow a map of his that led to a gold mining operation on the west side of the Cavern Complex. Actually, I can't take full credit for the discovery. There was also Tammy who you already met, and Josh Knight, whom you haven't met."

"Tammy was with you?" questioned Jo.

"Yes, but not by choice," half laughed Bryan.

"You actually found gold?" she asked.

Bryan paused and threw a small rock. They watched it ricochet off of a boulder. "You're the first one I've shared this with outside of the inner circle. Just keep this to yourself until this is fully out in the open. I may need others to raise their voices if something should happen to me. And besides, no one will probably believe you anyway." After a pause he continued. "Gold! Yes, enough to double the world's known quantity of the precious metal."

"What? Are you serious?" demanded Jo.

"Absolutely! And that's only the tip of the iceberg."

Jo squirmed and pushed herself back against the rock wall.

"That's a pretty tall tale," she commented. "But, that would explain why there is so much military security surrounding that project. If what you're saying is true, then no wonder you have had to watch your back."

"There was a landslide blocking access to the Cavern from the western side of the Sierra," continued Bryan without acknowledging her comments. "Over a year ago Josh and I found the 'backdoor,' which was another way in. We became separated and I was trapped up there. Josh went for help and nearly died in a blizzard. Tammy was brought up to the Marine Base to help them find me. And with her help they did get me out alive."

"Wow, this is better than any Hollywood movie," replied Jo thoroughly impressed.

"At this point the Government was all over this like—bees on honey," Bryan continued. Jo smiled. "Matter of fact this wasn't the first time they took possession of Camino's gold, which is a whole nother story," he added. "But what they were after was the source of the gold and I led them right to it. I had a personal reason for tracking down the Captain, not the gold. But anyway, we better get back to work, I could talk all day."

"I don't think I can go back to work after hearing this," confessed Jo.

"You'll get over it. It's just yellow metal. Life goes on," commented Bryan.

Finding their way into a very remote part of Deep Springs Valley, Rick made the decision to return the next day to complete cataloging of one unique vertical panel. It had the appearance of a sentinel or an ancient trail marker.

So the next morning they left before dawn and arrived while everything was still in shadow. Jo would have to do the climbing by herself that day. The sun was just breaking over the peak above them as Jo put her gear on to commence the climb. Rick and Bryan asked her to be extra careful.

Bryan sat nearby as Jo hiked and hand-climbed her way up the back side of the rock panel. The air was already getting warm as she anchored herself and rappelled down the rock face. Jo called out that some of the markings were quite unique. But after several minutes, Bryan heard her fussing about something.

"Is everything okay up there?" he called out.

"My rope is stuck. The carabineer has flipped and locked up my rappel line," she called down jerking at the line again.

"Okay, try this trick. While pulling yourself up on the rope, push off and see if it flips back," he suggested.

She tried a couple of times but nothing happened. "No go," reported Jo.

"I'll be up," announced Bryan. "This is why there should be at least two climbers working together," he commented to Rick who was showing some concern over the situation.

Bryan climbed up an alternate route to come out above the petroglyph panel. He looked down to see Jo hanging below. She saw him and waved.

"Be careful with your arm," she warned.

Bryan set his rope and tested his weak arm. "Coming down, watch for debris," he announced. Sliding down he quickly reached her elevation.

"These things happen," he commented. Reaching over he grabbed the errant carabineer and pulled it around from behind her. "Go ahead and lift."

"Still stuck," she reported.

"You could have a small rock caught in there," speculated Bryan. "I'll give you a little boost. Go ahead and lift again."

As he lifted, the weight shifted putting more pressure on his left arm causing a sharp pain. The combined effort was enough to relieve the pressure and break the rope loose. Bryan grabbed his arm and grimaced.

"Oh no, you must have hurt your arm," realized Jo.

"I think so," he replied. "You'll be able to finish okay. I'm going down."

"Shall I go down with you?"

"No, just finish up. I'll be okay."

"Are you hurt?" asked Rick as he came down.

"I'll be fine. I think I pulled something," he replied holding his arm. "Jo is free again and she should be able to finish without any more problems."

"I'll get you some ice for that arm," stated Rick heading over to the vehicle. After a few minutes he brought the ice and a bag of trail mix that he shared with Bryan.

Once down on the ground Jo expressed her regret for causing his further injury. He brushed it off and said it would eventually heal.

"The only thing that it's going to affect is a small job that I had planned on doing in a few days," he commented.

"You mean climbing wise?" she asked.

"Yeah," he replied.

"Well, maybe I can do it for you," offered Jo.

"You don't know what you're asking," stated Bryan.

"Why, is it super-secret or something?" she whispered in a mocking way.

37

"I've already told you more than you should know," he replied in an under tone.

As they were talking, Rick had headed down to the truck with some of the gear.

"O-oh, so it's having to do with this Government thing," she realized.

"Indirectly it does."

"I wouldn't have a problem with it," Jo related.

"I'll have to think on that—there's a risk," related Bryan.

"Hey you two let's get packed up," called out Rick from down the trail. "It'll be dark when we get back and I'm already hungry."

"Yeah me too," they both chimed in.

It was quite a lengthy trip back to Bishop from their remote location in the rugged mountains along the Nevada State line.

Bryan thought about Jo's offer, but how could he work it out? It would be unthinkable on his part to consider just the two of them going down alone. Tammy could be the answer. That evening he would call Tammy and see if she was free for a weekend jaunt.

Tired as he was the call still had to be made, but whether she would be at the apartment he didn't know. It did not take long to find out as a voice answered at the other end.

"Hey there sweetheart," greeted Bryan.

"Thank you for that Bryan, but you should probably tell that to Tammy," answered Rachel.

"Oh no, I'm sorry," he apologized. He could hear her telling Tammy that he called her 'sweetheart.' Tammy laughed.

"Hi honey, how are you doing tonight?" she asked.

"I'm a bit tired and I hurt my arm again today, but otherwise I'm doing great," he answered.

"How did that happen?" asked Tammy.

"Jo got stuck on a rock face and I had to go up and rescue her," explained Bryan.

"You were not supposed to be doing anything like that," she complained.

"I know, but it happened. I couldn't leave her up on the rock all night," he replied.

"I think it's time you quit," Tammy recommended.

"Yeah, that will be happening soon enough. This was just a fill in for a few days," agreed Bryan.

"Or was it to be with your climbing buddy?" she teased.

"No, but her services could be valuable."

"Services?" queried Tammy.

"Here is the deal. Since the Government has decided to call my bluff on the Camino agreement, I need someone with climbing ability to go down into the well at the Alamo. And crawl through the tunnel to photograph the Grinstad wall. But to make that work it will require your help. Do you understand what I'm asking?" he inquired.

"I understand what you're saying. Thank you for considering our relationship to be a higher priority," she commended. "I would love to be with you. But, I just can't right now," replied Tammy.

"Sorry to hear that. Well, maybe Josh could join us for a couple of days," considered Bryan.

"That would be fine with me. But the reason this is all happening right now is—what?" she asked.

"Her availability, plus she volunteered to help," he answered.

"I guess it's a good thing. If it will help keep you safe," agreed Tammy.

"I guess." he replied.

"No guessing," responded Tammy. "This is a forever contract."

"I like that concept," commented Bryan.

"Does Jo know the risk involved?" she asked.

"Yes, but I have withheld certain details until we have a green light," he answered.

"Please let me know if Operation 'Grinstad' is a go," requested Tammy.

"I'll give you a call if it is a go," agreed Bryan.

"Nice hearing your voice, miss you, love you," she reassured.

After hanging up with Tammy, Bryan focused on what he would say to Josh to persuade him to go. Josh was initially doubtful, but Bryan convinced him that the weekend excursion would not interfere with his busy schedule. Finally he agreed. Bryan said he would make arrangements and call him back as to where and when they would rendezvous.

Bryan checked with Jo to see if she was still interested in joining the mission. She did not hesitate to accept. He informed her that it would take place that weekend and they would most likely be flying out of Stockton. She was dying to know where they were going and what part she played in this. Bryan said he would brief her on the way.

There were basically three things for her to prepare. First, pack light and do not expect an overnight stay. Secondly, pack the climbing gear in a travel bag. And finally, call home to let them know that she wouldn't be coming home that weekend.

Bryan could see the excitement building in Jo as the time drew closer. She kept fishing for more details, hanging on every word he uttered. Jo was imagining that this was like one of those spy movies. He concurred that there would be some similarities and she would have to keep all of this to herself.

They learned that there was a vehicle swap being planned between the Inyo and the Stanislaus Forest Service motor pools. Bryan tracked down the employee who was going to make the run over to Sonora. His name was Trent, and he was someone Bryan had seen before, but never met. Arrangements were made with him for a ride over and back, offering at the same time to share with the driving. It took a bit of effort to convince him to leave at three in the morning.

Thursday evening Bryan made all of the confirming telephone calls to give everyone the green light. And thereafter Jo made her call; leaving her family wondering what she was up to. Did she have a new boyfriend or something?

The final day of the week seemed to fly by as they finished up work on two small sites near Westgard Pass. Rick had no idea what was afoot with his two crew members, except there seemed to be a heightened sense of friendship between them.

At three o'clock they were off in the wee hours of the morning in the two-seater pickup truck. Trent elected to drive to start things off. Jo just curled up on the back seat and slept. They met only four cars on the road over the mountains at that early hour into Tuolumne County.

Arriving a little late, Trent dropped them off at Josh's home. They made arrangements to meet up on Sunday for the return trip. Thanking him, they waved goodbye as he drove out. Then Bryan rushed to get things loaded into Josh's pickup. Josh soon came out carrying a duffle bag.

"Jo, I want you to meet the legendary Joshua Knight, and Josh this is Jo Flynn," introduced Bryan.

"Nice to meet you," replied Josh. "And I'm not legendary," he laughed.

"Bryan tells me some incredible things about you," she remarked.

"Oh, I don't know about that," he downplayed.

Preparing to go Jo scooted to the middle. Once on the way, Bryan began his briefing on the order and timing of the events.

"Our destination is San Antonio, Texas, and we will be going to the Alamo," he informed.

"The Alamo?" she questioned.

"That's correct, we will be going to the stone well that's in the granary, and that's where you come in Jo. You will climb down the well. Then enter a side tunnel that inter-connects to a second well that's been capped off from the surface. Continuing on you will come into a hewn out room," continued Bryan.

"Does anyone else know about this?" asked Jo.

"Including yourself there is only four of us, as far as we know," answered Josh.

"Who is the fourth person?"

"Tammy," he replied.

"Once you're in the room you will notice pictographs on the walls. There will be a map and writings. The writing on the left wall is our primary objective, but you will photograph all panels in the room," further explained Bryan.

"Do we have a camera?" she asked.

"We do, and I'll go over it with you before we enter the operational zone," he answered.

"O-oh, 'operational zone'," she repeated. Josh Smiled. "But will there be any difficulty with the staff when we try to enter the well?" she wondered.

"I think what Bryan has in mind is that we'll be creating a diversion while you enter the well," spoke up Josh.

"Exactly," confirmed Bryan. "We'll have everything timed out so we can get in and out before the place closes."

Well below Jamestown, the sun had risen above the crest of the Sierra casting a golden glow across the Valley onto the distant Coast Range.

Josh and Jo seemed to hit it off; talking all the way to the outskirts of Stockton. Finally arriving at the airport Bryan suggested they do a final equipment check before heading into the terminal.

Once inside they could hear continuous announcements concerning various flights boarding and some arriving echoing through the hallways. Bright sunlight shone through the tall plate glass windows into the lobby area. They did not have to wait long before the announcement came that their flight was now boarding.

After finding their assigned seats and stowing their carryon luggage in the overhead compartments they were able to settle in. Jo asked if she could have the seat with the window view. The boys said that would be fine.

"You know this is kind of strange," she commented looking out of the window.

"How so?" asked Bryan laying his head back.

"Well, here I'm with two guys, going who knows where on some strange adventure."

"You're not giving up on us, are you?" asked Bryan sounding concerned.

"No no, but it's strange for me to be doing something like this with people that I have only recently met. But something about you Bryan, caught my attention, and I've met Tammy and Bryan's mother, and now I've met you Josh. You all make me feel like I've always known you and can trust you like family," she explained.

"I hope you still have that same rosy outlook when we get done with this operation," commented Bryan.

"Just ask Tammy what she went through with us. But after a while you couldn't keep her away," added Josh.

Jo smiled and settled back in her seat as the plane taxied for takeoff. Passing over the green fields of the valley their route soon skirted the eastern foothills as they flew south. While in flight Bryan was able to sleep for a short time while Josh and Jo quietly conversed.

By eleven in the morning they had touched down at the San Antonio Airport. So far everything was pretty much on schedule. This was familiar territory to Bryan. There were memories here. He noticed that some of the seating and counters had been changed around, which gave him pause for thought. In that things never remain the same. A person has to continually make new memories.

There was finally time to stop and eat since they were starving. This gave Bryan the opportunity to run through the plan one last time, and acquaint Jo with the camera and flash unit.

"Jo, you are the star of the show, everything hinges on your success," stated Bryan.

"No pressure there, right?" replied Jo.

"This is not a life or death situation, but it is important that this gets documented," related Bryan to put things in perspective.

"Okay, let's do this, and get back home," she replied.

A cab soon arrived and delivered them to the Alamo site. The first things to catch their attention were large stone monuments, honoring those lost in the battle at the Alamo. These were set in the wide landscaped strip that fronted the Alamo complex.

After viewing the monuments, Bryan turned towards his companions. Remember, we're tourists—act like tourists," he reminded. "Pretend to be boyfriend, girlfriend or something."

Josh and Jo eyed each other. And so it was they played the tourist part slowly walking through the museum just as Bryan and Tammy had done some eighteen months before. Bryan pointed out the painting that showed the two wells which led to the original discovery. The number of visitors began to thin as they made their way into the granary. The next phase was just to mill around the landscaped enclosure and wait for the first opportunity.

After about ten minutes the coast was clear. The grate over the well was now paddle locked. Bryan anticipated this possibly and brought a small pair of bolt cutters. While he cut the lock, Josh and Jo stood so as to block the view of others if they should appear. Bryan and Josh did the same for Jo as she put on her climbing harness and a small pack. Bryan connected an anchor to the well frame and laced a short rope section through the loop.

Suddenly, there were two people in the entrance way in the far corner. They were looking at something along the back wall. As quick as they appeared they disappeared.

Josh opened the grate and Jo sat on the wall with her feet dangling into the well while she connected up to the rope. Tightening everything up and securing her headlamp she spun around and entered the well. Closing the grate the boys placed a couple bags to hide the rope anchor.

Jo turned on her light which lit up the individual stones inside the well. And she now noticed the foot and handholds that led downward into the black void. Jo glanced upward toward the light and then gradually descended another twenty feet until there appeared a large concrete patch in the wall. This was not what she was led to expect. Dropping lower she discovered that the handholds had stopped and she could now see debris and water in the bottom of the well.

Jo now realized that Bryan's tunnel was now sealed off. This confirmed in her mind that Bryan was truthful about everything he had told her. But what a disappointment this would be to him.

Ascending back to where the tunnel would have been she gave it a kick, but it proved to be solid. The concrete looked fairly recent. Continuing up to the top she asked to be let out.

"That was quick," commented Bryan.

"You okay?" asked Josh.

"Yes, I'm fine," she replied. "But, the tunnel has been sealed off."

"Are you sure?" asked Bryan.

"Yes, it's been walled off with concrete."

Josh helped her get the equipment bagged up. "So, what are we going to do now?" asked Jo.

"I wish I knew," answered Bryan sounding disappointed.

"Is there any other way in?" asked Josh.

"No, I don't believe so. The second well is out under the pavement," recalled Bryan.

"I don't know if you noticed it or not, but there is a patch in the asphalt out front," remembered Josh.

"Really? This is not looking good," Bryan commented. "Let's go take a look."

Working their way out of the Fort, Josh led them to where he had seen the patch. "This is the spot," pointed Josh.

"We're standing almost directly opposite where the well in the granary was located," estimated Jo.

"Let's go see what we can find out before this place closes," suggested Bryan heading back into the museum.

Asking at the information desk provoked a laugh from the man behind the counter. Apparently, inspired by a television program called "Unsolved Mysteries," the attempt was made to dig up the second well because there was a rumor that treasure had been hidden at the bottom of it. But after digging down a number of feet they hit a concrete plug. A couple attempts were made to break through, but it was too massive.

Bryan next asked if any work had been done on the well in the granary. Unsure he went into the backroom to ask someone. They could hear them conversing. Then the curator came back out curious why he was asking about that.

"Well, I was wondering if there was an inter-connecting tunnel between the two wells?" asked Bryan. Josh was a little concerned about throwing that possibility out there. But he realized they had to know this already.

"It's strange you ask. Hardly anyone knows about that. How is it you do?" he asked.

"The painting over here that shows the two wells made me curious, and when I realized that one ended up outside the Fort and one inside, I got to wondering," explained Bryan.

"Hmm," was the man's response.

"My only question is: Did someone verify they were connected?"

"The assumption is they were connected, but the thing of it is that a section of the tunnel collapsed before anyone who check it out," the man answered. "Probably because of the jack hammering that they were doing," he added.

"That must have been how the side tunnel was discovered in the first place by the sound traveling into the granary well," conjectured Josh.

"Probably," was the reply from the curator.

"Okay, thank you," replied Bryan in a disappointed tone.

Leading them back outside away from the building he stated, "The operation is a bust, and there's nothing we can do, but head home. Thank you two for helping me on this. And I want to especially thank you Jo for trusting in me," finalized Bryan.

"Bryan, up to this point I had just an inkling that what you told me was true," she replied. "But today I have seen it with my own eyes. So, what you described up on the mountain near Sonora Pass must be real too."

"It is real," confirmed Josh. "Welcome to the club."

5

FIRE ON BLACK MOUNTAIN

As the last rays of the sun slowly surrendered to the night the plane left the tarmac at San Antonio. Bryan was troubled by the series of recent events and it wore on him. As he studied the distant lights through the window Bryan considered the fact that he didn't have a clue what his next move would be. How was he to connect the dots?

It was different with Jo. She was like a kid in a candy store. There was no end to her questions and excitement. Good thing Josh was along because Bryan didn't really want to talk all that much.

Near eleven o'clock that night they disembarked in Stockton and drove the return route back up into the foothills. Josh returned home, and it was prearranged that Jo would bunk out at Tammy's mother's house for the night.

It was mid-morning the following day before everyone gathered back at the Anderson's for breakfast. Mrs. Anderson was busy making flap-jacks as the guests made their way in.

"I am so glad you're back safe," Tammy said giving Bryan a hug.

"It was quite uneventful," he replied. "Who's that with you?"

"It's Jo, who do you think?"

Apparently Tammy had redone Jo's hair so that it was no longer in a ponytail, but beautifully made up. Josh then came in and was amazed by the transformation in Jo. He couldn't keep his eyes off of her.

To Jo the rustic log cabin décor and the friendly family atmosphere made it the kind of life she would like to be part of. Catching her eye just before entering the living room she spotted the paintings of Captain Camino and White Feather. Seeing this, Bryan walked over to introduce her to them. After his mother restored White Feather's painting, she also had the Captain's picture brought up so they could be displayed together.

"That's where you get your good looks from," stated Jo.

"He's already taken!" was the voice from across the room. Jo laughed. "So, this is the famous Captain Camino."

After eating they all gradually reconvened back in the front room to share their experiences and to visit.

Later that morning Bryan's father came in for lunch. Over hearing the discussion he commented that maybe it was time for Bryan to focus on other things.

Tammy kind of agreed, reminding Bryan of what he had told her earlier about how it was time for them to start building their own life.

Josh had already moved on to other things, but he was always open to a new adventure.

But for Jo, she had a completely different perspective on the whole matter. This was exciting, and was something that had to be figured out.

As for Bryan, he was not ready to quit yet, but realized that he would soon be reaching a breaking point. His plan had been to quit his temporary position on the archeology team if they were successful, and Bryan truly believed that was going to be the case. But since it did not happen that way, he decided to stay with this assignment and gather more information.

Before heading back, Bryan decided to take another look at the photographs of the composite map formed by the box. As well as the one land grant that seemed so nebulous. Matter of fact he felt no qualms in revealing these new discoveries if they were held in confidence. Bringing these out he laid them out on the table so others who see them.

"The Captain is missing, but he has left us a way to follow him," he announced. "Here are photos of a map that was integrated into the construction of the box that was found in the ice cavern, as well as a number of land grants that were found in the box. Some of which are still of unknown location or extent."

Jo picked up the photograph that showed the modified sun symbols resting on curved lines that formed a wave. "This was at Spy Rock," she excitedly spoke holding up the photograph.

"That's right," confirmed Bryan.

"You have been holding out on me; this is new stuff," commented Josh.

"The discovery of the map is new. The Captain's box itself was the map," explained Bryan. "Let me get the box and I'll show you." As he left the room to get the box, Tammy was looking at a couple of the old land grants holding them up to the light of the window.

"Bryan, look at this," she called out as he came back in. "Notice the faint water marks in each of the corners of this document," she pointed out holding it up to the light. Their eyes met in realization that this was all too familiar. They laughed.

Jo smiled at the deep connection they seemed to have. It was the kind of relationship that she also hoped for.

"Tammy, good eye," commended Bryan. "It's the same symbols that are on the box," he realized.

"That would suggest there is a definite connection," called out Mrs. Anderson from the back of the room.

"What was it about this box that you were going to show me?" asked Josh.

"Oh, yes," Bryan responded. "See the individual small boards that make up the box, and then all these scattered lines and symbols?"

"Yeah, I see them," affirmed Josh glancing over at the photographs. "When put together in the right sequence it forms the intended image. That's genius. Bryan, you have not lost your gift."

"The real genius is the one that originally figured it out and made it," replied Bryan.

"This could be like the analogy of a door and a key. The land grant is the door and the key to unlock the door is the map," reasoned Jo.

"Or it may be the other way around," commented Tammy.

"Either way, they must work together somehow," said Bryan.

Josh jumped up and began excitedly pouring over the photographs. Everyone laughed.

"Relax Josh, this mystery isn't going to disappear tomorrow," stated Tammy.

Tammy questioned Bryan privately about what his thoughts were concerning his current status with the Federal Government. She expressed her fear based on Jo's report of the man that approached her.

Bryan felt that since they were casting doubts about the reality of Captain Camino they probably wouldn't do anything against him at this time. As long as he made no provocative moves there would be no reason for them to act against him. Perhaps it was a good thing for him to continue to work out in the open public. In some ways his comforting words put her at ease. However, Bryan wondered if the Feds had any idea about his recent trip to San Antonio.

About one in the afternoon Trent arrived in a long white van anxious to get back over the hill. Saying their goodbyes before leaving, Bryan noticed Josh and Jo talking. They parted smiling.

Bryan took the wheel for the trip back to Bishop, while Trent took a turn napping in the back, listening to music on his headphones. Jo shifted herself into the corner of the passenger seat facing more toward Bryan asking him questions about Josh. What it was like growing up with him and any romantic interests he may have.

"Jo-o? You're not interested in Josh are you?"

"Well, if he's anything like you, sure," she answered. That comment made him a little nervous.

He took a deep breath, as she continued. "How about we re-read the description of the mystery land grant to pass the time?"

"Sounds like a good idea," Bryan said feeling relief.

Traffic was light on the highway heading up out of Sonora. Numerous construction signs were going up everywhere in anticipation of roadway realignment that was soon to start. Jo was silent as she methodically read through the description.

"From what I can gather," she reported glancing back to make sure that Trent wasn't listening, "the eastern boundary of this grant is the 'great river'."

"It has to be well south of us, probably out in the Southern California desert somewhere," suggested Bryan.

"Out in the Mojave? Now that's one thing I do know about," reminded Jo. "There is really only one good possibility in the entire desert region, and that is the Colorado River."

"That's true, but that's a stretch of some three hundred miles all the way to the Sea of Cortez," he commented.

"Here are a couple of more clues which you no doubt have already considered," she continued. "The northwest corner of the land grant is a high mountain peak with a small forest at its summit and the letters 'ILD' marked into its eastern flank."

"I must admit my ignorance with any of the southern peaks," confessed Bryan.

"One possibility could be Mount San Jacinto near Palm Springs," proposed Jo.

"Doesn't that have the tram that goes all the way up to the top of the mountain?" he asked.

"It is, and there's a forest up on top," she added.

"The only problem, it's a very long way from Palm Springs to the Colorado River," realized Bryan.

"There are many other peaks scattered throughout the desert," replied Jo. "Some are in the Chocolate Mountains, the Turtles, the Old Woman, and the Granite Mountains just to name a few."

51

"Does anything else stand out to you?" he asked.

"Well, the distance to the southwesterly corner of this grant is twenty leagues due south to a granite mountain peak, also inscribed with the letters 'ILD'," paraphrased Jo.

"That's about fifty or sixty miles if I'm figuring correctly," calculated Bryan.

"Twenty leagues are far less than twenty thousand leagues," she joked.

"Yeah, especially if you're under the sea and you happen to be a certain Captain Nemo," chuckled Bryan.

"The real Captain left everything vague enough that it required another key," realized Jo.

"Read me what's written on the back of the Land Grant," he requested.

"Okay, 'May the journey of the first part be a pleasant one. You will be well supplied on your arrival.' And the next paragraph further down says: 'Let the sand sing and you find the forests in the sky and descend to the river below.' And at the bottom it simply states: 'The outlet is at the sea,' " read off Jo. " So, 'The forests' and 'the river' would seem to match what it says on the opposite side. But, I still don't see anything new," she commented.

"The first sentence mentioned 'the first part,' " recalled Bryan.

"That's correct," she confirmed.

"I wonder if it's referring to side one of the map?" he speculated.

The vehicle slowed as they ascended Twain Harte Grade. Bryan shifted down. "You want me to get out and push?" she teased.

"Oh, would you?" he asked smirking.

"Brya-an, be nice," she replied.

"Grab the photographs next, so I can see what your take is on the map," he said.

"Okay, I did look at these earlier. But the map seems to be less yielding to clues than the land grant," she commented.

"This is what I do. I just step back, look at the whole thing, and then I look at the individual segments. You try it," suggested Bryan.

"Alright, the map is two-sided. This symbol here in the lower right-hand corner matches the symbol in the upper left-hand corner of the opposite side. Therefore, this must be side one and the other is obviously side two," concluded Jo.

"Yes, yes, Jo, I already have them marked side one and two, see there," he impatiently pointed.

"Oh, okay," she laughed. "The sun symbol on side one is upright, and on the other side it is downward, for what reason I do not know.

"I'm not for sure either," Bryan agreed.

"Tammy made a good discovery when she found these images on the land grant," Jo commented.

"Tammy doesn't miss much, she's pretty sharp," agreed Bryan.

"Smarter than you?" she asked.

Bryan smiled. "No, but I definitely want her to be on my side," he laughed. "I think of our relationship as being complementary."

"You speak correctly," she commented. "No wonder she loves you so much."

"It wasn't always that way," he reflected.

"Hmm," contemplated Jo.

Changing the subject quickly Bryan asked, "I want you to tell me, what things on side two of the map stand out to you?"

"A number of things," she answered. "The bird head in the upper left hand corner and to its right is a set of wavy lines. Then a couple of mountain peaks, and an apparent river, that runs vertically to the bottom of the map. Lastly, there is a large bird with the downward sun in its beak in the lower right hand corner. But, what do these symbols really mean?" she wondered.

"Focus on these two mountain symbols." pointed Bryan. "What do these indicate?"

53

"Mountain peaks with trees at their summit," Jo thought out loud. "One of these could be the northwest corner of the land grant," she realized.

"That's what I'm thinking too," agreed Bryan.

"There has to be more to this; and what is this leading to?" questioned Jo.

"No one alive knows," he answered.

"This is a pretty area up here amongst all the cedars and pines," she noticed finally looking around at the gallery forest they were now traveling through.

It was late afternoon as they neared Bishop. Trent woke up and was the first to notice a large pillar of black smoke billowing up in the southeast beyond Bishop. Pulling into the Ranger Station they noticed increased activity. Forestry trucks were busily being loaded with fire gear and a low boy with a caterpillar tractor was being prepared for transport.

Rick rushed out of the barracks with bags in hand. "Get your gear together we're headed for fire camp," he informed. Bryan and Jo looked at each other acknowledging the change of events.

Fire camp was being set up in a rural park area near the town of Big Pine. During fire season all employees no matter what agency they worked for were expected to participate either on the front lines or at camp. The three of them were assigned to help with getting the camp set up. Initially, after arriving on site they were put under the direction of the Camp Boss, Martin Beal. Jo was assigned to the First Aid Dept. and helped to get it up and running. Rick and Bryan were put in charge of setting up tables for the kitchen and a garbage station. Soon a number of generators and light stands arrived and these were made ready for operation.

In the meantime, the fire continued to rage in the foothills and mountains on the east side of the valley. Bombers dropping fire retardant making their runs could be heard powering in and out of their flight path. Radio chatter sprang to life as the communication system and the Command Station came on line. Bryan helped with getting the fire maps up on the display boards.

Through conversation it became known about Bryan's previous experience working with the Forest Service on the Stanislaus and his rock climbing background. Glancing around he noticed Rick wasn't to be seen. Someone must have grabbed him for another assignment.

In the background Bryan could hear the Sector Bosses reporting in, giving location and progress of the fire crews under their direction. The reconnaissance aircraft suddenly broke in and announced an emergency situation on the west slope of Black Mountain. A man and woman hiking or climbing were pinned down on a ledge with the fire closing in on their position. The pilot asked on the availability of a rescue crew being deployed.

"Standby," was the reply. There was brisk conversation between the head brass at the Command Table. Using another radio they connected up with the Fire Dispatcher in Mammoth Lakes. A rescue crew was available, but it would take two hours for them arrive.

"We don't have two hours!" exclaimed the Fire Boss slamming his fist down. He eyed Bryan. Going back to the radio he pushed the transmit key. "Recon One, do you copy?"

"Recon One, over."

"Is there a need for a medical evac? Over."

"That's a negative, it appears they are just frightened," he crackled back.

The Fire Boss waved Bryan over. "Did you say you had climbing experience?" he questioned.

"Yes," Bryan answered.

"Have you passed all the safety training, first aid, and the usual protocols etc. etc.? And do you have necessary equipment here?" he additionally asked.

"Yes, yes, and yes. And my partner is also here I might add," replied Bryan.

"Okay, I'm going out on a limb on this, but find your partner, gather your equipment, and be ready to be air lifted to the site," instructed the Boss. "Once you find them, get them off the ledge to a safe location where the chopper can land. You'll be given a portable radio to call it in. Now go!"

Bryan made a beeline for the First Aid tent. He spotted Jo and an older woman sorting supplies. "Jo, drop everything, we've been asked to go on a rescue mission!" he excitedly exclaimed.

"Rescue mission?" she questioned.

"Yes, two people are stranded on the west side of Black Mountain and the fire is closing in. We have to move quickly," he answered.

Informing Rick of the sudden change in venue, they acquired their climbing gear and reported to the heliport at the southern end of the camp.

"I've never been up in a helicopter before," protested Jo. "And besides you are not a hundred percent yet. Tammy made me promise to keep you out of trouble."

"Jo! I'm not going to force you to go, but consider this—the other rescue team is two hours away and they will not get here in time," he explained. "Besides, if you have learned to cope with the risk of rock climbing I think you can handle a helicopter."

"Alright!" There's never a dull moment around you is there?"

A fire dispatch technician outfitted them with an additional first aid kit, a portable radio, and a number of fire blankets. The helicopter signaled his approach. The dirt blew as a large Bell helicopter came in from the south and turned sideways to touch down in the designated landing zone. The door flew open immediately even before the dust had settled. A copilot or one of the crew waved them on over.

"Stoop down low," ordered Bryan.

While the rotor blades were roaring with some intensity above them they scurried over to the open door and stepped in. Finding two seats facing forward they buckled themselves in as the door slammed shut. There was a brief flight check as the pilot communicated with Fire Command. Powering up they felt the immediate lift and the subsequent movement forward. Jo gripped Bryan's forearm and closed her eyes.

Bryan shook Jo. "Open your eyes, you're going to live," he encouraged.

Jo felt buoyant as the craft ascended and swept northeasterly toward the Inyo Mountains. Radio traffic was heavy especially from the incoming bombers. The pilots had to time their penetration into the air space on the east side of the valley. After three or four minutes a clear window of opportunity presented itself. The helicopter banked right and accelerated through drifting smoke. Light dimmed and brightened as they passed through these particulate filled clouds. Breaking into the clear the foothills were just below them.

"You may want to take a look at this," called out the copilot asking Bryan to step up into the cockpit. Unbuckling himself he stumbled forward. "Black Mountain is dead ahead," he informed.

Bryan could see the mountain looming up in front of them. It appeared that the west and the north slopes had suffered some kind of catastrophic landslide in the ancient geological past. The slopes were sparsely populated with small trees and brush. Smoke was blowing out of Black Canyon being driven by updrafts ascending the canyon wall. The potentially explosive fuels ahead of the fire were being preheated.

"The couple we are looking for should be on this side of the mountain, above the main drainage swale," continued the copilot.

The fire now was coming around the mountain, toward the hikers. Just to the north the White Mountains towered above them. Portions of a meandering trail were discernable wrapping around to the west side of the mountain.

"There they are, on that ledge of sorts," spotted the pilot.

Bryan could see that they had made their way off the main trail under the brow of the mountain.

"So, where do we set you down?" he asked.

57

"Time is of the essence, therefore it would best if we came in from above," reasoned Bryan.

"Their location is not that far below the top of the mountain," commented the copilot.

"It won't be long before the fire will reach them," Bryan realized. "Just drop us off at the top of the bluff."

"There's a fairly flat area over to the right. I can put you down there," he observed.

Bryan glanced back at Jo and considered the dangerous situation they might be plunged into very shortly. Had he erred in including her in this? Bryan went back to his seat and informed Jo they were landing. He added they would be rappelling down the face of the mountain to the bench where the two were located.

"You're nervous about this aren't you?" she noticed.

"A little, but those people down there are absolutely defenseless. The fire is closing in quickly," he answered.

"Maybe they'll put our names on a plaque if we don't make it," reflected Jo.

"We'll make it," Bryan assured.

"I promised Tammy, we have too!" she exclaimed.

"Get ready, sixty seconds to the drop zone," called out the copilot.

Gathering up their stuff, they momentarily waited. Feeling the helicopter touchdown, the copilot rushed back and opened the door for them. Dragging their gear with them they stepped out on the ground and made their way beyond the circle of the helicopter's confluence. Bryan gave them the all clear. Powering up they slowly rose and turned toward the west and finally southeasterly skirting the Inyo Range.

"Let's set up our rappel anchors," directed Bryan.

"Transverse cracks only, right?" added Jo.

"That is correct; score three points," he replied.

"If I get enough points what can I cash them in for?" she teasingly asked.

Carrying their gear to the edge of the cliff they peered down the eroded mountainside and through the intermittent smoke to eye the ledge far below. Bryan also took note that the sun was dipping quickly. He figured there was only about two hours of daylight left.

"Here are some nice ones," she called out.

Hammering in two sets about six feet across, they next laid out their ropes and connected up.

"Everything secure?" asked Bryan.

"All secure," she replied.

"Petroglyph crew to the rescue!" Bryan called out as they began their descent. Jo laughed and followed.

Reaching the bottom of the 300-foot ropes they re-anchored and descended again. A sudden gust of wind dislodged the two fire blankets that Jo had tied on and they went flying to who knows where.

"I hope we won't need those," yelled Bryan over the wind.

"I hope not either," she replied.

In short order they had reached the target ledge. Smoke and hot air whipped by them as they placed their gear into their packs.

"Okay, let's hit the dusty trail," she called out.

"Hey! That's my line," protested Bryan.

If his recollection was correct the man and woman should not be that far. The fire radio crackled with increased activity. Progress was initially slow as they made their way over a number of rockslides. But, in less than ten minutes they found them huddled up behind a rock outcropping.

"Hello! Anyone home?" called out Bryan.

"Yes! Thank goodness," replied a woman of about 28 years of age.

"You're here to rescue us, right?" asked the man who was about the same age.

"That's the plan," answered Jo.

"The fire is right on our heels. We need to make tracks out of here as quick as we can," informed Bryan.

"But first, here's water," offered Jo.

"Oh, good," they responded.

After exchanging introductions they identified themselves as Kyle and Pamela. Bryan noted they were wearing hiking shorts, which gave them little protection from the fire. Blowing cinders and charred bits of vegetation began dropping out of the wind and smoke.

"This is not looking good," Bryan called out. "We have to go!"

Bryan led them through the rock and brush that choked their escape route. The couple seemed a little dazed, but kept up a good pace. Jo followed in behind them. The mountainside terrain changed to a more moderate slope with an increase in the number of trees and underbrush. Bryan had in mind to contour downward away from the fire until they could find a half level landing site, but so far nothing of the kind had presented itself.

Jo noticed heavier black and brown smoke coming from above and behind them. Loud crackling could be heard as the fire got into a pocket of brush not that far back. Passing down through the trees which were predominantly piñon pine she inadvertently touched one and got sticky resin all over her hand. She realized this could be conducive to an explosive fire.

Breaking into a small clearing Jo could see Bryan talking with someone on the radio. Kyle and Pamela sat close by resting and catching a quick drink.

"We advise you to seek shelter just beyond the rock ledge that is southeast of your position, over," informed the voice on the radio.

"10-4, we'll hunker down and let it pass," replied Bryan. Facing the others he had grave news. "The fire is about to overtake us. We'll have to use the fire blankets to give us protection from the fire and the heat. But first let's get to the rock ledge and make a stand there."

Making their way toward the rock outcropping, the intensity of the fire above them was flaring up. Hot wind and smoke was enveloping them as they made their way over the rocky spine.

Coughing and stumbling their way through the remains of the ancient volcanic dike was proving to be difficult.

"Bryan, have you forgotten that we're down to just two fire blankets?" questioned Jo under her breath so the others could not hear.

"No, I have not. We'll have to share them the best we can," he replied. Jo didn't think they were big enough to share.

Soon they found themselves in a very rocky area away from the heavier fuels. Sparks were flying like crazy peppering down everywhere.

"We better make our stand here," judged Bryan. "In behind this rock ledge will serve as a partial fire screen." Removing his pack he gave Kyle and Pamela one of the highly reflective fire blankets to cover themselves with. "Let's use our packs for padding. It might make it a little bit more comfortable," he suggested.

"We're going to have to really snuggle up to fit under the one blanket," observed Jo.

"Yeah, I'm afraid so. I'll tell you what. I'll lay on my side with my back toward you. That'll probably make this situation a little better," suggested Bryan.

"That will work," she agreed.

They next helped the couple get situated. Recommending that they take another drink to keep themselves hydrated. In addition Bryan soaked a couple handkerchiefs and rags with water to be deployed over the nose when the smoke got unbearable. Wrapping the blanket around them they helped them to see how to hold it down tight.

Unfolding the remaining blanket with the reflective surface out, it was now their turn to get under. The air temperature surrounding them must have risen some 20 degrees as the brunt of the fire raced toward them.

"You manage your side of the blanket and I'll manage mine," said Bryan settling in.

"Can I ask one favor?" she asked.

"I didn't eat any beans today, you know that," he replied.

"What? No, I was going to ask, can I sling my arm over you so I don't roll back?"

"Sure, just don't tickle me," he laughed.

"No, of course not," Jo replied.

Bryan heard chuckling and then coughing. He asked Kyle and Pamela how they were doing. They said it was increasingly hard to breathe, but were finding them quite entertaining.

Nearby trees were exploding into flaming torches as the main front bore down on them. Hot cinders rained down and the hot breath of the fire intensified. Bryan could feel Jo's firm pressure as she clung onto him. The heat was like a blast from a furnace racing around them. The fire radio crackled to life with activity. They could hear the approach of a plane from the south. The roar increased and passed overhead then faded away.

"The cavalry has arrived," yelled out Bryan.

Almost immediately the sound of fire retardant raining down upon them was heard. Then after a few moments it seemed that the fire was abating.

"Let's wait for a few minutes to make sure we're in the clear," mumbled Bryan.

"I can't take this much longer," confessed Jo.

"Us too," agreed Kyle.

"Is the worst over?" asked Pamela.

"I believe it is. Breathing does seem to be a little easier. But it's prudent to wait and make sure," answered Bryan.

After a bit Bryan peeked out and it seemed to him the fire had indeed been knocked down in their vicinity. "I think it's safe, you can come out now," he reported.

"Must we? This is so cozy," commented Jo. Kyle and Pamela laughed.

"Jo! Do you want to stay on this mountain all night?"

"No, of course not," she replied releasing her grip on him. "But, I must admit I'm getting hungry."

"Us too," seconded Kyle.

"When we get back to Fire Camp you'll eat like kings," Bryan announced.

It was good to see everyone alive and in good spirits.

In the dim light that still prevailed they could see black and white ash splattered with reddish-pink fire retardant. The wind had also noticeably died down giving them some relief.

Without wasting any time he radioed that they were safe and needed directions to be picked up. As they waited for instructions they packed up their gear and prepared to depart.

"Bryan, look at this," noticed Jo examining the bank next to where they were lying.

"It's petrified wood," realized Bryan.

"Like a whole tree," she said excitedly.

"A mighty large tree," he confirmed.

6

SWANSEA

When they finally reached Fire Camp it was well after dark, and they did indeed eat like kings. Bryan and Jo were heroes for the day, getting their thirty seconds of fame on all the newscasts.

One consolation was that they had the next day off to rest up. Their families were all excited after hearing the news reports. Bryan noted that Tammy again had mixed feelings about the whole thing saying, "You and Jo seem to be getting along pretty well together." Bryan had to downplay it, but secretly he too worried about her intentions at times.

Bryan was curious about the tree fossil they had seen on Black Mountain. It made no sense to find such a thing on that dry sparsely treed mountain. Talking with a "forester" he found out a little background on the subject. Back in geological time, the White and Inyo Mountains were the dominant range inland from the coast and received all the moisture that came in off the Pacific. Among the ancient trees that grew in these mountains were the Sequoia Gigantea, all the common pines, firs, and cedars. Basically, all the trees that now grow on the western slope of the Sierra. However, when the Sierra Nevada rose out of the earth's crust and blocked the majority of the moisture from getting to the back range, things began to change. The luxuriant forests of those mountains began to die. Only the hardiest vegetation survived in the rugged heights including the ancient Bristlecones found in the White Mountains between 13,000 and 14,000 feet in elevation.

This was intriguing to him that giant Sequoias grew in these mountains eons ago. The geological forces that formed the Sierras no doubt had also built up the White and Inyo Ranges. If these geological forces had a similarity, then perhaps the dispersion of gold bearing strata was also corresponding.

But he realized the Owens Valley floor was over 4,000 feet in elevation. If the gold bearing strata of the Sierra is found at the 2,500 foot level then one would have to go down 1,500 feet to reach that same elevation along this range.

Maybe that is why in isolated places where geothermic forces are present gold is able to surface. This was exciting to think about. He hadn't considered anything like this in a while that intrigued him like this, except for the Captain's hidden map formed by the wooden box.

After their day off they went back to work at the Big Pine Fire Camp. The fire was now forty percent contained, but was expected to be controlled in another two days. Jo was asked to return to First Aid where her services were dearly needed with all the injuries coming in.

Somehow, the impression was they were a couple and Bryan was given an assignment nearby ferrying injured fire fighters back and forth between the heliport and First Aid. This struck Bryan. Maybe Tammy was right, it was time to move on before things became more complicated, even though the best of intentions were in place. This wasn't going to be easy he told himself, but better now than later. Bryan figured he would have to work the week out or give them a full two week notice if they needed it. He would have to break it to Jo in a way that wouldn't cause her too much duress. At the same time this would probably put him back on the FBI's watch list.

It was about ten in the morning when the first flight came in with two injured men from off the fire line. A motorized cart was pressed into service for him to transport ones to and from the heliport. Running back and forth every so often people would stop and congratulate him on a job well done.

He realized he hadn't seen Jo all morning. Approaching noon, a nurse came out and flagged him down before he could leave. "Jo needs to talk to you about something important," she related waving him inside.

"Okay," he reluctantly responded stepping out of the cart. Walking over to the First Aid tent he peeked inside.

"Oh good, Bryan, there is someone here you need to talk to," informed Jo setting some bandages down.

"Who would that be?" he asked.

"His name is Stanley, he's an injured fire fighter who knows a lot about the petroglyphs and the different sites," she answered.

"Well, we do too," flatly stated Bryan.

"Listen to him, he has insight that has been handed down from generation to generation," insisted Jo. "He's part Paiute."

"Fine, I'll be back shortly," he said turning to leave.

"Bryan, are you alright?" she asked. "You seem different today."

"I'm alright, how about you?" he responded.

"Top of the world," smiled Jo.

"That's good, I'll see you in a few minutes," repeated Bryan.

Jo thought to herself, what it's like when you get to know someone and you're able to distinguish subtleties of their personalities. It seemed obvious something was bothering him.

It wasn't long before Bryan returned mentioning he was on a lunch break. Jo immediately took him back to the patient area finding Stanley sitting on a cot. His right foot and ankle was noticeably bandaged up. He was a bit taller than what Bryan had expected, and had dark hair, blue eyes and a tanned complexion.

"Stanley, this is Bryan, and Bryan this is Stanley," she introduced. "Bryan is very much interested in your knowledge of the petroglyph sites and certain symbols."

"I'm glad someone is taking an interest in them, and will hopefully do a better job in protecting them," first said Stanley.

"We've been locating, cataloging, and photographing many of these sites," acknowledged Bryan.

"You're not the first," he added.

"I'll be back in a few minutes," announced Jo. "You guys keep talking."

"What background do you have with these sites?" asked Bryan.

"I'm half Paiute and half Swiss," he declared.

"Swiss?" questioned Bryan.

"Yes, my father was from Switzerland?" explained Stanley. "He was drawn to the desert even though he grew up near the Alps. My mother is Paiute; and it was from her side of the family that I learned about these places from a very young age."

"So I take it, they took you out to these places," stated Bryan.

"With my grandfather mostly," he answered.

"What did he tell you about these sites?" asked Bryan.

"These were like migrational hubs or camps that were three to six days apart. They served through the seasonal changes as the food and water sources went through an annual cycle in the Great Basin as it's called now."

"How about the symbols themselves, what purpose did they serve?"

"They were in a sense like information boards, with solar and lunar calendars, directions to the prime fishing and hunting grounds, as well as distances to the other camps."

"There are two symbols that I'm especially curious about," informed Bryan. "Let me draw them out for you. I'll get a pencil and a piece of paper." As Bryan sat back down and got himself situated he asked Stanley about his foot.

"I took a tumble off the trail and ended up with a bad sprain and a gash just above my ankle. I'll live another day," he shared.

"That's good to hear," responded Bryan as he began to draw. "There's this one with the top half of the sun situated on curved lines, and the other is the opposite with the bottom half of the sun facing down." At that moment Jo came back in.

"The 'upright sun,' as you call it appears in most of the sites, from north of Mammoth Lakes all the way down into the Mojave. According to my grandfather it represented a place of great riches, like 'the splendor of the sun,' " informed Stanley.

"What about this one?" pointed out Bryan holding the paper up.

He shook his head. "I personally have not seen this one, but I've been told about it," he reluctantly answered.

"But, what does it mean?" directly asked Bryan.

It seemed he was again hesitant to talk about this one. "From the talk of the old men it was associated with darkness, the subterranean, danger, a place of death," he recollected.

"What about the two curved lines that are common to both?" further questioned Bryan.

"Sand," flatly said Stanley.

Bryan turned toward Jo. "Sand," he repeated.

"Yeah, makes sense to me," thought Jo. "Like sand dunes," she motioned with her hands.

"You were not the only one who had been interested in that particular set of symbols. There was a man who came and visited my grandfather many years ago; he was an anthropologist by the name of Von Trigger. He disappeared in the desert and was never seen again," added their informant.

"Thank you, Stanley. I believe what you have shared with us will at some point prove valuable," appreciated Bryan.

"I have to go now," announced Jo. "But I was wondering, how far south can this one symbol be found?" she asked pointing to the upright symbol.

"I have seen it at Swansea, but I understand it is also found down in the China Basin, but don't hold me to that," he answered.

Bryan thanked him again as he got up and wished him a quick recovery.

"Join me for lunch?" she asked Bryan. "My treat."

"Sure, but I'll pay for myself, thank you."

Walking over to the cafeteria they got in line. After making their selections they found a spot at the end of a table.

"Wasn't that worth the price of admission?" she asked a little proud of herself.

"Barring some verification, I would say this could very well help us on the trail south," he agreed. Bryan felt that this was making what he had to do more difficult.

"We did good, right?" again inquired Jo.

"I like your sense of teamwork," Bryan confirmed. "But there is something I need to talk to you about," he continued.

Hearing the serious tone in his voice she straightened up and did not smile. "What?"

"As you know I took this job to stay close to the Camino Project, but that has changed. And in the meantime I've been trying to figure out what my next move might be. So, I've made my mind up that I'm going to give notice," he disclosed.

"What! You're quitting? You can't. What am I going to do?" she protested seemingly upset.

"You're going to be fine," calmed Bryan. "Finish this summer job and get your degree, just like you wanted. It's all going to work out."

"You've been the only breath of fresh air down here," Jo related shoving the tray to one side still visibly upset. "Josh said I was in the club so to speak. But now, I probably won't be seeing you guys anymore. I'm going to miss this whole family thing."

"Not true. You're still on the inner-circle on this. And you are still our Southern California expert. It's just I have some other irons in the fire that I have to take care of," related Bryan.

"I can understand that, but I feel like your abandoning me," she responded.

"You are a good person and I want you to stay on the team. But we do have to show some balance in our lives. My family has been trying to get me to pay more attention to my real future and stop pursuing the Captain across the continent and through time," he answered.

"But that's what is so exciting. Think of the treasures and the monetary rewards that are at hand," she countered.

"The reality is that there has been only a small return in all the time and danger that has been invested in the pursuit," explained Bryan.

"But this time, from what I can gather the Federal Government has no idea about this new development. You're home free," pointed out Jo.

"Not quite, there is a good chance they will again observe my movements. You and probably Josh may be above any kind of suspicion," he commented.

"But without you what can I do?"

"Keep following the sites south mapping the sun symbol as far as you reasonably can. Rick informs me that we'll be visiting the Swansea-Keeler Group perhaps later in the week," Bryan answered.

"I wish you could stay on for a while longer," she stated.

"Well, I'll be here at least through the end of the week. Josh and I will make ourselves available on weekends. I need to spend more time with Tammy," explained Bryan. "Here, eat your lunch," he encouraged scooting her tray back to her.

"Thank you, but it's still going to be hard without you being here. I was hoping that somehow this summer would never end," Jo whimsically shared.

The remainder of that day and the following day Jo kept pretty much to herself. She realized that her heart had allowed herself to become interested in someone who was not available. He was already engaged to Tammy, and it would be wrong to hurt him or her.

On Thursday with the fire wrapping up they were free to return to their project. Rick voiced his disappointment on Bryan's coming departure, saying he had hoped things would have worked into a full time position. Bryan thanked him for that, but explained he had his eye on forestry as his career goal. He also talked privately with Rick asking him to keep an eye on Jo seeing that she was taking his departure a bit hard.

As anticipated they were off to the Swansea site, southeast of Lone Pine to survey this extensive collection of rock art. This was deemed as a multi-cultural petroglyph site, due to the presence of Eurasian symbology. They had opportunities to conduct solar observations on inscribed calendars and festival markers. The entire area was located within a dolomite or limestone formation.

Driving and hiking to the extremities of the rock inscriptions proved to be tiring under the baking sun.

"This could take more than a month," concluded Jo after they returned to the vehicle. Gradually, Jo was adjusting to the idea that Bryan would soon be leaving and consigned herself to being more independent.

"We should be able to get temporary help to finish out this year's work," stated Rick.

"If you get into a pinch and need a second climber sometime in the near future, give me a call. I may be able to make myself available for a couple days here and there," volunteered Bryan.

"This must have been a major encampment," realized Jo.

"With Owens Lake nearby, I would say this was a major draw for fifty miles in either direction," considered Rick.

"What a shame, look at the Lake now. It's just a dust bowl," commented Bryan.

"Just up the road is Cerro Gordo, which had the richest silver mines in the whole state at one time," revealed Rick.

"Is it still active?" asked Jo.

"No, but as I recall there's still quite a few buildings left up there," he answered.

Dust was visible scurrying across the dry lake bed as the wind picked up. The old lake was several miles across reaching almost to the foot of the mountains on the far side. Why would the people of that time congregate on this side of the valley and not on the Sierran side? To Bryan it seemed the landforms were more gentle, and not so steep or difficult. Maybe that would explain why. Additionally, there must have been adequate water and no doubt fowl and four-footed game were plentiful here on a seasonal basis.

"As we go, we'll have to differentiate between the various panels, culturally and chronologically," stated Rick thinking about the task that lay ahead of them. "Bryan, you're going to miss all the fun," he added.

"If I could clone myself, my twin would love to stay," replied Bryan.

"I like that idea," responded Jo. "Now wait a minute, why can't you stay and your twin go?" she asked after a pause.

"Because I have things to do, but my clone has no such responsibilities," he answered.

With that Jo couldn't contain herself and started cracking up. Both Rick and Bryan couldn't help but laugh along with her.

Later as Bryan was leaving he promised to keep in touch. Making an arrangement with Jo to have her call once a week and to keep track of any expenses she might occur.

Jo returned home that weekend and shared more of the adventure she had on Black Mountain, but little about the previous weekend. Only mentioning they had explored a well looking for a lost tunnel. It felt good to be back at home in Apple Valley with its rolling hills and horse ranches.

During the quiet time it gave her an opportunity to think about her future and take stock of where she was at.

Returning back to work she felt empty knowing that Bryan wouldn't be there. Nevertheless, she figured she had to press on.

The first two days of the week Rick and Jo worked alone at Swansea, but on Wednesday a temporary employee was hired out of Bishop. Her name was Helen, a mother of two, who desperately needed the work. Jo and Helen seemed to get along well enough. Blonde-haired Helen gave Jo an earful on motherhood. She warned Rick to keep the blonde jokes to a minimum. He laughed.

Some of the first groups of petroglyphs they encountered had solar calendars associated with them. A closer examination showed that these had been reworked or repatinated some years in the past. Taking a break between cataloging and photographing, they observed shadow movement or a "dagger of light" on the inscribed calendars. More extensive observations needed to done on a seasonal basis and during times of equinox.

Progress was slow on the project due to the long drive from Bishop each day. The week seemed to go quick enough for Jo, but there was nothing to report to Bryan on Friday. Taking a deep breath, she realized it felt good to talk to him again. He was busy at home working with Josh. They were preparing to get the foundation for Bryan's future home built.

During the following week, Jo finally ran across the symbol of the 'upright sun' just as Stanley said they would. But something new came into play. A whole different kind of inscription was found. Rick reminded them that this was a multi-cultural site. Bringing out a book on previous sketches he pointed to the match which was thought to be of Arabic origin. There was a stick figure with a cross, probably denoting a pick, and a Kufic silver mark.

"Silver?" questioned Jo.

"Yes," replied Rick. "Remember, what's just up the road?"

"Cerro Gordo," answered Helen. "The richest silver mine in these parts."

"There is also a reference here for a similar inscription down the valley at a place called Little Lake. It shows an ingot of silver with an assayer's rectangle and again the Kufic mark for silver," noticed Rick.

"That's interesting," commented Jo. "I don't suspect we'll be visiting that site?" she asked.

"No, that's not in our scope of activity this year," he replied.

"Hmm," responded Jo. Her curiosity was peaked on two counts. One was concerning Cerro Gordo and the other involved this new location at Little Lake.

7

YOU CAN'T TAKE THE CITY
OUT OF THE GIRL

Bryan felt good to be back among the tall pines and greener vegetation once again. He wanted to put everything aside that concerned the Camino Project and all its challenging legalities. Bryan wanted to concentrate on getting his personal life back on track. Tammy was glad he had finally quit his job, but she still seemed to be distant and preoccupied. Nevertheless, he planned to spend some time with her including a day in Berkeley.

Two immediate things were on Bryan's mind. The first was to see if Tammy had any problems with a couple minor changes to the house plans. Secondly, he needed to meet up with Josh to finalize the plans and get the building permit issued. Then they could break ground and get the utilities stubbed in and the foundation poured.

But from time to time he couldn't help but think about Jo and Rick, wondering how everything was going with them. Bryan definitely felt he did the right thing by quitting, but still felt a commonality with Jo in her interest in all things outdoors.

Among all the other activities Bryan still wanted to help his dad around the ranch to the extent that he could. In general his dad's business had diminished. Now he was relying heavily on contracts with the Forest Service.

Bryan spotted Graffiti their golden retriever sleeping in his favorite spot on the front porch and petted him on the way into the house. Crossing the living room he paused in front of the paintings of Captain Camino and White Feather. "Where have you gone?" he asked.

"They have gone to the place that is the eventuality of all mankind," answered his father who happened to be passing by in earshot.

"Yes, that is true," agreed Bryan. Ultimately he would not have cheated death. So, why did he make his next venture so secret, where only a select few or perhaps just one could follow? What was his new endeavor? Whatever it was, it must have been something big. "My goodness, I was born too late to get in on the ground level of this one," he verbalized. But again he wouldn't have Tammy and Josh, and that was not negotiable.

Next day Bryan met Josh at the house site just around the knoll from the present ranch house with a view of the mountains. Josh had not delivered his backhoe to the site yet, but a load of form boards on a flatbed trailer was sitting to one side of the clearing. Josh and a young assistant were shooting elevations on the ground at the corners of the foundation.

"It's hard to believe that this is all coming to pass," spoke up Josh after peeking through the level.

"How so?" asked Bryan.

"When you guys first met, you fought like cats and dogs, remember?"

"Yeah, but I think at some point we realized that what we wanted was the same thing," answered Bryan. "Are you suggesting I call it off?"

"No-o, of course not. I'm happy for you two. It's just interesting how things turn out sometimes."

"Speaking of which, Jo has been asking about you," Bryan informed.

"Oh yeah? What did she say?" he said nonchalant.

"She was asking if you had any romantic connections," disclosed Bryan.

"Really? She seems nice, but maybe a little bit on the wild side," commented Josh.

"Once you get to know her, she might be a keeper," responded Bryan.

"Say, you're not trying to set me up are you?"

"No, but I need you to go down with me on a weekend or two and give us a hand on 'the trail south' as we have come to call it," he explained.

"I'm really busy right now," pondered Josh. "But, I would love to hit the old 'dusty trail' again as we had in the past. However, I'm not sure about Jo though."

Bryan smiled, thinking about Josh's statement on how surprisingly things do turn out sometimes.

Jo decided to call a day early in anticipation of securing help to go with her on Saturday. She was curious about Cerro Gordo and what could be found at Little Lake, since there seemed to be a link with the Swansea site.

Bryan was surprised when she called, thinking that Jo might have lost interest. He thought she may be onto something, but he already had plans with Tammy and wouldn't be able to make it this coming weekend. Bryan said he would check with Josh and see if he might be available.

Josh was at first uncooperative, but the more he thought about going up to the silver mine, the more it intrigued him. Finally, by Friday he had agreed to meet her.

Bryan was up early Saturday in the cool of the morning taking care of a few chores. He noticed in the eastern sky low clouds drifting silently north, and figured monsoon moisture was moving up out of the Gulf of Caifornia.

His plan was to pick up Tammy from her mother's and take her over to their house site. He wanted to show her that they had finally broken ground. Bryan even purchased a bouquet of flowers to surprise her and a few perennials that could be planted to commemorate the occasion.

But when he went over to get her, she was not there. He was told she had called and would not be arriving until midmorning. That took the wind out of his sails. Bryan explained that he had a surprise for her, but it could wait. The flowers will keep for a bit longer he told himself.

So he decided to go back to the building site. Grabbing a handful of lathe and a roll of flagging he staked the location of the electrical service and the layout of the water lines. It wasn't long before Ralph, Josh's part-time laborer came by and unloaded some additional lumber and stakes. Then he distributed the form boards around and began chalking the foundation excavation.

An hour later Tammy drove up, surprising him. She must have guessed where he would be.

"Welcome to the Anderson homestead!" Bryan called out. "I wanted to surprise you about the groundbreaking on the house," he added coming over to give her a hug.

"That's wonderful," she replied looking around. "I see you have somebody else working out here on the project."

"That's Josh's worker getting things prepared for the foundation," Bryan explained. "Are you okay?" he asked holding her at arm's length.

"I'm just tired I guess," she replied.

"Here, I have something that will cheer you up," Bryan announced. Opening the door on his truck he grabbed the bouquet of flowers and presented it to her.

"Wow, Bryan, that's so romantic," responded Tammy. Hugging him again she pressed her head against his chest. "I don't deserve you," she stated.

"If I have anything to say about it, I think you do," he replied. "Come on let me show you around. Oh, by the way look here in the back of the truck, these are perennials. I thought we could plant them to commemorate the groundbreaking."

"How thoughtful," she reacted. "I feel so bad I didn't contribute towards this."

"No-o, this was to be a surprise," he reiterated taking her around.

For Tammy it felt good just to cuddle with Bryan and watch a few lazy clouds float by and look again through that imaginary window of their future house that had such a grand view.

Tammy wanted Bryan to know that she understood how disruptive the pursuit of her degree has been on their relationship. This was something she wanted to accomplish before they settled down and appreciated his support to make it happen.

But there was something wearing heavily on her. She had been warned against telling him, but her love for him steadied her course.

Before leaving, Tammy picked out a nice spot to plant the flowers in half sun and half shade. This symbolic gesture made Bryan feel that this was the beginning of good things that would happen here.

The following day Bryan was looking forward to being with Tammy again. She had planned a little celebration at her apartment in Berkeley for achieving a bachelor's degree. There was a time when he had a real aversion to anything having to do with the City, but gradually accepted that it was not all a "den of iniquity."

Turning off of University Avenue in Berkeley onto a small side street he closed in on Tammy's apartment that she shared with Rachel. Parking was always a problem, but this morning that was not the case.

Catching his notice was the variety of pastel colors on the buildings and residences in that part of the town. It reminded him of some kind of artistic renaissance movement. Through a narrow garden path Bryan made his way up a flight of stairs to the second story. Turning left to the first apartment he knocked. While waiting he looked over the railing to spot a bubbling fountain directly below.

Tammy peeked out the door. "Wonderful, you're here," she said giving him a hug and smiling. "Come in, I have just a couple of things to do and we can head up to the University."

"Bryan!" called out Rachel from the kitchen. "Good to see you. You're looking good."

"Thank you," he replied. After a pause he asked her: "You're still not telling Tammy to play hard to get are you?"

"No," she smiled. "I think we're well passed that."

Bryan couldn't help but notice how neat and orderly everything was. Tray's and glasses were already set out, no doubt for the gathering that was planned for that evening.

Tammy soon came back in putting on her earings and took note of what Bryan was wearing. "You're wearing that this evening?" she asked.

"Ah, yeah, it's okay, right?"

"Well, it is a little on the informal side," replied Tammy. "But we'll make it work."

"I like it when you use the word—we," smiled Bryan.

"We-e, can take my car since I have a parking pass," recommended Tammy.

"Let's go, I would like to see this edifice of higher education," he remarked.

"Bryan, be nice," she replied scooping up her keys. Saying their goodbyes to Rachel they were off.

The University and its distinguishing beaux-arts architecture, which had its roots in the Roman era stood out as they approached on the main avenue. Walking in through the arched Sather Gate, Sather Tower with its bell and clock tower which loomed over the whole campus came into view. Tammy waved at a couple acquintances as they passed along. Many of the dated architectural buildings of the period were draped in ivy and were beginning to show their age. UC Berkeley was the flagship of the whole California University system. As Bryan soon found out in some of its satellite facilities, high tech research was in progress. Such as at the Lawrence Livermore Lab where a huge fusion reactor was being assembled.

As he opened a door into one of the large buildings Bryan thought to himself how he was not intimidated by all of this, but was actually proud of Tammy for being accepted here and excelling in the field of communication. Some of the classrooms he found were actually moderately sized auditoriums.

"This is a far cry from the old two-room schoolhouse up in Tuolumne," commented Bryan after meeting one of Tammy's professors.

"Thank goodness, we've progressed beyond that backwoods mentality," he commented without hardly looking up.

"Quantity is not always quality though," Bryan fired back.

Tammy interceded; and after concluding her business made a mad dash for the door. In an adjacent building she had to turn in some paper work to a receptionist. She looked at Bryan and the way he was dressed and then at Tammy. As if saying: What are you doing with him?

"Tammy have you made up your mind if you're going on the FCTA study course in Spain?" she asked.

"Ah, no not yet," Tammy slowly responded glancing at Bryan.

"It's an opportunity you should not pass up," she encouraged.

"Yes, I know."

"Spain? Tammy what's this about Spain?" questioned Bryan.

"I'm sorry, I planned on telling you. But, it's best we talk about it in private," she answered.

From there they cut across the campus where Tammy had a short meeting in the Administration Building. In the meantime Bryan wandered through some historical exhibits in the adjoining rooms. Bryan in someways felt lost in this academic world, but felt reassured that his real purpose in life was still out there among the mountains and forests.

He sat down on a bench and just closed his eyes for a moment. In his mind's eye everything around him vanished and all he could see was Tammy's beautiful face and sweeping hair.

He felt a certain satisfaction that he had found a real treasure in her. But at the same time he wondered what was this business about Spain.

"Wake up, sleepy," came a familiar voice awakening him.

"I was just closing my eyes for a minute," he informed finding Tammy smiling down at him.

"Are you hungry yet? I know the perfect spot," informed Tammy.

"Sounds good, lead the way," he readily agreed.

Navigating through the maze of buildings and landscaped areas they came to a food court. Nearby were a few tables by a small stream called Strawberry Creek that naturally flowed through the University where they were able to find a pleasant spot to eat.

"Tammy, I must say I'm impressed with what you have accomplished here. I hope you're happy in achieving what you had set out to accomplish?" asked Bryan.

"Yes, for the most part," she answered. But it seems like there is always pressure to do more. I guess it's part of the self-perpetuation of the educational system."

"You are so pretty, I can't wait till we can finally set the date and get married," expressed Bryan. "But, what is this about Spain?"

"It is an opportunity to study abroad for six months, all expences paid," she explained.

"Six months?" questioned Bryan.

"Yeah, I know, this came up kind of sudden. I realize this is going to make it difficult for us," acknowledged Tammy.

"But you just got your degree, what more do you want? How would this benefit us?" questioned Bryan. "Are you seriously considering it?"

"I have thought about it, because it is one of those once in a life time opportunites," she confessed. "Bryan, I love you and I don't want this to be a deal breaker for us."

"Well, I don't have the insight into this as you do, so you'll have to make the decision. I just hope it's the right one," he replied.

"Yeah, I know," she acknowledged.

Tammy had one more stop to take care of some loose ends with her classes. From there a trip to the local grocery store was next on the list.

"We haven't been out shopping together in a long time," realized Tammy as the automatic door opened allowing them to enter the store.

"I think we better re-think our hunter-gatherer relationship," laughed Bryan.

"In some of these large stores you have to be a hunter and a gatherer," replied Tammy.

Back at the apartment they found Rachel busy in the kitchen preparing some finger foods for the gathering.

"One of these days, Bryan, if you let me, I would like to help out putting together a book detailing all about Captain Camino and the unraveling of the mystery," inquired Rachel.

"Yes, perhaps one of these days," agreed Bryan smiling while glancing at Tammy. Unknown to Rachel was the fact that the mystery was still unraveling.

"Bryan, you just relax, watch television or something as we get things ready," suggested Tammy.

"Okay, I'll be right here if you need me," he replied.

Sitting in the easy chair he took the remote and did a little channel searching while listening to the chit-chat of the girls in the kitchen. There was something soothing about that. Catching a part of the conversation they were apparently discussing someone that was not going make it that evening. Clicking between channels he found a comedy, a woodworking program and a local baseball game to select from. But somewhere along the line he must have dozed off.

"Time to wake up," came a call from the other room.

"Oh, I must have nodded off," he realized.

"Guests will be arriving soon, you could wash up if you like," advised Tammy.

"Probably a good idea. Before long I'll have to take a number to get in," replied Bryan getting up.

Soon the guests began to arrive, which included fellow students and friends. Including an older couple that were professors at the University. Bryan was curious if they taught in the same curriculum, but apparently they did not. He was told that was one thing that has kept their marriage viable.

Bryan found initially the discussions were very philosophical and in many respects quite interesting. But after the influence of a couple of drinks it seemed the demeanor of the conversations began to deterioate. A few hilarious stories were being circulated at the expense of some of the other guests.

"Say, I understand you're a cowboy," inquired a tall fella with chin whiskers. Apparently he was a fellow student of Rachel's.

"Not in the classic sense," laughed Bryan. "I do work with horses though. I also do forestry related work and this summer I've been employed as an associate archeologist," he added.

"That's incredible, you're a regular outdoorsman," concluded the young man. "It's amazing that you and Tammy have anything in common."

"Superficially that might seem to be the case, but I think we connect at a deeper level," expressed Bryan.

The young man quickly disappeared back into the crowd to get his drink refreshed. Almost immediately a friend and fellow student of Tammy's named, Angela, came up and introduced herself.

"Nice to meet you, Bryan. I imagine you're proud of Tammy?" she asked.

"Absolutely," he answered.

"Isn't it wonderful that she is going to Barcelona on that special grant," stated Angela.

"I was under the impression that she hadn't made up her mind yet," replied Bryan.

"Oops, maybe I shouldn't have said anything," she realized.

"Angela, I'm hoping they also teach truth and ethics in this place of so-called higher education," commented Bryan walking away.

He was disturbed by that last conversation. Surely Tammy would have discussed it further with him before making a final decision. Sipping on a drink he hung out by himself for a couple minutes.

It seemed that Tammy was having a good time with many of her friends. She did have a lot in common with many of them he realized, but it appeared that a couple of her male friends were being a little over-friendly. One came up and put his arm around her, which seemed to be just a congratultory gesture, but when he kept it up that's when it began to get under Bryan's skin. Tammy didn't seem to mind the attention. He didn't want to make a scene, but decided to waltz over to the countertop next to their location. Leaning against the wall he made eye contact with the offender. Seeing Bryan's stare, he backed off and withdrew his arm. Tammy took notice of the situation and glanced at both of them. Without saying anything Bryan turned away to start up a conversation with one of the professors.

It seemed as the evening progressed the behavior of some of the guests made him feel increasingly uncomfortable.

"Bryan, are you enjoying yourself?" asked Tammy making the rounds.

"You seem to be enjoying the company of your guests," commented Bryan without answering.

"They are just friends; don't be so jealous," she answered.

"I didn't appreciate, whats-his-face putting his arm around you," he shared.

"Don't take it so personal, there's nothing between us. I must admit though he is a bit clingy at times," reflected Tammy.

"There is talk going around tonight that you have already accepted the offer to go to Spain," stated Bryan.

Tammy let out a long sigh. "The truth is I have," she confessed. " I have not been able to figure a way to approach you on this without hurting your feelings."

"You should have told me the truth from the beginning. Not feeding me half-truths," he insisted.

"You're saying you don't trust me? And yet you can go off on your quazi-government assignments out in the middle of the desert with Jo for weeks at a time," pointed out Tammy.

"Look, I quit because of you. Things can happen when people are together over a period of time," he responded. "It's not you, it's them I don't trust." Bryan noticed that some of the guests were now beginning to take notice of their conversation as their voices became more elevated.

"I'm sorry you feel that way, but they are my friends," she defended.

"Tammy, you do what you think is right. If that means going to Spain, then you should do it," finalized Bryan. "And if you change your mind and want to consult with me on anything let me know." At that he abruptly began gathering his things.

"Bryan, I don't know what to tell you. You can get so self-centered at times," argued Tammy as he headed for the door.

Bryan made no reply as he gave her one last glance before making his exit.

"So much for that 'connection at a deeper level,' " came a comment from one of the guests.

She ignored that comment and went into her bedroom crying. Rachel went to check on her when she heard something hit the wall and break. She froze and stepped back into the living room figuring she better let her settle down first.

8

CERRO GORDO

Early Saturday morning while driving over Sonora Pass Josh reflected on his and Bryan's past adventures in that area. This included the unnerving appearance of Ben Coleman at Deadman Creek, and the midnight sojourn to Leavitt Lake and the Sierra crest.

Other places that provoked old memories was at Bridgeport and at the Mono Lake Overlook where he told tourists that Bryan was a secret agent coming in on the helicopter. Josh smiled reliving the expressions on their faces. But now there had to be new experiences, ones that he himself would have to make.

Before meeting Jo at the Ranger station he stopped for fuel and a few snacks to carry with them. But Josh soon found out that Jo had things more than prepared for their day of activity. She had prepared a picnic lunch with many extras.

"Wow!" exclaimed Josh. "Forget the silver mine, we're good to go right here. There is one thing though," he stated in a serious tone.

"What?" she asked.

"I hope you can make a better sandwich than Bryan. I've been through some tough times with that boy," answered Josh.

Jo laughed as she gathered a few last things. "You're funny," she remarked.

As Josh and Jo were loading up, she received a call at the barracks phone. "What now?" wondered Josh as he waited. She quickly appeared announcing that her cousin, Heather, would meet them at Lone Pine.

"That's good, but you haven't said anything to her about what we're looking for, have you?" asked Josh a bit concerned.

"No, she thinks we're just going to do some exploring and have a picnic," she replied.

"How are you explaining us?" he further asked.

"Oh, I hadn't thought of that. Well, you're a friend that I met while at work, which is basically true," she answered.

Josh shook his head and replied, "O-okay."

Finally getting on their way in Josh's truck they headed south with the windows down, as it was already getting warm. A few clouds were finding resting places in the Inyo Range to their left and in the higher peaks of the Sierras.

"Before we go up to Cerro Gordo, I want to stop at the Swansea site and show you the 'upright sun,' " stated Jo.

"Is this the furthest south that the symbol has been found so far?" inquired Josh.

"Yes, it is, but the map shows there will be more. Matter of fact at some point the map shows an abrupt turn to the east," she answered.

"This whole desert region down here is as big as some planets," remarked Josh. "So you think Cerro Gordo could be a place to look next?"

"It may or may not, but there is a link with another site called Little Lake that has potential. I also would like to check out today," responded Jo.

"What link?" Josh further inquired.

"It's an Arabic symbol that is believed to denote silver. According to a previous survey something very similar has been found at Little Lake," she answered.

"So there is a possibility that the 'upright sun' symbol may be there also," he reasoned.

"I like the way you think," responded Jo.

Before long they had made their way past Big Pine and skirted along the east side of the Alabama Hills to finally arrive in the small town of Lone Pine. Jo directed Josh to Joseph's Market where they were to meet Heather.

"Before she arrives, we need to remind ourselves to be careful about what we say in front of your cousin," reminded Josh. Jo readily agreed.

They didn't have to wait long before a young woman wearing sunglasses driving a small sports car came driving in. Heather was a bit shorter than Jo with auburn hair. Josh did not believe that was her natural hair color. However, popping up her sunglasses revealed the most stunning green eyes. Jo made the introductions and they were quickly off again down the road with Jo sitting in the middle.

"Did you see that road sign, Whitney Portal? That must be the way to Mount Whitney," realized Heather.

"Yes," confirmed Jo.

"Oh, I was just reading that Lone Pine used to be called Los Uvas, which means "the grapes," added Heather without taking a breath.

"Wow, Heather, you seem to be on a roll this morning," commented Josh. Jo eyed him and smiled.

Turning east on Highway 178 they sped across the valley toward the rugged Inyo Mountains, and after crossing the Owens River they turned south to skirt the foothills. Immediately noticeable on the hillside above was the glaring white deposits of the Dolomite Mine, part of the overall limestone formation that included the petroglyph site.

A little further, a glittering white dry lake became visible south of their location. They told Heather this was what was left of Owens Lake. She wanted to know what happened to it. Jo informed her that it was because Los Angeles is very greedy, and very thirsty.

Jo asked Josh to slow up since their turn off was just ahead. The well-worn dirt road that departed left, wound its way up and over a hill through the sage brush. Coming to an unmarked wide spot in the road they parked and prepared to hike in.

"This is what I wanted to show you, Heather, the kind of work that I do," stated Jo. "It's just up this narrow unmarked trail."

Jo acting as their tour guide led them along the path to a nearby rock formation. Josh toted a camera along to document the significant rock symbols for Bryan to see later. Jo gave them a quick explanation of the different symbols that were etched on the rock faces including the mountain sheep motif and the functioning of the solar calendar.

"This is interesting, but I don't see how you put up with the dirt and all this heat, it's so hot," commented Heather.

"It does, and other things too, but it's the discovery of new things that keeps me going," explained Jo.

When it came to the 'upright sun' and the Kufic silver mark along with the stick figure having a pick, Jo pointed to these giving Josh a meaningful glance when doing so.

Josh snapped various pictures that included Heather and Jo. He had to keep reminding Heather to smile. Hiking back to the truck they refreshed themselves and got back on the road.

The route that led to Cerro Gordo was called The Yellow Grade Road due to the color of the minerals found along the route. The year of its construction was 1868. It wound its way up through the hills and the higher canyons some seven and a half miles to arrive at the mining site. The road was narrow in places causing Heather to feel a little anxious.

"Josh, you drive with such confidence," declared Heather. "I would probably panic if I had to drive."

"Actually, this is not as bad as some," downplayed Josh.

"I noticed that about Bryan too, you guys drive like you know where you are going even though you've never been there before," echoed Jo.

Josh smiled. "Look, at that formation up ahead," he pointed.

"It's all crunched up, how strange," commented Heather.

"Looks like black limestone or something," thought Jo.

On some of the curves it was possible to look back down into the playa of Owen's Valley many miles away. Further along more and more shafts and prospects began to show up. Rounding the corner of a truncated bluff, Cerro Gordo's buildings and all the mining facilities came into view sitting restfully at the base of Cerro Gordo Peak.

"This must have been some big time operation in its day," summized Jo.

"There is almost no spot on this mountain that was left undisturbed," observed Josh.

Approaching the weathered buildings, a historical plaque came into view. Parking in a flat area across from the main buildings they walked over to read the historical narrative.

Cerro Gordo in Spanish meant "Fat Hill" and was first worked by Mexican prospectors in 1865. The site is 8,500 feet above sea level; and was the scene of the richest silver mine in California. At its peak there was a population of 3,000, which rivaled the pre-Los Angeles cow town called "El Pueblo." Silver bullion was shipped primarily by wagon, and for a short time by railroad, and even by two ferry boats that crossed the once-upon-a-time blue waters of Lake Owens.

"Look at this," pointed Josh. "It took 8 tons of charcoal to smelt twenty five tons of galena sulphate and carbonate lead ores."

"What is so significant about that?" asked Jo.

"You know how much wood it would have taken to produce just one ton of charcoal?" he asked in return.

"Lot's," answered Heather.

"They must have cut down every tree within fifty miles," reasoned Josh.

"There are quite a few other ruins of kilns scattered through out the district," recalled Jo.

Walking back toward the buildings a sign directed all visitors to check in with the caretaker at the hotel. Apparently the American Hotel which was originally built in 1871 was restored in recent years. Though restored the two-story structure retained its rustic nature. Josh opened the door for the girls, but no one was in the small lobby area. The walls and shelves were full of mining pictures and memorabilia. Josh called out but there was no answer. He then heard a noise from the adjoining room.

"Hello!" Josh spoke up again approaching a doorway to the left. He spotted an older man with a slender build working at the far end of the bar. Josh realized this was a saloon. Stepping into the room he caught his attention.

"Howdy, I didn't hear you come in," he responded. "I'm Mike."

"This is Jo and Heather," introduced Josh. "And I'm Josh."

"Visiting for the day?" asked Mike.

"Yeah, we were curious about Cerro Gordo and came up to look around," answered Jo.

"Jo has been working just down the hill at the petroglyph site," informed Josh.

"Oh yes, but I'm afraid you won't find anything like that up here. The whole mountain has been thoroughly worked over," replied Mike.

"This was a saloon, wasn't it?" asked Heather.

"Yes, and it still is. There are 156 bullet holes in the floor to prove it," he answered.

"Miners' life must have been pretty wild," commented Jo.

"That it was," he agreed.

"We like to look around if that's alright?" asked Josh.

"By all means knock yourself out. Just watch your step," warned Mike.

Walking out Heather eyed the painting of a nude behind the bar. Josh paused to look at what Heather was looking at. Jo stepped between Josh and the painting, blocking his view.

"Eyes forward, mister," insisted Jo.

Mike laughed. "Oh, by the way, we offer a wedding package, honeymoon suite, the whole works," he called out after them.

"Okay," laughed Josh. "We'll keep that in mind."

"You wouldn't seriously consider that?" objected Heather.

"No-o, of course not," he replied after stepping outside.

They continued on around to the other buildings that were being maintained in various stages of arrested decay. One of the larger buildings was a barracks. Further on a smaller structure in ruins proved to be the assayer's office.

Look at this," spoke up Jo standing next door in front of the remnants of a small wooden building.

"What do you see?" asked Heather. "The sign says 'Lola's Palace of Pleasure,' " she read.

"How convenient is that?" remarked Josh.

"No comment," replied Jo realizing what it was.

Josh looked up at the peak behind the mines and observed a major communications array stationed on top. The seeking of riches at this location had turned a corner he thought to himself.

Before leaving they dined heartily on Jo's well prepared picnic lunch as they sat in a shady spot with a view.

"So, Heather, what are you doing with yourself this summer?" asked Josh.

"Learning sign language," she replied.

"Really, is there a big need for that?" he asked.

"Absolutely, more and more all the time."

"What I find interesting about sign lanuage is the cleverness of the signs that are used," commented Jo.

"Do you have to spell out everything with your hands? he asked.

"No, it's not quite like that," answered Heather. "There are hand symbols for expressing words and complete thoughts."

"That makes sense. Not to change the subject, but Jo, weren't you talking about visiting a place called Little Lake, today?" asked Josh.

"Yes, it could be the icing on the cake so to speak," thought Jo.

"How can you guys think about food after such a big lunch?" questioned Heather.

"That is true, I might fall asleep on the road down the hill," commented Josh yawning. "Does anyone else want to drive?"

"No way!" they responded.

"Okay," he chuckled. "Jo, thank you for a nice lunch. It was worth the price of admission."

"Thank you kind sir for noticing," she replied.

Heather felt comfortable enough to take a turn sitting in the middle on the trip back down the hill. On the way a view of Owens Lake appeared and disappeared as they wound their way back and forth down the canyons.

"How is Bryan doing?" asked Jo in a kind of subdued tone looking out towards the infinite sea of mountain peaks.

"Oh! What is that?" interrupted Heather pointing off to their left on a knoll.

"That's probably one of the towers for the Salt Tram," thought Josh.

"Oh yeah," she realized recalling a picture in the lobby of the Hotel.

"Bryan is doing fine," finally reported Josh. "He has been busy helping his dad, and getting started on his new house."

"How is Tammy?" asked Jo in a matter-of-fact tone.

"Very busy, I think she has bit off too much in my opinion," he answered.

"What do you mean?"

"As you know she has been pursuing a degree at Berkeley. But I believe it's gotten to be more involved than she first thought. Just between us, I think Bryan is getting a little frustrated. Originally, it was Bryan who wouldn't commit to a relationship, but now it seems that Tammy is the one delaying. I am not saying its intentional or anything." explained Josh.

"Women have the right to do things for themselves too you know," commented Jo.

"True, but there's nothing better than being barefoot and pregnant is there?" teased Josh. "Ow!" was his reaction after Heather elbowed him.

"That goes for me too," added Jo. "You're getting too personal."

93

"I was kidding," he laughed. "But you're right, I shouldn't have said that."

The girls made no reply giving him the silent treatment. Josh was enjoying a restfull moment from the constant jibber-jabber of the girls.

Finally reaching the bottom of the Yellow Grade they headed south on Highway 136 passing by the junction of Highway 190 which led into Death Valley. Continuing on their course skirting along the east side of Owen's lake they drove through a small whistle stop on US 395 called Olancha. A service station and a store that advertised beef jerky made up the bulk of the town.

Why was there so many places in the desert that sold jerky? Josh wondered. Was there some sinister plot behind that? He silently chuckled to himself.

"Look at that cloud," pointed Heather. "It's like spun glass."

"They're called lenticulars," informed Josh.

"That's a strange term," she replied.

"Lens-shaped clouds are caused by strong upper level winds," he explained.

"I think I like spunticular better," Heather said matter of fact, causing everyone to laugh.

Josh didn't mind being with the girls, but he realized he really missed Bryan's company. He reflected on the years that they grew up together and the many adventures they had. Maybe it was his ingenuity that always kept him interested. The pursuit of Captain Camino had taken them throughout the Sierra Nevada and now into the vast Mojave Desert. Perhaps someday they would be down in the Sea of Cortez diving for clues. That thought seemed refreshing to him as hot as it was.

Suddenly the highway passed over a large concrete-lined aqueduct that dog-legged to the east and continued south.

"What was that?" asked Josh.

"Southern California's water supply," informed Jo.

"Oh, okay," he realized. "The infamous leach of the Sierra Nevada."

"What's that supposed to mean?" asked Heather.

"It's just that they have bled the eastern Sierra dry over the years. You probably have heard the phrase 'Save Mono Lake.' Just look at Owen's Lake back there, to name another."

"True, but Mono Lake has been partially restored," defended Jo.

"Yes, but just partially," he emphasized.

"You're sounding an awful like Bryan," pointed out Jo.

"Who is this, Byran? When do I get to meet him?" asked Heather.

"I don't know. I reckon you would have to go through a security check, or something," answered Josh.

"What-t?" whined Heather. "You have my interest peaked. You guys talk about him like, he's some kind of national treasure or something."

"Well, maybe not quite that extraordinary," commented Jo. He is human and in some ways vunerable," she reflected.

Passing a large red volcanic cone on their left, a sign indicated they had reached Little Lake. On the same side of the road along a reddish-brown volcanic bluff was a shallow lake that paralelled it for quite some distance. Apparently, this was Little Lake. It was about a quarter mile wide and a mile long.

"According to my site plan there should be a driveway coming up on our left very quickly now," informed Jo.

"This could be it," thought Josh activating the turn signal.

A sign indicated that they were now entering into a private duck refuge.

"Follow the dirt road along the lake to the south end where there should be a place to park," continued Jo.

A number of vacant picnic tables were grouped together under a stand of small trees near the undeveloped parking area. The hot sun beared down on them as they followed a trail to an area along the bluff just south of the lake. Hats, water, and the map were prerequisites for the hike. The angle of the sun eliminated all shadows along the walls of the red volcanic bluff making it easy for them to pick out any inscriptions.

"I hope it's not much further; its just plain cooking out here," complained Heather.

"Not much further," encouraged Jo.

After several hundred more feet they spotted the first of the petroglyph panels just above a short talus slope.

"What we're looking for should be in this first panel," believed Jo studying the site plan.

"Let's go up and take a look, but keep an eye out for critters," warned Josh.

"What inscription are we looking for?" asked Heather.

"The assayer's rectangle, remember …," reminded Jo.

"These rock faces are like natural chalk boards so to speak," commented Josh.

"Without the chalk," agreed Jo. "Actually, stone on stone."

"Somebody had to have a serious notion about these things to put in all the work to inscribe them," stated Josh.

"Over here, you guys, I think I've found what you are looking for," called out Heather from further down the cliff.

Stumbling across the talus slope they neared Heather's location which was well removed from the main panel of glyphs.

"Yes, yes and yes, all the elements are here. This is the silver glyph that matches the one at the Swansea site," verified Jo. "Very good, Heather," she commended.

From that location their gaze wandered up the rock face to a section of the cliff that angled to the right, where they saw something even more familiar. Jo and Josh's eyes met with the simultaneous realization that here again was something of significance. It was the 'upright sun,' facing east. This was definitely a change in direction. Two rays radiating from the sun were thought to indicate how many days journey it was to the next site. While Heather continued looking around the corner they took pictures of both glyphs.

"Jo, I want you to pose for me," stated Josh as he fiddled with his camera.

"What are you saying?" she questioned.

Josh laughed. "No, I'm not shooting a swimsuit edition. But stand under the sun and hold your arm and cup the sun in your hand, like this," he demonstrated.

"Like this?"

"Yeah. Hold up your arm a little higher. Now smile. Good, that'll be great for our scrapbook," informed Josh.

"You want me to take your picture?" she offered.

"No-o, I'm not as pretty."

Jo thought about that comment for a moment. "Josh, there is one more glyph I would like to look at before we go," she requested.

"It's getting kind of late. Can we find it quick?"

"Yes, I believe we can. It shouldn't be too much further," encouraged Jo.

"What is it we're looking for?" he asked.

"It's officially called the Desert Flood Panel, but more commonly just the 'Flood Glyph,' " answered Jo.

"Flood?" questioned Josh.

"Yes, it is one of the great mysteries of the desert," she added.

"Heather! We're moving on," called out Josh.

"We need to find a large boulder that has a unique cluster of drawings," disclosed Jo as they scrambled down the slope.

Heather soon joined them as they searched the immediate area away from the volcanic bluff among the scattered outcroppings and boulders.

"Jo! Come and look at this one," called out Heather after a few minutes.

"Be right there," replied Jo from some distance away. Walking in that direction she inspected the boulders and ledges on the way.

"Heather! How do you do it? You really have a knack for finding these panels," stated Jo realizing she had indeed found it. Josh soon joined them. It was located on a very large boulder that commanded a view of the Lake. The rock art was not at ground level, but at about ten feet up on the vertical face of the boulder.

"This is supposed to be between 500 and 1,500 years old," informed Jo.

"What are these drawings depicting?" asked Heather.

"I have my little cheat sheet here and can decipher the symbols, but I want you guys to tell me what the story is," she challenged.

"Oka-ay, but no guarantees," agreed Josh. Heather just shook her head.

Jo began by pointing out, "Look this is a depiction of extensive rain leading to a great flood with no land visible anywhere. Notice the rake-like symbol that represented rain. Next, the 'Vessel Glyph' shows a stick figure on a boat and the waves are depicted right here," she pointed out.

"What's that just above the boat?" asked Heather.

"That's the 'Bird Glyph.' Apparently, there is some significance with a bird or birds, the man, and the boat. And finally, on the left over here is what is called the 'Dispersion Glyph,' where from a location things began to spread out again," explained Jo.

"I think I know this one," thought Josh. "Heather, what do think?" he asked.

"I don't know," she shrugged.

"This is very similar to Noah and the Flood," Josh answered.

"Correct!" replied Jo. "It is interesting that most researchers ignore the Biblical account when interpreting ancient rock art, but this is a perfect match."

"This is interesting," thought Josh. "So, that means it must have been handed down through the generations."

"When people migrated across the 'land bridge' from Asia to this continent they must have carried these accounts with them," added Heather.

"It's safe to say this is pretty unique," concluded Jo.

"We better get going," reminded Josh checking his watch.

Hiking back to the parking area they were soon on the road returning to Lone Pine recounting the day's discoveries. Heather thanked Jo for inviting her up for 'a day in the sun' and their mini-adventure.

"Josh, it was nice meeting you despite your comment about being barefoot and pregnant," she stated.

"Likewise, Heather. I hope everything works out for you in the sign language field," he smiled.

Jo and Josh waved to her as she departed in her sports car headed out of the parking lot to disappear down the street.

"Well Jo, shall we head home?" asked Josh.

"Home? And where is that?" she asked in a whimizical kind of way getting into the passenager side of the pickup.

"The ranger station, then to Columbia, I guess."

"You can't go all the way home tonight," objected Jo.

"Well, I don't know what else to do, except to get a room for the night in Bishop or something," he answered.

"No-o, maybe you can catch a few winks in one of the extra bunks. I'm sure the others won't mind. There is hardly anyone there during the weekend anyway," she suggested.

"Aren't you going home this weekend?"

"Actually, I haven't even thought about it," realized Jo. "But no, it wouldn't be worth it. There isn't enough time."

"How about dinner then? We can talk about the sun symbol with the two rays we found at Little Lake, and what may lay ahead," suggested Josh.

"That's a nice idea," she responded.

9

INTO THE GREAT MOJAVE

Two days had passed and Josh had not heard from Bryan or Tammy. This in itself was not unusual, but he was anxious to share what they had discovered over the weekend. Stopping by the Anderson's he was met with a bit of a shock. Bryan had come and gone. Apparently, he and Tammy had a falling out. When Bryan returned home, he packed up a few things and had taken off for parts unknown. His parents were quite concerned.

Josh was perplexed on what to do. Usually, Bryan was there to figure things out. He left no message, and no way to contact him. Talking with Tammy's mother didn't help either. Tammy had called and told her about the argument they had over the special grant that she had received. Also that Bryan was quite upset and had stalked out. Apparently, she had tried calling Bryan, but he had already left.

Suddenly, Josh felt all alone. His closest friend had now vanished. Where could he have gone? Out in the desert, or maybe Bishop? I know, I'll call Jo and see if she has seen or heard from him, he thought. In some ways he was drawn to Jo, but could he depend on her? Bryan seemed to put full trust in her. Hopefully, she knows something as to his whereabouts. He just wanted to find Bryan before he did something foolish. So he determined to call her that evening at the ranger barracks.

"Josh? What a surprise to be hearing from you so soon. I know you just miss me, right?" she teased after hearing that it was Josh calling. He didn't reply to that. "Is everything okay?" asked Jo.

"Actually, no," Josh answered.

"What happened?" she asked.

"Bryan and Tammy have broken up, and he has disappeared. Have you seen or heard from him?" he inquired.

"Oh no! I haven't. You're fooling me," answered Jo in disbelief.

"I'm afraid not," replied Josh. "Everything has fallen apart."

"I suspect he has headed for the desert," he revealed. "We need to find him before he does something crazy."

"How are we going to find him?"

"By pursuing the clues ourselves, maybe only the way to catch up with him," suggested Josh. "I have no doubt he is out there already looking for Camino's trail. Bryan feels hurt and I know he will just isolate himself."

Wow, this is all kind of sudden," replied Jo trying to think of what she could do. "Okay, let me figure something out. I have copies of the maps and documents here. Plus, I think this Friday is my day off," she realized.

"I have two concrete pours scheduled for this week," stated Josh. "I could be there Friday if I hustle."

"Okay, let's try for that," Jo agreed. "Call me Thursday to verify."

After hanging up, it all began to sink in. How should she feel about Bryan and Tammy splitting up? One part of her thought it was good. But on the other hand she had to consider Bryan's and Tammy's happiness.

Josh felt good about the call. He was glad Jo was taking the lead since she was up to speed on the map and the clues. All he had to do was get his work completed by Thursday. Easy said, but in reality making one pour and setting the forms on another would keep him working until dark. Then he would make the second pour early in the morning.

Jo pondered their next move. From Little Lake it was a two day journey on foot or horseback to the east. Digging out the Geological Survey maps that covered the area from Little Lake to the east she measured off twenty miles to see about where it would land.

"Oh my goodness!" she exclaimed. "This could definitely put Bryan in danger if he tries venturing out there."

The spot was located right in the heart of the China Lake Naval Weapons Restricted Area. But something on the map just north of her scaled distance was something that caught her eye.

"Little Petroglyph Canyon," read off Jo. "Another glyph cluster," she realized.

That night she went to bed pondering what to do and fell asleep thinking that this might slow Bryan down and give them an opportunity to catch up. It might be a good thing. At the same time she feared for Bryan. Additionally, he was not aware of the Little Lake discovery and the change in direction. Unless he would guesstimate this departure on Camino's map himself.

Next day Rick came to the rescue having heard of Little Petroglyph Canyon and two or three other sites in that vicinity. They were part of the Coso Volcanic Field which included some of the most extensive and best preserved glyphs in North America. Matter of fact there were established tours arranged under the direction of the Navy Base. The tours he believed originated at the Maturango Museum in Ridgecrest.

Jo made a phone call late in the afternoon to inquire about the guided field trip and to her surprise was able to reserve two spots on the tour that very Saturday. This was basically the end of the spring tour season as the heat would soon become unbearable.

After hanging up she was kind of impressed with herself. But, in reality if Josh hadn't called when he did or if Rick had no knowledge of the petroglyphs or the tour, they would have missed out on accessing that area until fall time. So with a more humble opinion of herself Jo went about taking care of more mundane matters.

She couldn't wait for Josh to call so she could share the good news. Jo kept watching the time as it dragged on. Concerning Bryan she had an idea to bounce off Josh as well.

Finally, he called. It was kind of late in the evening. Josh had worked late to put the finish on a slab of concrete. Jo could tell by his voice that he was tired.

"Do we have a place to go?" he asked.

"Yes, and it's all arranged," informed Jo.

"Picnic lunch and all?" asked Josh.

"You must be hungry," she laughed. "And yes, I'll fix something. But we have to be in Ridgecrest no later than eight Saturday morning to go on a tour into the China Lakes Weapons Center to look at our next glyph site."

"Wow, China Lake?" he questioned.

"Yes-s. You don't have a police record or anything, do you?" she asked.

"No, I sure don't," Josh replied.

"Great, then we are good to go," clarified Jo. "We should have no problems with the security check. There is one thing you could do on the way down though," she stated.

"Not shopping!" he protested.

"No," she laughed. "You know that café in Bridgeport that Bryan used to frequent?"

"Yeah, I think so. It's the one just as you come into town on the right," recalled Josh.

"Yes, that's the one. Go in there and ask for a waitress by the name of Katie. Ask her if she has seen Bryan in the last three or four days," suggested Jo.

"That's a great idea. You are really getting into this detective business," he commended.

"Frankly, I'm wondering what I've gotten myself into," Jo confessed. "I'll see you tomorrow and drive careful," she finalized.

Josh was happy to hear that he didn't have to leave before sunrise. He could leave midmorning and get some extra rest.

103

It was a beautiful day in the Sierra as he drove over the Pass. Everything was still green, and the sky bright blue. But it didn't seem right with all the trouble afoot. Again as he went along there were a flood of memories of his and Bryan's past adventures. What would be the outcome of this desert sojourn? He hoped they would be able to find him.

About noon, Josh rolled into Bridgeport and quickly located the café that Bryan used to frequent. He decided to go ahead have lunch there as well. Finding a corner booth he settled in, taking note of the waitresses. Initially, there seemed to be two of them wearing matching light pink uniforms. After a minute or so a dark haired woman about thirty years in age approached him. He could see that her name was Joyce by the tag on her uniform. Josh decided to go ahead and order before asking about Bryan. When his order did arrive he asked if Katie was working that day.

"Yes-s, who shall I say is asking?" she inquired.

"Tell her, Bryan's friend," he answered.

"Okay," she acknowledged.

After two or three minutes a young waitress came around the corner drying her hands.

"You know Bryan?" she asked coming up close.

"Yes, he's my best friend," confided Josh. He noticed her bright blue eyes. "Have you by any chance seen him in the last few days?"

"Matter of fact, yes. It must have been about four days ago," she recalled. Katie had a concerned look on her face and proceeded to sit down in the booth opposite him. "He seemed upset and somehow sad. Is he okay?"

"I don't know. He disappeared last Monday. Did he say anything that could be a clue to where he was going?" Josh further asked.

"Well, before he left he said that he may not be back again and 'you might be able to see him on the evening news,' " she remembered.

"Really?" asked Josh.

104

"Yes, and he asked me if I wanted to get married, but it wasn't like a direct proposal or anything," added Katie.

Josh shook his head. "Bryan and his fiancée broke up, and she happens to be my cousin," he explained.

"I'm sorry to hear that. He used to come in here on a regular basis and was usually upbeat and encouraging. I didn't always agree with him on some things, but he was always very nice. Matter of fact I always looked forward to seeing him. But this was not the Bryan I knew," she shared.

"Thank you for the information. I hope we can find him quickly," said Josh.

Katie stood up and put her hand on his and asked him to let her know somehow. He said he would.

On the road again, Josh reviewed what he had just learned. Bryan had indeed come through Bridgeport and no doubt was headed south into the desert. He was feeling pretty down. But what was that comment he made, "You might see him on the evening news." What did he mean by that? What did he have in mind? Was he going to make a move against the Feds? How could he do that? He wondered.

It was mid-afternoon when he finally rolled into Bishop. He briefly thought about the visit they had made there two years previous, when they met up with Ben Coleman's landlady.

Pulling into the Ranger Station he parked and walked over to the sidewalk and stood there for a moment looking around, wondering what he was doing here. Three months ago he knew nothing about Jo, petroglyphs, or the Mojave Desert. What was the common thread in all of this? Bryan and the mystery of Captain Camino continued to drive this whole scenario. He reminded himself that Bryan was the reason he was here.

Josh inquired at the door for Jo and she quickly came out to greet him.

"I can tell this is wearing on you," observed Jo.

"Yeah, this whole thing has me baffled and worried."

"I agree. Did you get to talk to Katie?" she asked.

"Yes, Bryan did stop at the café in Bridgeport and it sounds like he was pretty depressed. He also made some comment about making a big splash on the media or something," informed Josh.

"I wonder what he meant by that," pondered Jo. "So, there is a good chance he is somewhere down here."

"I believe that is the case," he concurred.

"We have our work cut out for us," she commented. "Oh, by the way, I have a bunk reserved for you on the men's side. Grab your stuff and put it in the barracks. Then meet me in the dining room and you can tell me more about Bryan and Tammy."

"And I want to hear about this China Lake thing," stated Josh.

Once Josh brought his gear in and got situated he made his way around the corner to find the cafeteria. He found Jo waiting at a table with a folded map sitting to one side. Josh plunked down on the opposite side from her.

Resting her elbows on the table she leaned her head toward him. "Now tell me, what is going on with Bryan and Tammy?" she asked.

"You don't have any ulterior reasons for asking do you?" he inquired.

"No, I just want to know!" she begged.

Josh shared what few details he had come to learn from Bryan's parents and Tammy's mother. The disagreement from what he could gather was over an opportunity for Tammy to study abroad under a grant of some kind.

"Umm, there must be more to it. I don't think that in itself would cause such a meltdown," commented Jo.

Josh shrugged his shoulders not knowing what more could be behind it.

Jo then filled him in on what to expect on their trip to Ridgecrest the following morning. She also mentioned that one of the girls in the office was willing to help on the gas if they could take her to Ridgecrest.

"That should be okay," he replied, "as long as she doesn't bite."

"You are so funny," she laughed.

"You know this is kind of strange, meeting you here, going places, and doing things. Like dating, but different," stated Josh.

"Yeah, I guess. You mean like we've been washed up together on some remote beach after a shipwreck?" she asked wondering what Josh was really thinking.

"I'm not saying we are victims of circumstance, but if I had to choose, there is no one else I would rather do this with," replied Josh.

Early the next day, Margaret, who was going to join them, arrived early. On the way they got to hear about her duties at the office and her family who lived in Ridgecrest.

Jo suggested they stop at places along the route to inquire if anyone had seen Bryan or his vehicle in the last four or five days.

One business had surveillance tapes that viewed the parking lot and the adjacent highway for the previous seven days. Due to the time constraint they informed the store manager they would have to come back.

"That's pretty smart of you to ask about the camera tapes," stated Josh as they climbed back into the pickup. "You always seem to know all the right questions to ask."

"It was just a thought," she dismissed.

Forty-five minutes later they finally rolled into the unremarkable town of Ridgecrest that laid low in the bottom of Indian Wells Valley. Scattered palms seemed to be the one thing that accented all the neighborhoods that they passed through. Margaret directed them down one of the main avenues and then onto a side street. Thanking them, she gave them directions to the Museum.

The Maturango Museum at the north end of town was quite easy to find. Its brown architecture allowed it to meld right in with the desert background. Arriving a few minutes early gave them an opportunity to glance around the Museum's various exhibits, displaying natural and cultural depictions of life in the northern Mojave Desert. Stuffed coyotes and owls peered down on them from the tops of the display cases.

The people who had come for the tour assembled in a large side room as they waited for the guide to make an appearance.

"It's so nice to see a young couple like yourselves coming out on this tour," commended a middle-aged woman.

"Yes, thank you," answered Josh standing there with his arms folded. "The only problem is I don't think Jo loves me anymore. She said we were on the rocks and wanted to come out and show me."

"Josh! That's not true," protested Jo kind of embarrassed.

Josh couldn't hold a straight face any longer and began laughing.

The woman looked at Josh, then at Jo, and back again to Josh. "Oh-h, I think we have a major joker in the crowd today," she chuckled.

"Yes, more than I had realized," added Jo.

"We'll have to keep an eye on this one," commented the lady.

"I think so-o," agreed Jo.

At that moment the tour guide and his assistant came in. They introduced themselves and reviewed the guidelines that everyone would have to abide by, since they were entering a military reservation. They all received identification badges that would have to be worn at all times. Josh learned that an exhaustive background check had been done on each one of them, which included the verifying of all the personal information provided on the application. Josh realized he had not filled out an application. Jo had made all the arrangements.

A caravan of several cars and pickups collected behind the tour guides vehicle in the parking lot. Soon they were meandering their way through the local streets to eventually come out into the open desert north of town.

Within a short distance the caravan reached the main security gate for the Navy Base. A large sign above the gateway clearly designated this as the China Lake Naval Weapons Center.

Numerous warning signs were posted on the approach to the entrance. One such sign mentioned "deadly force" may be used against anyone trespassing without proper clearance. Guards with side arms checked everyone's identity badges and made vehicle searches. This made Josh a little nervous. Jo didn't seem to be bothered at all.

Once through the gate the caravan passed a number of buildings following a paved road that led north across the desert floor toward the mountains.

"Jo, how is it that I was able to pass their security background check without making out an application?" asked Josh.

"Since I work for the Government I do have a little clout," she explained.

"Yeah, but they have no idea who I am. I could be a spy from some foreign power," he stated.

"Josh, you ask too many questions. I trust you and I want you to trust me. There are some things I can't tell you right now," replied Jo.

Josh was a little taken back by her statement. Who was she in reality?

After fifteen miles the pavement ended near a dry lake bed and from there a well-graded dirt road led northeasterly up into the canyons.

Along the way were a number of odd-shaped objects and structures that made them wonder what the military was testing out here. Suddenly, just ahead of them two jets flying extremely low rocketed across the roadway at an excessive speed, and quickly disappeared out of sight.

The road grew rocky as the caravan entered a rugged canyon characterized by a brownish-red volcanic landscape. Jostling their way for several miles they finally came to a parking area that was situated below the beginning of a major side canyon.

"I guess we're here," announced Josh.

Shouldering their packs they all gathered at the end of the parking area where the trail head began. The group was once again reminded not to stray, but to stay within the confines of the Canyon. Someone in the front of the crowd pointed toward something moving in the brush not far away.

"Oh yes," spoke up the guide. "There are wild mustangs running loose on this preserve. As long as you stick in a group they shouldn't pose a danger," he explained.

A last check was made on trail essentials such as hats and water. Finally, they were off single-file up the rocky trail.

It wasn't long before they had made their way up the moderate slope to enter Little Petroglyph Canyon, which originally was called Renegade Canyon. Almost immediately the group began seeing a maze of Native American inscriptions on both sides of the canyon. The guide emphasized that here in the Coso Range was one of the most extensive collections of ancient rock art in the world, not only in diversity but in number.

The group stopped at predetermined locations so the guide and his assistant could explain the significance of certain motifs. Prominent as with other sites was the hunting theme depicted by bighorn sheep being pursued and ambushed by hunters. The drawings showed the use of the bow and arrow, long darts, and the atlatl, which was some form of hand-held catapult device that would launch spears. Some images showed what some believed to be mythological figures that had oversight of the hunt, as well as bountiful plant resources, and the cycle of life. On certain panels, group dancing was shown with the participants holding hands and wearing feathered headdresses. Also captured on rock were mountain lions and dogs. All of this stirred everyone's imagination about the people who had inhabited the Cosos centuries in the past and the life they lived.

After a while they were allowed to explore on their own up to the point where a security fence was installed. The guides walked about answering questions and pointing out things to the different groups of hikers.

"Okay," spoke up Jo. "Here's our chance."

"What side would you like?" asked Josh.

"I'll take the left," chose Jo.

Josh hustled across to the opposite side and quickly worked his way up through the pockets of inscriptions and panel collections. Almost immediately he caught sight of a curiosity of stones encircling a small basin of sand. Josh called Jo over to ask her about it.

"That was quick," she remarked working her way over.

"I didn't find anything yet, but I was curious about this," pointed Josh.

"Oh, this is called a tinajas. It's a natural depression for holding water. Thunderstorms would replenish the water in them. The sand would trap the water so it would not evaporate so easily," explained Jo.

"Oh, okay," replied Josh. "Sorry for disturbing you."

"Yeah, don't let it happen again," teased Jo.

The north wall along where Jo was working was exceedingly hot. Even with a wide-brimmed hat it was beginning to affect her. She was guzzling water faster than normal and feeling a little faint.

Josh was well ahead of all the visitors when he first spotted the fence and a sign further up the draw. After a half hour or so he reached the fence, but did not find the inscription they were looking for. Glancing back down he could see that Jo was still a ways back.

The sign mounted on the fence declared that no access beyond this point was allowed. He noticed that this was pretty much the high point with the canyon falling off to the east. Beyond the fence Josh thought he spotted another tinajas or whatever it was called, and an odd looking column of rock behind it.

When Jo finally caught up with him, she did not look good. "Are you okay?" he asked.

"I think I'm a bit dehydrated," she answered. "Do you have any water left?"

"Yes I do. But you'll have to put your lips on mine," answered Josh handing her the canteen.

"What? If I didn't know any better I would think you are flirting with me."

"Good thing you know better," he stated in a matter of fact tone.

"Thank you, that's a life saver," she said returning the canteen to him.

"Do you happen to have your field glasses with you?" asked Josh.

"I do indeed," replied Jo. "Did you see something?"

"Beyond the fence, right at the pass is one of those tin-ajas things and may be something else," he pointed. Taking the glasses he focused on what appeared to be a stone basin against the canyon wall. Looking up from there a realization struck him. "This is where Bryan would normally have an epiphany," he shared.

"What are you talking about?" she asked.

"Three years ago when we were following Camino's clues we were stumped until Bryan realized the significance of the 'sun' symbol on the cliff wall above a pool of water," explained Josh.

"Let me see those glasses," demanded Jo. "You're right, it's on that spire of rock standing above the tinajas," she confirmed.

"How many rays on the sun?" he asked.

"A-ah, looks like four this time," answered Jo. "And may be something more," she added.

"What?"

"An owl's face, if I'm not mistaken."

10

DOG NAMED TRAMP

Driven by frustration or by a madness he did not fully understand, Bryan wasn't sure how many days it had been since he left home. He had received information that Josh and Jo had traced Camino's trail to about thirty miles west of his location. They apparently had turned the corner as shown on the map. His objective was to find what was next depicted on the map as a bird head or a helmet.

Bryan situated himself northeast of Trona and east of the Slate Range nearing the south end of Death Valley. The impressive Panamint Range loomed up running north of his position with the eleven thousand foot Telescope Peak being the crown jewel in this western wall of Death Valley.

All that was left of the old mining town of Ballarat was a number of old buildings and scattered ruins. The population had been reduced to only two individuals who ran the small general store. It was here that he bought needed supplies and received some insight on the surrounding area. Bryan heard all about the local legend, Seldom Seen Slim, the last of the old miners that frequented the west flank of Death Valley.

He inquired about any petroglyph sites in the immediate area. The only ones that they were aware of were to be found in the Naval Test Range in the Cosos or within Death Valley National Park itself.

With the Military Test Range to the south and the National Park to the east there wasn't much territory left that wasn't under the watchful eye of the Government. However, it was the military area that posed the real problem if he had to enter it. His first inclination was to check out the western approach of the Panamint Range then go inland.

Josh just about fell out of his chair after hearing an evening news report. "Underground explosions and cave-ins reported near the historic Alamo site have officials in an uproar," stated a news correspondent.

"What? What?" he stammered.

"Authorities are looking for a woman and also two male accomplices who reportedly rented equipment, including ground penetrating radar, and hired laborers to access manholes and underground tunnels very close to the main entrance to the Alamo. For what purpose no one knows. As you look behind me you can see the large sinkholes that have developed," continued the reporter who was at the scene.

Josh glanced at the clock on the wall. He thought he had better call Jo right away. It was still early evening and she should be off work. As usual it took a minute or so for her to be found.

"Hello, Josh?" she answered with kind of a fondness in her voice.

"Yes, I'm sorry for disturbing you, but have you heard the news?" he asked.

"News? No, is it about Bryan?" she asked.

"No, there have been huge explosions outside of the Alamo. Large sinkholes have developed out where the second well was located," Josh expounded.

"Wow, when did this happen?"

"A couple of days ago, while we were traveling or out on the desert," answered Josh.

"Any leads in who they were?" she asked.

"Not yet," replied Josh.

"Hmm, this is baffling. Do we really know where Tammy is?" questioned Jo.

"Now wait a minute, you're not suggesting that Tammy is behind all this?"

"Well, has anybody been able to contact her since she left?"

"No, not that I'm aware of, but that's not Tammy, she wouldn't do that," he answered.

"There must be something big going down. A tall woman was here the day we went down to China Lake asking questions about us," revealed Jo.

"What was her description?"

"From what I was told she was dressed in a dark suit, had auburn hair, wore sunglasses, and showed credentials that identified her as an FBI agent," she replied.

"FBI?"

"Yes, but I know for a fact she wasn't," stated Jo.

"And how do you know that? It's not the first time we've been investigated you know," questioned Josh.

"Well, I'm just convinced that she wasn't," was her contention. "Oh, by the way, I went and looked at the tapes from the mini-mart."

"Anything to report?"

"No, but he could have slipped through after dark or went another way," she replied.

"Jo, I'll try to contact Tammy and see if she will help us," stated Josh.

"I hope you can, unless she has switched sides on us," pondered Jo.

Just north of Ballarat, Bryan followed the natural lay of the land and ventured into Surprise Canyon. After several miles he came to Panamint City which was the site of an old silver mining operation. Ruins were scattered throughout the sage covered landscape.

Nothing here looked remarkable in any way. The mountains or the rock formations gave no hint of anything that was associated with a bird or hawk.

Traveling south of Ballarat on a rough unimproved road there was one more point of access into the Panamint Range just north of the military proving grounds. Signs at this turnoff marked this well-worn dirt road as Coyote Canyon Road and Goler Wash.

The road up Goler Wash was rough and basically nonexistent in places. Sections were layered in gravel or were right down on bedrock. The Wash varied from twenty to one hundred feet in width bound by fiery red walls. The canyon wound its way up into the mountains, giving no place for Bryan to get a view of the surrounding territory.

A bit further the Wash began to open up and a fairly new sign indicated he was entering Death Valley National Park. A fork of the primitive road veered right and continued to follow Goler Wash to an obvious dead-end.

On the main road a rustic wooden sign showed that Mengel Pass was another fourteen miles. It wasn't long before he arrived at the rugged pass. The roughest part of the rock strewn road was just below the summit.

A large stone cairn was located right in the narrow Pass. At its base was a concrete stone impressed with the name Carl Mengel 1868 – 1944. Was this some kind of burial monument he wondered?

At this point Bryan considered that he was going too far north of where Camino's trail should have passed. What to do? Bryan realized the area to the south and east of Goler Wash was where he needed to investigate. Only one problem, there was no access from this side of the Panamint Range.

There were two routes that could take him to the opposite side of the mountains. He could continue on this same course into Death Valley and down into the mountains just north of Fort Irwin.

The other option was a one hundred and fifty mile loop around the southern end of the range. There was no contest, he would continue north from Mengel Pass into Death Valley.

Next stop was Butte Valley, but first a rough section of road had to be navigated to get down off the summit. It was a slow process rolling and bumping over rocks and through gullies to finally break out into gentler slopes. It was now smooth sailing.

This ten mile long valley was lying in a north-south direction surrounded by barren mountains. But one thing that was unique to this basin was Striped Butte, a massive angular chunk of mountain rising out of the desert floor. Alternating bands of light and dark rock are what gave this monolith its name.

Curious wild burros grazed nearby on scattered sagebrush in the diminishing sun. Part way into the valley, Bryan spotted a nicely maintained cabin on a rise that overlooked the upper end of the basin. It appeared to be presently unoccupied. A small sign above the door designated this as the "Geologist's Cabin." Inside he found that it was well stocked with supplies and a few pieces of furniture that made it somewhat homey. A note on the wall made the point, that the food and supplies were available for use, but asked that something be left to compensate.

Another small handwritten sign posted on a window frame simply stated: "Watch for the face on the Butte." Someone had written just underneath in faint pencil, "during evening."

He went back out and brought a few things in to spend the night. While sitting at a table by the window he ate a simple meal and watched the lengthening shadows spread across the valley, but no face was visible yet. What an interesting place to return to someday he thought to himself.

Bryan wondered what Tammy was doing about now. He imagined her standing on some balcony looking out over the villas with a rising Spanish moon. A romantic scene no doubt, but not meant for him.

It was bad enough to break off contact with Josh and Jo, which no doubt were causing them all kinds of grief. But it was necessary so he could move about undetected. Which brought to

117

mind where was he now, as compared to their last position. Bryan dug out his photographs of his great great grandfather's map and found the one that covered the general area where he was. Comparing those with a modern map seemed to confirm that he was indeed north of the trail's guessimated alignment. In an easterly direction, the route actually appeared to dip south. On that alignment it could possibly pass into one of the military bases.

In one photograph that covered side one of the Captain's map, in the lower right hand corner was the shape of a distorted figure he had seen before, but never really scrutinized. It seemed to have no connection with anything, it was just there.

Bryan reviewed his route that would take him through the mountains down into Death Valley. It would be another hot day tomorrow, so he figured he would light out at first dawn.

Back outside again, Bryan reorganized his gear in the truck after all the jostling coming over the Pass. Turning around Bryan noticed that Striped Butte was being transformed into a porcelain white shape. The low sun was shining directly on its south face.

"Wow, this is weird. It must be the 'face,' " realized Bryan. It was a distorted grotesque head and face rising out of the earth looking towards the southeast. It was that same odd image he had seen earlier on Camino's map. Bryan went back in and pulled the photograph back out of the folder.

"I wonder if there is a connection?" he questioned. The distorted shape had that same grotesque face. Looking out the window and comparing with the map convinced him this was a match.

"So what is this telling me?" wondered Bryan. The face on the map pointed toward the bird head symbol. Could it be as simple as that, just a directional reference point?

"Okay," he realized. In his mind he envisioned the intersection of two rough alignments. Taking out a modern map of the region, Bryan drew a pencil line that projected the approximate alignment of the 'face.' Since the north-south location of Camino's trail was unknown that would equate to a broad band that extended easterly. Drawing two parallel lines across the mountains in which the trail should track, he noticed they intersected the 'face' line near the north end of Fort Irwin. This gave him confidence that he was closing in on the bird head.

As the sun prepared to set, Striped Butte once again became just a salt and pepper layered mountain sitting askew on the desert floor. That was unique. He knew it and Captain Camino had also known it.

A couple wild burros had made their way up close to the cabin flapping their ears and looking his way. "Beggars," laughed Bryan. Looking through his grub sack he came up with a couple of soft apples. Stepping outside he threw each one an apple. They snatched up their prize and trotted off.

It was so quiet. The only thing stirring was an occasional gust of wind. As the stars came out, Bryan decided to retire early in anticipation of starting at first light. Bryan slept like he hadn't in weeks. He felt safe hear in this remote location.

The next morning it did not take him long to pack up and get on the road. The sun was just breaking the horizon as he drove by Striped Butte. Its dull grey appearance in shadow gave no hint of the metamorphosis it went through at twilight the previous day. Soon it was small in the rearview mirror as the rocky road left the valley and ascended through a narrowing canyon to a subtle pass.

The route now turned east and began a descent into the great basin of Death Valley. After many miles he passed a sign that indicated he was now at sea level. Continuing down this road put him below sea level as he arrived at a paved two-lane highway near the ruins of Ashford Mills. From here Highway 178 ran north to Furnace Creek and the Park visitor center. In the opposite direction it abruptly turned east toward Shoshone. It was at this departure that a rough graveled road continued south into some of the most remote areas of the Park.

The mountains in the north and east were now getting hazy as the temperatures began to soar. In the narrowing valley, the route began paralleling the Amargosa River which at that time of the year was more like a creek. Stirring up the dust for twelve miles Bryan finally came to the access road he was looking for, Owl Hole Springs. The map referred to the mountains to the west of him as Cabeza de bú ho.

After traveling several miles he skirted around the southerly edge of this mountain range and passed a sign that indicated he was now leaving the National Park. There was a sliver of land about two miles wide that was neither in the Park nor in the Military Reservation. It extended west for some twenty miles at which point it stopped at the eastern boundary of China Lake. Bryan's plan was to go back in as far as he could and set up a base camp.

He kept wondering, what could be designated by a hawk or bird; and he further hoped it was not located within the Army Base. The road drifted ever closer to Fort Irwin's boundary and forked. The southern fork, marked as the Randsburg Road abruptly stopped at an unmanned gate decorated with all the usual signage indicating that deadly force would be used on trespassers. Owl Hole Springs Road continued west through no man's land.

Bryan was thinking that there had to be more clues. This was as vague as searching the dark side of the moon with a flashlight. Had he missed something?

After passing a mine access road on his right there was no more forks or turn offs for nearly ten miles. The route had angled back into the Park. Crossing numerous washes and circling back around to the northeast he found himself on top of a mountain at a microwave station. This was the end of the road.

A high chain-link fence with a barbed wire top surrounded the site. Banks of solar panels supplied power to the facility. The views from this location were tremendous; but there was nothing in the mountains shapes that stood out to him. A great basin opened up just below. Significant ranges of mountains appeared in the Military Reservation to the south.

Even at this elevation the heat was beginning to wear on him. There was nothing to be done from this location. A possibility was a side canyon about two miles back at the edge of the mountain complex. Proceeding back down Bryan found a way to transition off the road into the wash. The sand and gravels were compact and didn't present any driving difficulties. About a half mile up the wash he came to a narrow side canyon. Barring a flash flood this would be a good place to hide and set up a base camp. Shade was the primary requirement for the campsite. By tucking the pickup into the narrow channel and using some brush he was able to hide it from aerial view.

Bryan decided to wait a little while before going out on foot to do some reconnaissance. He filled in the time by setting up camp and gathering some dead brush for a possible fire. Temperatures in the desert were known to plummet at night. Finding a nice sized limb Bryan was also able to fashion a walking staff.

Time went slow waiting for the sun to drop and for shadows to start streaming across the basin. He took an early meal. Turning on a portable radio, stations from far away Las Vegas and Los Angeles drifted in and out intermittently. Bryan begrudgingly chuckled to himself after hearing a traffic report that all lanes were blocked on the 405. He felt there was no place for humor in his life at this time. Making sure the bread wrapper was secure he put the food away. The dry desert air would quickly turn the bread into a rock if it wasn't properly sealed.

Bryan got to thinking about the fact that no one knew he was out here. If he broke his leg or was snake bit, there would be no helper for him.

Not wanting to wait any longer he shouldered his pack, grabbed his staff, and began walking up the wash below the bluff. This whole mountain complex was primarily red granite which contrasted greatly with the grey-white of the gravelly wash. There were large rocks randomly scattered throughout the wash. These large stones showed signs of being periodically moved by flash floods that would roar down the canyons after a thunderstorm.

According to his map there was a dry lake bed further on towards the west. That area would have to wait until tomorrow. Additionally, there was another dry lake on the opposite side of the ridge in an adjacent basin.

After walking a while Bryan felt he had a good grasp on the land and decided to head back in the declining sun. In the opposite direction the jagged ridge above was quite reflective along its crest. He thought he heard a coyote sounding off nearby. They shouldn't bother him.

Back at camp Bryan built a small fire to heat up some food as night came on and the stars began populating the sky. Sitting by the fire reflecting on better times he thought he glimpsed something beyond the circle of light. Was it a coyote? Actually, it was not that uncommon to have a curious animal snooping around. Getting up Bryan draped a tarp across the truck bed and tied it down. He thought this would be a positive deterrent to animals that might bother him. The pickup bed would prove to be ideal for sleeping up off the ground away from scorpions and snakes.

Retiring, Bryan let the fire burn itself out. He slept lightly, as it was his first night in this strange place. At one point during the night he thought he heard growling a short distance away.

Next morning it was all quiet and nothing appeared to have been disturbed overnight. After eating a basic meal he locked up all the extra food in the cab of the truck. Bryan carefully prepared his pack for a long day including extra water. A brimmed hat and his walking staff were also essential for the day's trek.

So off again, he headed north along the bluff once more. The jagged ridge-crest above was casting spiny shadows clear across the wash. It didn't take long to pass the point to where he had scouted the day before. After a short time a moderate sized canyon opened up to his right.

It seemed to him that someone or something was following him. He had glimpses of movement from time to time. And again, just now, there was movement on a bank some distance back.

What to do? Continue on he told himself. Necessity dictated that he should at least inspect the initial part of the side canyon. It didn't take long to see what he wanted to see. There was a dry water fall and extensive granitic decomposition.

Coming out of the canyon he was startled by an animal, which ran down and across the wash. It looked like a dog or a coyote, but its markings were more like that of a dog. Standing out in the wash Bryan could see the head of the animal above the far bank watching him. This was strange; could it be a rabid animal? Whatever the case he had to push on, and at the same time be watchful.

Picking up the pace Bryan pushed further north, toward the dry lake bed. Passing a rock outcropping he suddenly turned to find a dog following him, a Border collie of all things. It stopped when he stopped; keeping its distance. He tried calling to it, but that had no effect. Pushing on, he checked every so often to find the dog maintaining that same distance.

Approaching the south end of the alkali lake bed, the dog moved from behind him to his left. Bryan intended to skirt the lake on the east side, along the granite ridge. But the dog suddenly started barking making motions to follow him. Bryan stopped and watched as he repeatedly ran and barked. There had to be a reason he is behaving this way. What's he doing out here anyway? Looking across the basin he wondered what was on the far side.

"Okay! You better not be taking me on a wild goose chase," called out Bryan.

Following the dog across the tip of the lens-shaped lake bed the hills beyond began to waver in the ever building heat waves. Half way up the slope on the far side of the basin he had to stop and take a drink. How has this dog survived out here? The dog trotted ahead and stopped periodically to wait for him. It appeared they were making a beeline for a particular ravine. It was evident that the mountains on this side were higher and had deeper canyons.

The heat was beginning to have a toll on him as they made their way into the rocky ravine. A faint trail climbed over a low ridge leading into a larger canyon. The Border collie was getting further ahead of him and finally disappeared somewhere up in the dry wash. After a few minutes he heard a bark, like a beckoning to hurry up. Coming around a large rock formation tucked in beside a cliff was a small cabin. There was a spring with a few willows growing around it near the back corner. The dog was waiting for him by the cabin.

"Well, you old tramp what is it you're going to show me?" spoke up Bryan as he approached. At the mention of the word tramp, the ears of the black and white dog perked up. "You like that name, Tramp?" Again he raised his ears. "So, that must be your name," he figured.

After removing his pack, he called out, but there was no reply. Bryan glanced in the cabin to find evidence of recent habitation. There was food on the shelves and someone's personal affects were evident. A grub sack and some of its contents were scattered about on the wooden floor. The dog had no doubt been feeding himself.

Tramp barked to get his attention, apparently to follow him once again. Leading him once again they followed a narrow trail up to an old mine entrance. The dog wanted him to go in.

"What is it?" asked Bryan.

He checked the shoring timbers at the entryway and found them sound. But further in there was a cave-in. As his eyes adjusted to the light he spotted a canvas bag half buried in the pile of rock. Pulling it out he found inside numerous small hand tools. Tramp sniffed the bag and barked. Bryan looked up at the big cavity in the ceiling and all the material that had delaminated and ended up on the floor of the tunnel. Climbing up on the pile he could only see a short distance. He called out, but there was no answer.

"This doesn't look good," commented Bryan perceiving that the dog's master may have been buried in the cave in.

Going back to the cabin he found a propane lantern and hurriedly returned to the mine. Climbing back up on the mound of earth he held the light high and looked further in. If someone was beyond the cave-in they should have been able to climb out. Finding a shovel just outside, Bryan dug into the pile where he found the canvas bag. But he really didn't want to find somebody's remains. Digging back in several feet nothing was found.

How many days had it been since this event occurred? Going back to the cabin he looked around for a journal or something. There was nothing of that nature, but there was a calendar on the wall. The days had been crossed off. The last date marked off was seven days before. Bryan stepped outside and looked down at the dog.

"Looks like, it's just you and me now."

11

THE FORTRESS

F ar as Josh could tell, Tammy had not made contact with anyone in ten days. Navigating through the phone system at the University took some time, but finally he talked with someone who said she was definitely in Barcelona, Spain, with the rest of the class. Josh asked that they relay a message to her to call home and that Bryan has been missing for almost two weeks.

He hoped she hadn't hardened her heart to the point of cutting off all contact with family and friends. This wasn't like the old Tammy they knew. Josh decided to wait a couple of days before contacting Jo and see if Tammy would respond.

Jo was in a quandary on what direction or priority she should go with. She had her position and certain goals, but now that Bryan and Josh had entered her life everything had changed. This mystery concerning Captain Camino was very intriguing. Why was she so drawn by it? Initially it may have been Bryan, but now it was more. And the way the government was using its power was wrong.

Was it justified for her to quit and drop everything and search for Bryan and follow Camino's trail fulltime? Perhaps Josh was feeling the same way. What about Bryan's mom and dad? If Tammy didn't show herself soon she was going to have do something.

In the meantime, what could she do? The trail marker at Renegade Canyon indicated that it was four days journey to the bird head as shown on the map and on the rock. What was represented by the image on the rock? Getting out the maps and a ruler she scaled what she believed to be four days distance on horseback and drew an arc with a pencil across southern Death Valley and into the Fort Irwin Military Reservation. Two mountain ranges were named, Avawatz and Cabeza de bú ho with no particular landmarks being designated.

The Avawatz range was wholly inside the military's restricted area. The other set of mountains was barely within the National Park. Jo needed to have someone translate what the Spanish name for this range was in English. So she asked around the station to see if anyone could translate it for her. It didn't take long to find one of the girls in the office who was bilingual.

"Cabeza, is head, bú ho is owl, and montaña is mountain or mountains," she was told. "It means Owl Head Mountains."

"Wow, thanks, that's going to be very helpful," replied Jo.

Walking back to the barracks she realized this must be it, the name and the location match. Matter of fact as she recalled the image on the rock did have the appearance of an owl.

Bryan wondered if this fella even knew he was on National Park land. A bag of heavy rocks in the cabin shed more light on why he was here. The clue to this was in a small blue pouch that contained a magnet. The rocks were meteorites. Apparently, he had been out on the basin searching for meteorites. Some of these could be just as valuable as gold.

A folded and taped topography map next caught his attention. It showed the two basins that made up the interior of the mountain range. Under the designation Cabeza de bú ho Montaña someone had written in Owlshead Mountains. Could that be what that phrase means? If that was true he was at the bird head, but where? The contour lines on the topo map made the unique shape of the surrounding mountains very plain. The whole mountain complex being about twenty miles across was very distinctly the head of an owl.

The spiny ridge running down the middle made up an elongated beak, separating the two basins which contained the two dry lake beds giving the appearance of eyes. He was west of the left eye. Still the question remained was there something more here, or was it enough to just recognize this land mark and move on?

At that Tramp came in with his muzzle dripping wet reminding him to check out the spring that was adjacent to the cabin. Another memory popped into his head. On the back of the land grant was something about water or supplies. Whether it was pertinent or not he would check it out later.

Priscilla Wyatt looked out over a view of hazy Las Vegas after just receiving a phone call from her brother. He was wondering if she had heard from Bryan. Her thoughts drifted back several days to when she had questioned Bryan about what it was that he was involved with. She had asked, "I know the agreement was no questions asked, but can't you just give me a little hint to what this is all about?"

"No, that is if you don't want to go to prison," he answered.

"I'll take that risk with you," she replied.

"No," was his final answer.

"When will we see you again?"

"I'll let you know. Things are complicated."

That was their last conversation. She had a phone number in which she had used to contact Bryan, giving him information he had instructed her to gather. The phone number was the last link she had with him.

Curiosity was eating her up. Where was the phone located that was connected with that number? She tried calling it again to see if anyone would pick up, but no one did. Using directory assistance Priscilla finally tracked down its location. It was a pay phone in Baker, California, a small town in the Mojave Desert. Did she dare try to involve herself?

Bryan stayed in the shade next to the old cabin till the afternoon heat passed. Thereafter he hiked up the draw and into a couple of its branches, but found nothing remarkable. Tramp stayed close by the cabin while he was gone.

"Tramp, I've been neglecting you all day, I bet you're hungry," stated Bryan.

Looking through the grub sack and on the shelves he found some canned food that he could feed to the dog. He wondered what the dog would do when it was time for him to leave.

Bryan noticed a fire ring out front that he could use to heat up some grub. There would be no going back to base camp that night. He needed to ponder his next move given the new circumstances. After gathering a couple armloads of dead brush Bryan set out to get a fire going. The wood crackled and popped seemingly putting up a protest at its demise.

The shadows of evening began to fill the canyon; and a hawk sailed overhead. What a lonely spot this was, more remote than any place he had ever been. His thoughts wandered once again, wondering about Tammy, Josh, and Jo.

After eating and completing camp chores he settled down to review the maps and the land grant to help him determine what his next move might be. His great great grandfather's map indicated that beyond the Owlshead was a series of curved wavy lines, similar to the ones found on the sun symbol itself. What did Stanley say these represented? Sand dunes, if he remembered correctly. Beyond, there were two separate distinct peaks, one east and the other southeast of that location.

Bryan's modern map showed the Dumont Sand Dunes in a valley east of these mountains. As regards the peaks, there were too many mountain ranges out in the Mojave to know which one was which.

On the back of the mystery land grant was a series of poetic phrases, that didn't seem to go with anything, or did they? The

Captain would not have put these on here unless there was a purpose in it.

The English translation for the first phrase was: "May the journey of the first part be a pleasant one. You will be well supplied on your arrival."

Dropping down to the next paragraph it said: "Let the sand sing and may you find the forests in the sky and descend to the river beneath."

The first phrase seemed to indicate this was the end of the first part of the journey. But how would someone be, "well supplied"?

The second paragraph did have something that paralleled the map, the "sands," lofty peaks, and "the river beneath." There was something about those words, "the river beneath" that struck him. This could be stunning.

The light of day was dimming making it harder for him to read. Bryan tried using the light of the fire. How peculiar. He noticed that the letters from the reverse side of the land grant were forming new words with the ones on the side he was trying to read.

Getting these written down was not going to be easy. He determined that he would have do them one at a time, since they were difficult to read. Getting a notebook and a pencil he began making a list of the Spanish words that appeared in the light. The words in the first paragraph didn't take long to list, but the second one was much more extensive.

Normally, Tammy would translate for him, but since she was out of the picture, he would use the small Spanish to English dictionary he had recently acquired. After scribbling out the English equivalent, Bryan tried to make sense of it.

"Stand, left eye, follow, shadow, early morning, and lastly—fortress," he voiced out loud. Tramp raised his head wondering what Bryan was saying. "La fortaleza is a fortress," he double checked. Bryan considered that meaning and what the reality this would imply. Was there some kind of hidden compound in these mountains? What did the clues tell him to do? Stand at the left eye. It must be the left eye of the owl, if he was thinking right. That would be right out here in the dry lake bed. Then what? Follow a shadow early in the morning. Could it be that simple? After sunrise shadows from the jagged ridge that ran down the middle of the owl's face would be cast into the hills on the west side. But since it said shadow singular, there must be one prominent shadow that would guide the way.

A translation of the words derived from the second paragraph also proved interesting. Basically, it said: "Find great black bird that sits on black sands, within an immense cage. It nests along the western rise. The shadow of its eye descends into the great abyss. "

Bryan knew this referred to the images on side two of the map, the background trace and the bird shown in the lower right hand corner. This new set of clues was for the second part of the journey. It whet his appetite for what was to come, "black sands"—placer gold.

"I had a feeling that there was something more," he told himself. But did he have to come here to figure things out? Not necessarily, but that was how the order of things did come together.

"Well, Tramp, I guess we'll need to get up early and watch for a shadow," spoke Bryan. Tramp glanced up at him, and then turned away hearing a coyote far off.

Bryan knew he was a long way from finishing the journey. The description of the land grant included what he thought to be the Colorado River, but it was only by following the map and the individual clues that the exact location would be found.

Putting out the fire he decided to turn in. Bryan made a makeshift bed inside the cabin. As the moon rose above the adjacent hills a dull light flooded the canyon. Tramp slept in the doorway and cast a shadow across the floor.

Rising before dawn Bryan felt he was ready to sprint to the finish. Rushing around to prepare a meager breakfast for himself and Tramp he watched for the first hint of daylight.

"Tramp, you want to go on a hike?" he asked. The dog was attentive to his movements as he lightened his pack and filled up on water. Bryan donned his hat and shouldered his pack and prepared to leave. "We'll be back. Let's go for a walk," he coaxed. Tramp seemed to understand that word and followed.

Marching down the canyon they were soon out into the basin. It was an easy walk on the slight downgrade in the cool of the morning. Golden sunlight was finally hitting the tops of the mountains. Reaching the edge of the dry lake bed, Bryan found a clean spot to sit and watch the shadows. Tramp laid down beside him. Pulling out his field glasses he glanced around focusing on the mountains that were just coming into the light. This reminded him of the time he was with Josh and Tammy when they had waited for the *"Door of the Sun"* to appear.

It took almost an hour for individual shadows to start distinguishing themselves. There was one that was definitely taller, striking a mountain about a half mile to his left. As the sun rose the pointed shadows descended the rugged slopes.

"Tramp, I think we need to move down and keep an eye on that one shadow," stated Bryan. "Come on let's go."

After about ten minutes they were actually able to walk in the extended shadow towards the mountain. Because of the nature of the canyons running off at odd angles, it was probably a smart idea to begin working their way to the tip of the shadow. Bryan fixed its present position to landmarks on the mountainside and set off for the nearest canyon which was just to the right of the shadow.

The rocky gorge angled off to the left, uplifting in sections. It took a bit of hiking to meander around a large accumulation of boulders before he again spotted the shadow above him on the mountain slope. There was no choice but to continue up the canyon. After several hundred yards an intersecting ravine came in on the right. It was quite steep and fairly narrow.

"Whew! I'm tired. Tramp how about you?" asked Bryan stopping to catch his breath. The dog came up to him panting.

132

The steeply sloped walls of the ravine exhibited a blue-gray base rock resembling some kind of silver bearing ore.

Resuming the vertical course it wasn't too long before they came out onto a flattened ridge with a view of the entire basin. A few clouds were now noticeable in the south. Where is the shadow he asked himself? It was no longer above him. Searching off the edge of the flat, he spotted it downhill and north of his position.

"We must be close," Bryan told himself.

Mentally rewinding the sun and the shadow, he envisioned that it would have been above and behind him. As he turned around and looked up he could see a narrow ledge protruding out of the slope.

"Tramp let's go up and take a look," waved on Bryan.

Climbing the embankment brought them to a natural bench approximately fifteen feet wide. To his left small boulders and rocks covered the ledge. Looking in the opposite direction the ledge ran for about two hundred feet and abruptly ended. Bryan walked over to one of the rocks and sat down to take a drink. Tramp had followed the ledge around the boulders to disappear out of sight. After a minute or so he reappeared.

"Tramp! You want some water?" he called out holding up the canteen. Tramp barked at him. "What is it?" He barked again. Bryan recognized his—follow me, bark. "Okay, what did you find?"

Approaching the boulders, Tramp worked his way through the rocks to a cliff face. Bryan navigated through the boulders to join him. Tramp had his nose pressed up against the wall sniffing.

"What do you smell, boy?"

Tramp scratched the wall. Bryan rubbed his hand across the surface. It seemed there were cracks and seams in the face. Some were irregular, but they did have a pattern to them. Backing up a bit he surveyed the whole wall.

"Tramp, I think you're on to something here," acknowledged Bryan.

Examining along the wall he found on the far left side a vertical displacement. A four foot section was pushed out or maybe the adjoining section had sagged in. Perhaps earth tremors had caused this. But what Bryan saw next really got him excited. It looked like a keystone. It was a flat rock that extended out of the wall. If he was right, once this stone was removed the other stones would quickly follow.

"Let's see if this is real," spoke up Bryan.

Getting a grip on it he pulled and wiggled it until suddenly it jerked loose and slid out. A modest tap caused the stone above the hole to drop down. It too was easily removed. Soon a good sized hole had opened up. Taking out his flashlight Bryan peered into a dark cave.

"This is most assuredly the Captain's work," he concluded.

Tramp sniffed the air coming out of the hole. It didn't take long to dismantle a section of the wall.

Once inside it was obvious that this was indeed a natural cave that ran in about one hundred and twenty feet. The entrance had been purposely walled off to conceal its contents, a stash of supplies just as promised. Casks of what had probably been flour, sugar and salt, and shreds of something that resembled jerky were the most identifiable. Additionally, there was a natural spring at the back of the cave. Bryan realized this is what must have attracted Tramp, the smell of water. Further to the left was gun powder, remnants of rope, picks, pulleys and even two small ore buckets. He wondered where this equipment was destined for. Catching his attention next was a couple of shredded sacks of heavy dark material that resembled sand.

"Is this what they were mining—black sand? Wow, there could be a half million dollars of gold here," he estimated.

There was wall art on both sides of the cave. A large image on the right or northern wall was clearly the owl head with the "upright sun." On the southern wall to his left was the large "black bird" standing vertically, wings extended upward, its head facing to the right. Held in its beak was the "downward sun" as portrayed on the map.

134

Stepping back outside, Bryan realized there were sections of a low wall along the outer edge of the natural bench which proved to be a catch-all for all the rocks and debris that fell from above. This was a highly defensible fortress in its day. The view was magnificent from this location. Far mountain ranges in the east wavered in the heat waves.

There were no new clues here. This was just a way-station to serve those of that time. After taking a few pictures inside and out, he stacked the rocks back up into the opening in a crude fashion.

"Tramp, we're done here. Let's go back down," informed Bryan. "We'll hang in the shade the best we can."

Despite the sun and heat Bryan wanted to press on so he could get back to base camp before dark. Some of the clouds he had seen earlier seemed to be building into thunderheads. Hiking back down to the edge of the basin, they quickly made their way back to Cabin Springs, which seemed like an appropriate name in the absence on no other.

There would be a window of opportunity after the sun went down to hike across the basin to reach base camp before dark. But first there were a couple of things he needed to wrap up. His first thought was the prospector buried in the cave-in. There were two things he should do. Inform the County Coroner anonymously of the incident and post a message by the cabin door.

But what would Tramp do when it was time to leave? He couldn't leave him here. Tramp was closely watching him pack up. If he came he would need some additional food. Finding a number of canned goods Bryan made sure the dog was seeing him pack these.

Eating and preparing to go, Bryan contemplated the serenity of this place, the rustic cabin, the spring, and an absence of any distraction. What a place to hide out and write about this whole crazy adventure. Yes! Cabin Books that could be the shingle under which all of this could be written he pondered.

Finally, it was time to go. He dreaded this moment not knowing how the dog would react. Getting his pack on Bryan turned around and faced Tramp.

"Time to go, Tramp," he told the dog.

Sitting up Tramp made no move. Picking up his staff and another bag Bryan walked a few steps and turned back.

"Tramp, we're all done here, it's time to go," he motioned with his hands.

Tramp seemed to understand that. He looked up the canyon toward the mine and proceeded to follow.

"Good boy," praised Bryan feeling relieved.

It was an easy march back across to the owl's left eye and down the wash that led to his camp. Bryan looked across in the vicinity of where the fortress was located, but it was too difficult to pinpoint in the shadows.

12

SINGING SANDS

Josh was jolted awake by the phone ringing. What time is it? It's not even light yet, he realized as he rolled out of bed.

"Hello," he answered.

"Josh, it's me, Tammy," informed the voice over the phone.

"Tammy! It's about time. You really irked me disappearing like you did. What made you take off like that?" questioned Josh.

"I'm sorry! I thought I was doing the right thing," she stated.

"You have to be kidding?"

"No, they threatened Bryan's life and said if I didn't do as they said, they would carry it out," Tammy emotionally explained.

"When you say they, I'm guessing it's the Feds again, right?" he asked.

"Yes, they never really identify themselves, but you know it is," she answered. "It was all a sham to make it appear that I had left him for other pursuits. Then I was to stay away for a while. They set it up and all I had to do was say yes and tell no one."

"You unwittingly fell for it," stated Josh.

"I love him and I'll stand by that," she defended.

"Yes, but in doing so you caused Bryan to go off brokenhearted taking unnecessary risks. No one has seen or heard from him in two weeks," explained Josh.

"I know," she sighed. "I've ended up really hurting everyone. I'm coming home to rectify things. Pray that it's not too late," acknowledged Tammy.

"Think about this. Everything changed after the DNA test. Bryan lost his protection. So, it was their opportunity to eliminate the threat he posed. But, at the same time the Captain was found missing. There was more to the mystery—maybe more gold. They even returned the box and all the stuff to him. Because they couldn't make heads or tails of it," related Josh.

"My emotions clouded my thinking. I understand what you're leading to," she realized. "It was all a scheme to get Bryan motivated to solve the problem and I fell for it."

"Well, it's water under the bridge now. What's done is done," replied Josh.

"Will Bryan ever forgive me?" she wondered.

"I just hope he is okay," stated Josh. "There was some indication that he was going to make some big splash on the news or something."

"He didn't run to Jo did he?" asked Tammy.

"No, he has not made contact with anyone that we are aware of. It's almost like he's leapfrogged beyond us somehow. We have new clues, but he's never contacted us," he answered. "And regarding Jo, she seems to be just as concerned as I am about Bryan.

"She is probably hoping that he'll come to her," imagined Tammy.

"I don't know about that, but I think she is respectful that you two are still engaged," he responded.

"Okay, it's going to take me a number of days to get home. I'll call Mom and let her know," she informed.

"By the time you get back we could be back out on the desert. I'll leave a way for you to contact or find us," planned Josh.

After final goodbyes Josh hung up. It was good she called, but what a mess to untangle he thought. He had to call Jo and let her know.

Priscilla and her brother Cory were convinced that Bryan was into something big. Curiosity drove them to find out what. They had traced him to a phone booth in Baker, California that was adjacent to the Royal Hawaiian Motel. Arriving early in the morning they began asking around if anyone had seen him or his pickup around town.

Sitting in a small desert basin, Baker sat at the junction of Interstate 15 and Highway 127, being the official gateway into Death Valley. Comprising the business district were fast food chains, gas stations, and motels. It boasted that it had the world's tallest thermometer.

It didn't take long for them to find a gas station attendant who remembered Bryan and his pickup. The attendant apparently had worked on a tire of his that had a slow leak. All he could share with them was that Bryan had driven west when he left the station.

No one else remembered seeing Bryan. Cory had the idea to leave a description, a phone number, and the promise of a cash reward for anyone spotting him. Priscilla liked that idea.

Returning to Las Vegas, she recalled that he had mentioned something about working for the Forest Service. Doing a bit of research through the National Registry of Federal Employees, forty two Bryans showed up. Thirty four of them were back East, but eight were in the West. After numerous phone calls including one to the Stanislaus National Forest Supervisor's Office they hit pay dirt. Pretending to be someone else they were able to find out his last name and his background that included the search for a lost gold mine.

This was definitely intriguing. All they could do now was wait and see when he would reappear.

Josh contacted Jo with the news that Tammy was coming back to help find Bryan. Jo was somewhat surprised.

"I don't think we can wait till she gets back. We need to act now. I have located what I believe to be the 'bird head.' He may be there right now," voiced Jo with some confidence.

"Really, that would be great if we could catch up with him. We need some closure on this," replied Josh.

"How soon can you get here?" she asked.

"Wow, let me think. How about tonight?" he answered back.

"Good, I'll try calling Heather again and see if she can help us with the search," proposed Jo.

"That would be fine. We don't want people to get the wrong idea," concurred Josh.

"Great, I'll see you tonight," she responded. "Be prepared to stay for a while. We're going to see this through to the end."

Josh was struck by her sudden forcefulness. Was it the fact that Tammy was on her way back?

After arriving that evening Josh found out that their destination was the southern tip of Death Valley. Jo seemed agitated in some ways. She asked no further questions about his conversation with Tammy.

It turned out that Heather jumped at the chance to go with them, but was limited to two or three days. Jo confided in Josh that she thought Heather had a little bit of a crush on him.

"Well, I guess it's better than being disliked," commented Josh not taking it seriously. "Besides, she is not my type anyway."

"Who is your type?" she asked.

"Oh, someone who is more outdoorsy," answered Josh.

Jo turned away and smiled.

Getting an early start they rolled into Barstow about ten in the morning to meet Heather at the home of a family friend where she could leave her car. Heather sat in the middle and talked their ear off all the way to Baker. After stopping for a short time they were back on the road heading north toward Death Valley. Jo did all the navigating since she had access to almost every map ever made.

140

Nearing the south end of the Park, Jo directed Josh to turn off the paved road to take Saratoga Springs Road toward the west. After a mile or so they passed an area of sand dunes that Jo identified as the Ibex Dunes. Crossing the Amargosa River soon brought them to an even more primitive road, the Owl Hole Springs Road which was posted—dead end. Clouds were visibly building above some of the higher peaks in front of them.

"Thunder clouds," observed Heather.

"We're getting close," informed Jo as they rattled along.

"I hope so, if we break down out here it would take us a day or two to hike out," commented Josh.

About four miles further, a caravan of three vehicles approached sending up a dust cloud as they came. A white SUV that was in the lead slowed as it came close. They were able to read sheriff, written on the side of the vehicle. An arm extended out of the driver's side window directing them to stop. A white van with the designation coroner pulled up behind the SUV. Josh and Jo looked at each other thinking the worst.

"What are you folks doing way out here?" asked a deputy sheriff.

"We're looking for a friend," answered Josh.

The deputy looked kind of glum glancing back behind him. At that a helicopter passed over head coming down out of the mountains.

"How old is this friend of yours?" he asked.

"About twenty-one," answered Josh.

"We found the body of an older man back up in the Owlheads. Apparently, a prospector out on his own was buried in a mine cave-in," informed the officer.

"How did you ever find him way out here?" asked Jo.

"Well," he started to answer looking around for something. "We received an anonymous phone call that came in out of Baker about a possible fatality in a mine west of Lost Lake. We found the cabin and the mine. At the cabin was a written note. Do you recognize this handwriting?" he asked passing it over.

141

Josh looked, and thought it could be Bryan's. But before he could say anything Jo snatched it away and said it was not his handwriting.

"What's the person's name you're looking for?" asked the deputy wanting to write it down.

"Bryan," Josh started out.

"Marshall," spoke up Jo.

"Bryan Marshall, okay. I hope you find him. I don't want to come back out here," he finalized.

After their departure it took a few moments for what they just learned to sink in.

"That's not Bryan's last name," spoke up Heather.

"No, but we don't want them getting involved in this," answered Jo.

"That was Bryan's handwriting on that note," stated Josh.

"So, where is he?" asked Heather.

"Apparently, he has already been up in the Owlshead Mountains and has already left," concluded Josh

"He called from Baker. He is only a couple of days ahead of us," she realized. "This is good news, he is okay."

"There is no reason for us to go up into these mountains now. He has no doubt moved to the next feature on the map," thought Josh out loud.

"I agree," Jo pondered.

"What is the next feature?" questioned Heather.

"Sand dunes," she replied. "Bryan and I were both told that the wave-like lines similar to the ones shown east of the bird or now we can say it is the owl head were symbols for sand dunes."

They both looked at each other in realization of what they had just driven by less than an hour before, Ibex Dunes.

"You know what, the topo map also shows another area of dunes that's even bigger to the east of Highway 127," recalled Jo.

"Let's go check it out," Josh replied starting up the engine and turning around to head back.

142

At that moment there was a low rumble of thunder high up in the mountains. Some of the clouds had grown quite dark; and the wind picked up a bit.

"Must be monsoon moisture coming up out of the Gulf," commented Jo. "It looks like it had already showered here a day or two ago."

"Did you see in the note it said something about him rescuing a dog?" asked Josh not thinking about the weather.

"No, I just glanced at it," she replied.

"If that's the case, if ever we have to track him, there'll be a set of dog prints giving him away," thought Josh.

"Josh, you impress me," smiled Jo.

Two days previous, Bryan was at the very same location headed easterly on Saratoga Springs Road. Before heading back to civilization Bryan wanted to check out the Dumont Sand Dunes. On the way Bryan passed another set of dunes near the Ibex Range, which seemed to confirm that he was on the correct path.

Tramp liked to travel with his head out of the passenger window, but the weather had changed a bit that morning causing him to keep his head in. A south wind brought in clouds that produced mostly mist and an occasional shower. It was a welcome change.

Reaching Highway 127 he turned north a short distance to where a BLM sign directed Bryan onto a well-worn desert road that led directly out to the Dunes. Nearing a wide wash the road forked to the right crossing a mostly dry stream. On the other side was a closed pay station for campers and off-roaders that frequented the Dunes especially in the winter time. Stopping at an information board Bryan glanced at the maps, photographs, and interpretive displays. He noted that Sperry Wash Road continued on north of the Dunes into the hills beyond.

But what really caught his attention was a display entitled "Singing Sand Dunes." Diagrams and photographs documented how sand dunes were formed through the action of wind. Studies had been made on how sand moves through the desert. The technical term for their movement was called the Sand Transport System. A unique property of some sand dunes was their ability to sing, roar, squeak, and give off musical notes. All of this depended on the size of the sand grains as well as the shearing effect between adjacent layers of sand when driven by the wind or disturbed from their angle of repose. He had indeed found "the singing sands" as mentioned on the back of the land grant.

Bryan drove up to a trail head for a short nature walk in among some isolated dunes. He wanted to see if he could hear them sing. Due to the windy conditions he put on a jacket before they set out on the obscure trail. Tramp barked and ran ahead. It wound its way up to a saddle between two ridge-backed dunes. There was a fine spray of sand coming off the leeward side. Bryan could see someone in a dune buggy riding up and over one of the main dunes further to the south. He listened to the wind, but the sand was quiet.

Well, Tramp, I don't think the sands are going to sing for us today," concluded Bryan. "Let's go."

Bryan bolted down the dune giving Tramp a foot race back to the truck. Tramp barked chasing him, but Bryan lost it at the bottom and rolled in the sand. He came up laughing and Tramp came over to see if he was okay. Brushing himself off they walked back the rest of the way.

Crossing back over the wash, Bryan decided to drive up the road a couple of miles to look around. The road paralleled the wash until it made an abrupt turn into the hills, after that it went in and out of the gravelly wash.

Up ahead he spotted a vehicle off to the side with some apparent tire problems. A man about forty years old, stood there looking perplexed. Bryan really didn't want to encounter anybody, but he couldn't leave someone stranded either. Stopping behind him he got out.

"Need any help?" asked Bryan as he came around the vehicle.

"Yes, I am in kind of a pickle here. My jack went out on me and I can't change this flat," replied the man who wore a green plaid jacket and blue jeans.

"I can help you with that," he offered. "My name is Bryan."

"John."

"I have my Hi-lift jack with me so we should be able to get you back on the way," informed Bryan.

"Thanks, you're a real life saver," responded John.

It didn't take long for him to set the jack and get the vehicle raised up. While the stranded motorist removed the tire, Bryan glanced into the wash just beyond their location and noticed an unnatural mound of rocks that partially crossed the dry stream bed.

"Say, what's the story behind those rocks out in the wash?" questioned Bryan.

"Oh, that was part of the old T & T Railroad crossing," answered John.

"T & T?"

"Tonopah and Tidewater, built in the early 1900's from Ludlow all the way to Death Valley Junction. If I remember right, Pacific Borax originally put it through in the day," he further explained.

"All the tracks and ties are all gone now," observed Bryan.

"When World War Two started they needed the iron for the war effort and it was all used for scrap in 1942," he added tightening up the lug nuts. But there is one mystery that eludes explanation to this day."

"What mystery?" Bryan wondered.

"Well, my uncle some years ago bought a big chunk of property south of here," related John pausing as he thought about it. "He had never driven the whole property. Apparently it ran on for miles. But one day he decided to drive out and look around. In doing so, he came up over a hill and noticed out in a flat area there were two old railroad box cars."

"Wow, how interesting," commented Bryan.

145

"Now here's the kicker," he continued. "All the tracks had been taken up except for the ones that the cars were sitting on. It appeared they were parked on a siding. There was no getting into the two box cars because they were heavily chained and locked."

"What finally happened?" Bryan asked.

"He came back another day with some heavy duty tools and finally got the doors opened up. And guess what he found?"

"I wouldn't have a clue, maybe some explosives?" he guessed.

"No! Two brand new Model T's, perfectly preserved in the dry desert air. The only thing that deteriorated was anything that was made of rubber, like hoses and such."

"So who, when and why?" asked Bryan as he lowered the jack.

"That's the mystery! My uncle went to the railroads to see if they had any claim on those old box cars, but none did."

"That's very interesting," commented Bryan. "Somebody must have been up to something, but it didn't go down as planned."

"Bryan, I appreciate your help," John again thanked him.

"Sure, no problem," replied Bryan.

John also informed him that there was really no good way to proceed east from their location. He could go up to Tecopa Hot Springs and take a lot of back roads to get around to the other side. Or go back south to Baker, then east thirty miles, and back north again on the Kingston Road. After that revelation, Bryan turned around and headed back toward the Dunes. Just before reaching the highway he stopped to look back over the top of the Dunes to see the Dumont Hills and the Kingston Range rising high above them. Could there be a forest up in those peaks above the cloud deck? He would soon find out.

Heading toward Baker he thought about the phone call he would have to make to the Sheriff's Department. It also was time to refuel, refresh, and get a good meal before moving on. He didn't think anybody was even close to catching up with him, but he felt the need to press on.

The mystery of the Model T's kept coming back to him. There had to be a way to further research that he felt.

About noon Bryan rolled into Baker. The clouds had cleared, but the wind continued to persist. A sand storm was always possible. Gathering up supplies for another few days was the first order of work which now included food for Tramp. What was he going to do with the dog? He didn't trust giving him over to just anyone.

He decided to refuel and have a repair done to one of his tires before catching a hot meal. Staying away from fast food, Bryan picked a more traditional restaurant. Sitting in a booth having a good view of people coming and going he pondered what his future might be. He didn't want to think anything negative about Tammy, but knew he had to rebuild his life. I guess maybe it was true that you can take the girl out of the city, but you can't take the city out of the girl. Maybe he should just sail off into the sunset. Perhaps that's what the Captain had to do. There was no going back.

The waitress was nice. What was it about him and waitresses? They are paid to do what they do. It's not real. You can't really trust anyone. Leaving a nice tip and paying his bill he stepped outside and spotted a public phone.

It was time to call. As he suspected the call was recorded. They wanted more information, but Bryan said that's all he knew and hung up. He immediately left town, afraid they would be looking for him.

13

FORESTS IN THE SKY

Everything seemed to be in slow motion as Tammy made arrangements and boarded a trans-Atlantic flight back home. Nothing could go quick enough for her.

On the flight she wondered how she was going to convince Bryan, that she still loved him. He had a hard time trusting women anyway. What a fool she had been not thinking it through. They were close to building their dream home and starting their life together. Tammy was angry with herself, but especially against those that had put her up to it. This meant war. They no longer had any control over her.

Tammy had a feeling that Jo was just waiting in the wings for her to falter. How would she play into all this? Good thing Josh was there to balance things out.

Two days later after using a variety of transportation modes she finally made it home. But there was no welcoming party for her this time. In some ways it was comforting not having to face anyone. Tammy immediately went over to what was to be their home site. Gladly, none of Bryan's family was around. Nothing had really changed since she was there last. The thing that struck her was the condition of the flowers they had planted. The flowers had withered and the plants had died. She was choked with emotion and cried.

Cory's idea for a cash reward worked. It must have been about three in the afternoon that a call came in from one of the businesses in Baker. But it wasn't until five o'clock that Priscilla could get together with him. Then they had to head some eighty miles across the desert to Baker.

Priscilla continued to be intrigued about what Bryan was involved with. After they had helped him carry out a clandestine operation, she was led to believe that it was just the tip of the iceberg. But what could be so grandiose? Why was she sent to Bishop and Ridgecrest to gather information on two other people? Who were they? And why was no further observation necessary?

Cory and Priscilla were both quite tall and always attracted attention wherever they went. It was no different that day as they got out of their vehicle and looked for their contact. Once he was found they verified the sighting and questioned him on Bryan's purchases and his next movements.

They learned from what he purchased that he must be camping out somewhere. Secondly, that he was now accompanied by a dog. Next he went across the road to a restaurant and afterwards made a phone call from a booth just outside. From there he headed east. They thanked him for his help and paid him his agreed reward. Retiring to the car they discussed their options.

"Apparently, he is working out on the desert somewhere close," figured Cory. "But where?"

"Possibly east of here; but I wonder who he called?" pondered Priscilla.

"Well, we have the approximate time when the call was made, and the number is on the dial across the street," analyzed her brother.

"I like the way you think," she replied. "I'll call the operator and use the old 'I'm a law enforcement officer routine.' That should get results."

"Give it a try," he encouraged.

"Yeah, I think I'm getting the hang of this type of thing," she smiled putting on her seatbelt.

Cory drove them across the street to the phone booth. Priscilla stood there for a moment to get herself into the right frame of mind. She introduced herself as officer so-and-so with the local sheriff's department needing information on a phone call made from the very phone she was calling from. Surprisingly, the operator gave her the number without any hassle.

"Score three points, I got it," informed Pricilla.

"Dial it up," directed her brother.

"Okay, I'm on a roll," she replied with an air of confidence dialing it up.

"San Bernardino Sheriff's Department, how can I help you?" was the voice at the other end.

"Sheriff's Department?" questioned Pricilla stumbling over her words in surprise.

"Yes, that's correct."

"I'm trying to locate the person who called your office today at 2:15 pm. I'm a private investigator," she explained.

"I'm not sure I can give you that information. 2:15, let me see what that was about," was the response. There was a thirty second pause. "Actually, we're interested in this person also. Who are you?" asked the receptionist.

At that Priscilla abruptly hung up and kicked the phone booth.

Passing Ibex Dunes, two days later, Josh, Jo, and Heather soon arrived at Dumont Sand Dunes. Dark clouds hid the top of the mountains to the east. An occasional wind blew dust in a northerly direction.

"We're here," pointed Jo on a copy of the Camino Map.

"Looks like we are now more than half way," observed Josh.

"Maybe we can leapfrog through the next two landmarks and catch up with Bryan," she speculated.

"Two mountain peaks," he commented. "The second one is southeast of the first and from there it's more of a southerly direction to the final bird figure."

"One big clue that Bryan and myself had discussed in the past was that there are trees or perhaps a small forest at the summit of these peaks," recalled Jo.

"The timberline out here in the desert must be extremely high for that to be true," he reasoned.

"How high are these peaks to the east of us?" wondered Heather peeking out through the windshield.

Unfolding another map Jo looked for mountain elevations. "Looks like Kingston Peak is 7,323 feet high which would make that a logical candidate. But look here, Charleston Peak in the Spring Range that is north and east of here is more than 11,000 feet," she observed.

"That would definitely have some trees on it. Although it is a bit north," thought Josh.

"This is interesting, it's showing the Old Spanish Trail passing through Tecopa Hot Springs to our north and coming around the Spring Range," she excitedly discovered.

"Let me see that map a little closer," he requested. "If Charleston Peak is the first peak then the second peak could be either Black Mountain or McCullough Mountain just south of Las Vegas.

"Okay, but does it really make sense?" she replied. "Let me check one more thing. I have a map that is more historical, from the National Park Service. Well, isn't that interesting!"

"What?" asked Josh peering over.

"This particular branch of the Old Spanish Trail did run around the Spring Range coming out of Vegas over to Tecopa Hot Springs and from there down the Amargosa River passing this very location," she pointed out.

"Huh," remarked Josh. "Not that far off the beaten track from Owlshead either. Well, it might be a long shot, but things are adding up."

"There is very limited ingress and egress to Charleston Peak. So maybe we can surprise Bryan," she theorized.

"You sound like a lawyer," commented Josh.

So the decision was made to head north to Tecopa Hot Springs and from there to Vegas and then on up to Charleston Peak. Because of being re-routed from Owlshead, the consensus was they were ahead of schedule and it was worth the gamble.

Back on the paved highway it was a quick fifteen minutes to reach the small desert valley that contained the Tecopa Hot Springs. The small resort featured mud and mineral baths. It was a good place to camp and soak your miseries away.

"Jo, how do you feel about taking one of those beauty or mineral baths?" asked Josh.

"Why? Do think I need a beauty bath?" she snapped back.

"Well no, not for the beauty part. You're already there," he replied.

"Good recovery," commented Heather.

"Thanks, I think," smiled Jo. "But now you're saying I just plain need a bath. Do I smell that bad?"

"No, you're taking this all in the wrong direction," Josh tried to explain. "I just wanted to know if you were partial to that type of thing. That's all."

"I know, I'm just giving you a hard time," she confessed giving him a nudge.

The road from the Hot Springs proceeded over a minor pass before descending into Pahrump Valley. Almost immediately the huge bulk of the Spring Mountains rose up in front of them. It took them another hour and a half to get around to the opposite side passing through the north end of Las Vegas.

Once they worked their way up the winding road to the ski lift facilities and the trailheads they were able to get a clear view of the mountain peak itself. It was then that a realization hit them.

"Oh my, I didn't see it coming, how stupid!" exclaimed Josh.

"It's all my fault, I should have known better," replied Jo stomping the floorboard.

"When I was talking about the timberline I was thinking about a minimum elevation, not the upper limit of the timberline," he confessed.

About a mile distant was Charleston Peak. The top one thousand feet of the mountain was bare granite, being definitely above the timberline. Trees were abundant in places below that line, including a grove of Bristlecone Pines. It was quite apparent this was not a mountain with a forest at its summit.

"So, what I'm hearing is that this clue was more specific elevation wise than you guys thought," concluded Heather.

"That's exactly right," confirmed Josh.

"We've lost half a day on this little stunt," realized Jo feeling frustrated.

"It's getting kind of late," realized Josh. "We might consider a place to camp tonight, but I'm not sure where. Another option would be to stay overnight somewhere near Vegas."

"I don't want to give people the wrong impression, we stayed the night together in Las Vegas," replied Jo.

"I can think of two solutions," answered Josh.

Jo looked strangely at him. "What?" she asked.

"Well, we can make it legal," he answered. "Those love chapels are open twenty four hours a day."

Swatting him in the arm she replied, "That sounds like something that a guy would say." Taking him to task she asked, "You would really marry me—point blank, with all my baggage?"

"Of course not," confessed Josh. "I would have to get to know you a lot better. What baggage do you have?"

"Never mind, it's just a figure of speech," Jo rebuffed. "What's the other option?"

"I believe, there is a KOA right in Vegas according to a sign we drove by on the freeway this morning," disclosed Josh.

Heather commented, "That's not a bad idea, they have all kinds of different amenities. We wouldn't have to be out somewhere listening to the coyotes."

"Don't you like camping out in the great outdoors?" asked Josh.

"No, not really," she answered. "I'm even afraid to go out in by backyard at night."

"The KOA sounds like the option we better go with," agreed Jo. "Love chapels? Ha!" she laughed.

"You guys are silly," chuckled Heather.

Traveling back south into Las Vegas they eventually found the campground off the interstate. Camping spaces were quite small. There was just enough room for a vehicle and a couple of tents.

The girls were happy to have showers and get cleaned up. Afterward, Jo and Heather prepared a simple meal for them. Josh sat at the picnic table looking at a map of the region and came up with an idea of where to meet Tammy.

"We're going to be covering quite a bit of territory tomorrow," he realized.

"It's a shot in the dark as to where we will be later in the day," commented Jo.

"A good place could be the rest stop on I-15 near Kingston Road," proposed Josh.

"There are a lot of riffraff that hang out at those rest stops," commented Heather.

"But are there any public phones at the rest stop?" he asked.

"I believe there are," she replied.

"That might work," stated Josh.

He could tell Jo was still bothered about the possibility of Tammy showing up and the complications that might arise.

Josh felt that Bryan wasn't that far away. Hopefully, Tammy would be able to patch things up with him and defuse the situation. But what was at the end of the trail this time? Was there another colossal treasure or just disappointment?

Rising early, they were on their way down the Interstate headed for California. Once across the dry Ivanpah Lake bed, the divided highway ascended the next range of mountains. As they neared Mountain Pass there was abundant evidence of a major mining operation. This world renowned mine was producing many of the "rare earth" minerals used in the high tech industries.

"Molycorp," read off Heather as they passed a weathered sign. "Sounds like a good name for one of those evil companies you would expect in a disaster movie."

It wasn't much further to the Kingston Road turnoff and the rest area. The buildings and the information center all seemed to be relatively new. Landscaped areas were all orientated around native desert species. There were a number of open roof structures with picnic benches clustered under them. Walking up to the main building, Josh located a telephone.

"What are you going to tell Tammy?" Jo asked concerned.

"Well, basically that she can meet us here at this rest stop this evening," he answered.

"No guarantees," she commented.

"For some reason if we are detained we can call this number and give her an update," he added.

"There may not be any phones out where we're going to be," Jo reminded him. "Oh well, let's just go for it! We need to get going to make this day meaningful."

Josh made the phone call but the connection was quite poor. Tammy wanted to make sure they had all of Camino's documents and maps. Josh replied that they did have them. The call only lasted for about three minutes in which he tried to answer most of her concerns.

Getting turned around they made their way over to the narrow ribbon of asphalt that would take them north. They were alert to the fact that they could at any moment cross paths with Bryan.

Traffic was crazy on the Interstate. People were in such a hurry to lose all their money in Vegas thought Bryan. Leaving Baker it wasn't long before he had covered the twenty-nine miles to the Kingston Road exit.

He was grateful that the road north was paved and was not a graveled washboard that would shake your teeth out. There were mountains to the east and major hills to the west. The flat desert plain between was at least ten miles wide. Scattered among sparse sagebrush was an occasional Joshua tree along the narrow road. After twenty miles the valley narrowed at Shadow Mountain and Bryan spotted an unremarkable range of mountains in the far northwest that he figured must be the Kingston Range. Not much further the Excelsior Mine Road forked left heading in more of a northwesterly direction.

After some time the once distant mountain range with its lofty peak was now to his left. The route now began curving more westerly seemly on track to pass north of Kingston Peak. Reaching the foothills of the small mountain range the gradually deteriorating road ascended to climb through the hills. Mining prospects now became more frequent the further he proceeded. Gradually, the ridgeline of the Kingston Range came into alignment as Bryan reached a subtle pass, which he later learned was Tecopa Pass. Two water tanks and an old cabin marked the location of Horse Thief Springs on the left side of the road. Crossing a cattle guard and passing through an opened iron gate a dirt road forked right heading off to the north, northwest.

Continuing another half mile on the Excelsior Mine Road there was another tank and a rough access road that led along the edge of the ridge. After a quarter mile it ended at a landing, being impassable beyond that point. The sun was noticeably in the west, making him think that it might be better to camp there for the evening and make ascent first thing in the morning. There was a fire ring nearby if he needed it. It was convenient just to car camp that night.

"Well, Tramp, looks like it's just me and you again. Just us guys howling at the moon tonight," announced Bryan.

156

He decided to prepare his pack for the next day's assault on Kingston Peak. According to his calculations it was about three miles along the spine of the ridge and a three thousand foot elevation gain to the summit. If everything went well he could be up and down before the extreme heat set in. By the look of the terrain, Tramp should be able to go with him. He packed accordingly to the needs of both of them.

Later after making up their beds in the back of the truck, Bryan lying there looked up at the stars wondering if the others had given up on him, thinking that he was acting irrationally.

Bryan decided to have a good breakfast before "lighting out" as John Muir would have said. There was an established trail he soon discovered. An occasional foot mark was visible here and there in the sandy soil. Low sagebrush was scattered across the landscape. Tramp would run ahead and then would wait, unsure of where they were going. Rock outcroppings of granite appeared as they ascended up to and along the ridge. Views began opening up to the east the higher they climbed. Soon small fir trees began appearing along the route. Approaching a saddle in the ridge Bryan got his first good look at Kingston Peak. There were actually two saddles between him and the peak. At the first dip in the ridge line there were individual trees, but toward the second saddle there were actually groves of trees. On the final ascent to the top of the peak there seemed to be a more uniform spread of trees among the granite ledges and outcroppings. In a couple places Tramp needed assistance to get up over some of the bigger rocks.

Finally, after a tiring climb they made it to the rocky summit. The views were magnificent in all directions including prominent ranges well into Nevada. After resting a bit Bryan began looking around. The trees appeared to be white fir. Another unusual plant that caught his attention was something that had the look of something prehistoric—primeval. The twelve inch trunk was twisted and very course in texture. It was topped with foliage that resembled a spider plant. Bryan later learned this was the Giant Nolina.

157

Mounting the highest rocks he carefully searched their surface for what would validate that this was the first "forest in the sky." The area at the top of the peak was quite small, probably in the neighborhood of several hundred square feet. After a bit he found a carved shape on the vertical face of a nearby rock outcropping. It was quite weathered, but yet discernable. The 'downward sun' faced to the southeast.

Holding a hand over his eyes Bryan scanned the horizon in that direction. There was one definite mountain about forty miles distant that was on that alignment. Matter of fact he probably had driven past it on the way up to the Kingston Range.

Sitting on top of the rock slab, Bryan dug into his pack for a map. Tramp came over and plopped down beside him.

"Looks like we've found what we've come for," spoke up Bryan giving Tramp a pet. "Clark Mountain Range," he read off. "Clark Mountain is 7,903 feet in height." That had to be it since it was also high enough to support a small forest, being six hundred feet higher. I think we have everything we need from this place," Bryan concluded folding up the map.

Before leaving Bryan signed the guest book that was in a plastic case sitting on a rock mound near the summit. He figured that this shouldn't come back and bite him later.

The trip back down the ridge went much quicker. A breeze sprang to life coming up over the range from the northwest scattering the dust as they walked. Back at the truck they rested and refreshed themselves for about an hour and then drove off heading back the way they had come.

He contemplated what his next move might be while driving south on Kingston Road. Mount Clark must in fact be the northwest corner of the mystery land grant. No other mountains south of Kingston met the criteria. He was wondering if there is any reason why he had to climb the mountain this time. His great great grandfather's map showed the "great black bird" south, southeast of the second mountain peak. Bryan thought he would have to evaluate this further to make the final decision.

14

KOKOWEEF

J osh noticed that Jo had again grown quiet, no doubt contemplating their rendezvous with Tammy that evening. Relatively speaking it did not take them long traveling on Kingston Road to reach Tecopa Pass. A Bureau of Land Management Ranger who had been visiting the Excelsior Mine stopped to give them directions to the Kingston Peak trailhead. They questioned him if he had seen Bryan or his vehicle in the last few days. Apparently he had not.

Loading up on water they headed through the sagebrush to the ridge. Along the way Josh noticed some footprints, probably recent. A bit further, Jo spotted dog prints converging with the footprints. This told them that there was a high degree of probability that Bryan had indeed preceded them. Heather was not used to hiking in such strenuous terrain. Josh and Jo had to stop and wait for her a number of times. They noticed the increase of trees as they passed through the two saddles and on the way up to the top of the peak.

"Marvelous view from way up here," declared Josh.

"Look here," spotted Jo. "There's a plastic box sitting on a rock mound."

"Open it up," coaxed Josh.

"It's a climber's log or whatever you want to call it," Jo identified.

"Check to see if Bryan signed it," suggested Josh as he walked on around to the south side of the peak.

"Bingo!" she yelled. "Bryan did. He hid it at the bottom of the stack. Come here, he has written something."

"Really?" replied Josh quite surprised.

"The date was two days ago. He drew a 'downward sun,' and then writes, 'seventy feet west.' Bryan also scribbled: 'Off to Clark Mountain?' "

"Wow, what a revelation," realized Josh.

"I bet he didn't expect us to be reading this," commented Jo.

"Let's go look and see what there is at seventy feet west," he said.

"Made it!" declared Heather finally catching up to them once again.

Climbing up on the rocks it took a couple of minutes for them to find the marker. Josh noted he could see from that spot another prominent mountain chain.

"What mountain is that?" he pointed.

Digging out a map, Jo orientated it to an approximate north-south alignment. "That is Clark Mountain, I do believe. Elevation is 7,903, feet which is higher than this peak," she replied.

"Well, that would seem to be our destination as well," concluded Josh.

"Yeah-h, but we may have a leg up on this one," announced Jo.

"How's that?" he asked.

"We may not have to climb the next peak. There is an identifier on the east slope of the next mountain, that is if my understanding of the map and the land grant is correct," she explained.

"ILD, right?" understood Josh.

"Yes! It seems we're on the same wave length."

"That's saying something for people who haven't known each other very long," he commented.

"Gives pause for thought," smiled Jo repacking.

"Sooner we get down the quicker we can catch him," stated Josh.

"I second that motion," replied Jo getting up.

"Heather, are you ready? We're going to start heading back down," announced Josh.

"Yeah, I'm ready," she stated, "but I just got up here."

With a degree of enthusiasm they scampered down the ridge laughing and racing each other to get to the bottom of the saddle. Somewhat winded after that, their progress went much slower on the remainder of the return trip.

It was early afternoon and the heat was becoming unbearable as they once again hit the pavement driving south toward the Interstate and Clark Mountain.

"I hate to admit it, but I do stink," confessed Jo noticing how profusely she had been sweating. "Don't you dare laugh!"

"Why not," chuckled Josh. "We're the ones who have to endure it."

"Oh, yeah, as if your sweat is like perfume," she countered.

"Bryan owes us big time for putting us through all this," commented Josh.

"Are you saying that because of me?" asked Jo.

"No, if anything you and Heather have made this whole thing more bearable. But there is one thing that bothers me, if I can be frank?"

"What bothers you?" she asked.

"How you know certain things and have authority to amend security clearances, things like that," he said shrugging his shoulders.

"It's like I told you before. You have to trust me. I do work for the Government and I have been granted certain privileges," Jo tried to explain.

"Yeah, but you're an Archeological Assistant not the Federal Bureau of Investigation," Josh pointed out.

"Josh! Stop it! Little Petroglyph Canyon is a designated archeological site. I'm here because of personal choice. Matter

161

of fact I've put my position in jeopardy to be out here with you," answered Jo.

"I didn't realize," he apologized.

"It's okay, let's just get this thing done," she replied turning away.

"Jo, you must be really hooked on this Bryan guy, or whatever he's up to," commented Heather.

"Something like that," acknowledged Jo.

Josh reached over and put his hand on her shoulder. He could tell she was emotional. "I'm sorry. And you don't stink," he comforted.

She smiled at him kind of teary-eyed. "I'm sorry too for taking your head off," returned Jo.

"Now that's over, I need my navigator back," stated Josh.

"Yes, we need to figure out the best way to get to the east flank of Clark Mountain," she seconded.

"Find a way that doesn't require a four-wheel drive vehicle," he requested.

"It appears that the best route is just to circle around the Mountain counter clockwise via Interstate 15 up to the Yates Well Road Exit. From there we can take a couple of dirt roads up toward Benson Mine," outlined Jo.

"We need to find a good vantage point so we can use our field glasses," he stated.

"Hopefully, that will work," she agreed.

It took a little more than an hour to be on the approach to the Clark Range through the sagebrush and salt weed. The Benson Mine Road allowed them to get in close to the base of the mountain range with clear views of a large section of the east flank. The problem was that the sun had passed zenith and now shadows were beginning to creep in.

Taking turns they scanned the rugged sweep of the granite mountain. There were shapes and patterns repeated in the rock face.

"You said large letters, ILD, right?" asked Heather reaffirming what she was looking for.

"Yes, that is correct," confirmed Jo.

"It's hard to make out anything," conceded Josh.

"Toward the south end, there is something, but it is fragmentary," Jo commented.

"According to one of your maps there was another branch of the Spanish Trail coming out of Vegas that passed to the east side of this mountain and then over the Pass," he recalled.

"Yes, there were three variants of the route in this area," she concurred.

"I think I must have consumed at least a gallon and a half of water today," spoke up Josh guzzling down another bottle of water. "Most girls would have thrown in the towel by now," he added after a short period of silence.

"We're not like most girls are we, Heather?" asked Jo.

"Apparently not," she confirmed.

Some distance to the south Josh caught sight of a couple of faint vertical shadows in the cliff. He didn't say anything at first, but kept an eye on that location as he continued panning the other rock faces.

"I'm in no mood to climb this mountain," stated Jo feeling a bit frustrated.

"Maybe we won't have to," announced Josh.

"Why? What do scc?" she asked.

"Look, maybe a quarter mile south," he pointed. "There are shadows that resemble letters or parts of letters."

"Let me see," she requested taking the glasses. "Yes! Maybe so."

"Let's drive down this spur road and see how close we can get," suggested Josh.

"Let's hurry, this is getting exciting," she agreed.

It took a minute or two to roll through the swales and small washes to finally arrive a hundred feet below the letters. They were approximately ten feet high and stretched out to a total of about fifty feet.

"I wonder what the letters mean?" wondered Josh.

"Don't know, but it's probably Spanish," answered Jo. "It may have even predated Captain Camino."

"Sorry, I'm not much help with Spanish," informed Heather.

"I'm sure glad we found these," Jo reiterated.

"But we have not found Bryan yet," stated Josh.

"He has to be around here somewhere," believed Heather.

"May I be so bold as to suggest, we go find a swimming pool or something," proposed Josh.

"Ah, that sounds so good," they both replied.

"Primm is not that far," he recalled. "I will rent a motel room, and we can get cleaned up and take a refreshing dip before we have to go down to meet Tammy."

"Oh, that's right we have to do that don't we?" Jo realized.

"More the merrier, right?" he encouraged.

"I do like your idea about a swim," she finally answered without replying to his question.

Retracing their route across several miles of desert they arrived back at the Interstate. A couple miles north the tired searchers came to the resort community of Primm clustered on both sides of the freeway just beyond the state line.

Bryan pondered the evidence and came to the conclusion that Clark Mountain had to be the second peak with a forest on its summit. He even went to the locals to verify there was a petite forest on top and found out that none of the peaks to the south met that criterion.

He realized it was going to take another round of strategy to solve the final part of this mystery. Bryan felt he had to go somewhere out of the way and ponder his next move. He did not want to go back to Baker and show his face there again, but decided to cross the state line into Nevada. Primm was too new, catering to gamblers and all the other tourists. Up the road a few miles further was Jean, an older town that had many ma and pa businesses.

An older café called Gold Strike caught his attention, not too glitzy or too busy. Evening was coming on as he got out and made sure Tramp was okay before going in. Bryan tucked a folder of maps under his arm to review while he waited for his meal. He found a booth seat toward the back with a view of the front parking area.

Business was slow at that moment and didn't seem to improve much as the evening wore on. The food was actually quite good.

Bryan took a map and penciled out the approximate boundary of the land grant. The heart of the grant was Landfair Valley. But what was the "great black bird"?

"Say, I noticed you were looking at some maps," spoke up an older man wearing a white apron coming toward him.

"Yes, I was trying to figure something out," calmly answered Bryan.

"You're not into mining are you?" asked the grey-haired gentleman.

"Well, in a sense I am. It's in my family's history," Bryan replied.

"My name is Hank," introducing himself. "I used to work at the mine near Mountain Pass when it was owned by Molybdenum Corporation in the seventies. When the mine finally closed, I decided to get into another line of business, and here I am."

"Looks like they are very busy up there right now," commented Bryan.

"Yes, sometime after I left, Chevron bought into it and later Molycorp became the new owners who have substantially upgraded the facilities. In the rare earth minerals department they are the only mine in the western hemisphere," explained Hank.

"Rare earth minerals," repeated Bryan.

"You know doubt have heard the story about the River of Gold made famous by Earl Dorr back in the twenties and thirties?" he asked.

"No, I haven't. Tell me about it," requested Bryan folding up the map he was looking at.

"In a mountain south of the Pass is supposed to be the entrance to an underground cavern with a river along whose banks can be found black sand—placer gold!" he related.

This caused a pang to run through him. "What's the name of the mountain?"

"Kokoweef. Say, I have to go do a couple things, but I have two or three old magazines articles you can read if you're not in too much of a hurry," offered Hank.

"Yeah, I would be interested in reading a little bit about it," he answered.

"Be right back."

A few minutes later he reappeared with three old treasure magazines. Bryan overhead a female voice from somewhere in the back scolding Hank for trying to get someone else hooked on those old stories. How much truth was in these old articles he wondered. But this Kokoweef apparently was within the Camino land grant. And the part about black sands may have some truth to it. So perhaps the Captain's secret had already been discovered some years before. But why has nothing been said about it since?

As he read, the story began to unravel. It all began in Colorado in the early 1900's. Two Indian brothers by the last name of Peysert who were employed by Earl Dorr's father on his ranch, disclosed to Earl the existence of a cavern in the desert where there was gold. Apparently, they had lost a third brother to an accident in the cave and the body was unrecoverable. Indian traditions forbade them from returning to the burial place of their brother. They drew a map and gave it to Earl when he was in his early teens.

Another article claimed that a mining engineer visiting the Ivanpah area stepped off the train at a nearby railroad whistle stop happened to confront two Indian men trying to secure two failing sacks filled with black sand. He recalled they seemed to be agitated about something and wanted out of there as quick as they could go.

Earl believed the story and the map, and held on to it until he came of age and was able to go look for it himself. Evidently, he did find the cleft in the rock and the cave entrance that led deep into the underground. He later circulated the story that the entrance was Crystal Cave at Kokoweef Peak.

After the discovery, what followed was a series of bad events that led him to create a signed affidavit of the cavern's potential in 1934 that sought financial backing to re-access the cavern after the entrance had become blocked. The affidavit which was later published in the November 1940 California Mining Journal made a series of incredible claims.

Earl Dorr and a Civil Engineer by the name of Morton explored the caverns in May of 1927. They descended into a limestone cave system that was filled with stalagmites and stalactites to about two thousand feet below the entrance. At which point they discovered a chasm that was estimated to be another three thousand feet deep. A three hundred foot wide river flowed at the bottom of the gorge, but it remarkably varied according to the tides, narrowing down to just ten feet wide at times. During low tides, black sandy beaches were exposed which were very high in gold values. They followed this underground channel for some eight miles. At some point in their journey there was evidence of another entrance where light flickered in from above. The black sand that was packed out was assayed at $2,145.47 per yard at $ 20.67 per ounce. This was the basic claim made by the affidavit.

Reading on further in the article it stated that the return trip out of the cavern proved too much for Morton, and Earl Dorr had to pack him out, half conscious. It so happened that two fellas that Dorr had met earlier at Mexican Wells were curious about his activities up on the mountain. They came up to investigate about the time that Dorr and Morton made it back to the surface. The two men, one thought to be a prospector and the other of unknown character couldn't help but notice the black sand that they had brought up. This concerned Earl. After taking his partner for medical attention, he quickly returned fearing

167

trespass. The story goes that he dynamited the cave shut about three hundred feet down to protect his discovery. The blast evidently was catastrophic and collapsed a large section of the cave, making that point of entry no longer viable. The two men that met them at the cave entrance reportedly were never seen again.

This struck Bryan. Could one of those two men been the anthropologist that the firefighter at Big Pine had told him about? What was the name? Von Trigger? Yes, he was the one who also had been following the sun symbols. He was never seen again.

After that all other attempts of accessing the cavern through another tunnel or finding the second entrance had come to failure. Down to the bitter end he contended it was all true. His last effort was an unfinished shaft northwest of Kokoweef Peak that was located on a spur of the same fault that passed under the mountain and along the underground river. At the bottom of that shaft, through inch wide cracks, air movement could be felt. This no doubt was what he was chasing, hoping to break into the "great cavern" once again.

Soon Hank returned to see what he thought of the Kokoweef mystery. Bryan leaned back refocusing his tired eyes.

"Is there any concrete proof of any of this?" he asked.

"Not really. Everyone who had involvement in it are all dead now. There is a lot of circumstantial evidence and controversy though. One theory has it that Earl Dorr falsely claimed that Crystal Cave was the entrance to the cavern for the purpose of drawing attention away from the true entrance. Because of the strong possibility that was where the bodies of those two men who were nosing around were entombed."

"So, after all these years, no one has been able to prove or disprove if this cavern of gold really exists?" asked Bryan.

"No, except that deep well drilling in a few locations south of Kokoweef have dropped into voids and possible caverns. Air movement out of these drill points indicates that there must be other entrances," answered Hank.

"Hmm," considered Bryan. "Wow, that is quite a story. Did you ever go out and poke around yourself?"

"Oh, many years ago, but I'm no spring chicken anymore," he replied.

Bryan thanked him and promised if he ran across some of that black sand he would drop off a sack or two. On his way out he was able to talk the cook into mustering up some vittles for Tramp. The last hint of light softly lit up the mountains to the west as he disappeared into the night.

15

HOLE IN THE WALL

Do you guys have to go back in?" asked Josh coming out of the motel room.

"No, I think we're done," answered Jo. "Let's get going and meet your cousin if she is going to show up."

"Oh, I think she'll be there," he confidently replied.

After catching a bite to eat they were back on the road headed across the desert toward the descending sun. Josh glanced to his left into the great expanse of the Ivanpah Valley and wondered where Bryan was.

"Are you going to be able to work with Tammy?" asked Josh after a few minutes.

"I don't think that's the question you should be asking. Rather will she work with me?" restated Jo.

"We're doing this for Bryan whom we all love and respect, right?" reminded Josh.

"Yes, you're absolutely right. And however it turns out that's the way it's meant to be," she agreed.

"I've got to meet this Bryan," insisted Heather.

Once over the Pass it did not take long to reach the rest stop. A large number of trucks were parked in the diagonal slots in the center of the parking area. Passenger car parking was sparse along the curb in front of the buildings. Josh noticed a car that was similar to Tammy's a couple spaces over. Looking up he spotted a young woman wearing sunglasses sitting on a bench by the phone. Recognizing each other, Tammy smiled and came down the sidewalk to meet them. She was wearing a light yellow top and khaki shorts.

"Josh! And Jo, I'm so glad to see you. It seems it has been an eternity," greeted Tammy hugging them, but differently.

"It's good to see you too," replied Jo in a matter of fact tone. "I want you to meet Heather. Tammy this is Heather, and Heather this is Tammy," she introduced.

"It's nice to meet you. Are you related, or friends?" Tammy inquired.

"It's good to meet you too. And yes, we are cousins," replied Heather.

"So are we," said Tammy glancing at Josh. Then directing her attention to Jo and Josh she continued. "I know what you're probably thinking, and you're right—I really messed up," confessed Tammy. "I've wrecked everyone's lives in the process. And Bryan probably thinks I've dumped him and don't love him anymore, but it's just the opposite. I did it because I was afraid for his life. A person will do anything for someone they love, right?"

At that she broke down and started crying. Jo looked at Josh as if saying—someone has to do the right thing. Jo hugged her.

"It's going to be okay. It will work out because we're going to find Bryan and set things straight," comforted Jo.

"We are only two days behind him, more or less," shared Josh.

"Really?" acknowledged Tammy wiping her tears.

"We found a handwritten note of his today up on Kingston Peak that was dated two days ago," added Jo.

"You guys look tired," observed Tammy.

"It has been a long day," confirmed Josh.

"What's your plan for finding him?" asked Tammy.

"Let me get the maps and we'll catch you up to date," answered Jo heading back to the truck.

"Tammy, really how are you?" asked Josh.

171

"I'm all tore up inside," she answered.

"You'll soon feel better when we catch up to Bryan," Heather consoled.

"Yes, but how will he react to me when he sees me?" Tammy wondered.

"Bryan will come around, maybe a little stubborn at first, but he will," replied Josh hoping that was the case.

Jo returned and laid out the maps on a nearby table as they gathered around.

"Remember Camino's map?" asked Josh.

"How could I forget, I was there when Bryan and I first assembled it," responded Tammy.

"A treasure map? Wow, this is interesting," spoke up Heather.

Jo did not confirm Heather's comment before starting her explanation of their progress. "We have traced the route on this map to Owlshead Mountains as symbolized by the owl head, through the sand dunes to these two peaks that have small forests at their summits," informed Jo.

"This second peak is only a few miles from here, which just happens to be—," continued Josh before getting cut off by Tammy.

"The northwest corner of the land grant, right?" completed Tammy.

"Yeah, you got it," affirmed Josh. "Matter of fact we just confirmed that this afternoon."

"So the focus now is within this rectangular box that stretches all the way to the Colorado River," pointed out Jo referring to one of the maps she had laid out.

"In a sense he is now corralled," realized Tammy.

"Remember this symbol in the lower corner of the Captain's map?" asked Josh.

"Yes, the bird standing upright or perhaps in flight with its wings out and having the 'sun in its beak,' " recollected Tammy.

"This is what Bryan will be searching for next," spoke up Jo.

172

"If the owl head was a literal mountain then this full-bodied bird is also some natural feature or landmark," hypothesized Tammy.

"That's the way I see it too," agreed Josh. "Remember the *'Wandering Sky'* and the *'Door of the Sun.'*"

"Very much," Tammy replied.

"If the Captain's map is somewhat proportionate, then this mystery bird has to be a day or two south of us," reasoned Jo.

"From what I've read," commented Heather, "this whole area is loaded with all kinds of minerals, such as rare earth, gold, silver, and others."

"Most of this area between the two Interstates is also in the Mojave National Preserve under Federal protection," added Jo.

"Our primary goal should be to find Bryan and not necessarily solve the mystery," stated Tammy.

"But it may come down to solving it so that we can find him," countered Jo.

"Bryan may be the only one who can solve it," replied Tammy. "I would prefer it if we were with him before he tries something foolish."

"So what are we going to do?" pondered Jo motioning with her hands.

"Well, from a practical standpoint, Cima and Ivanpah are points where many of the roads intersect," pointed out Josh. "I would hate to just sit around and watch these crossroads for a chance meeting."

"Especially in this heat," agreed Jo.

"So maybe what I can do, if you guys station yourselves at one of the crossroads, is that I can drive around the loop," he proposed.

"That's not a bad idea," praised Tammy. "But does Bryan know you are right on his heels?"

"No, he has no idea," believed Josh.

"Then we have the advantage of surprise," concluded Tammy.

"But not the advantage of intellect?" questioned Jo.

"Perhaps not, but we have him physically boxed in if we act quickly," Tammy replied.

Jo could see how determined she was to make things right.

"I wish I could stay and see how this works out," commented Heather.

"That's right, we have to get you back to your car," remembered Josh.

Tammy discreetly asked, "Josh, what are our sleeping arrangements?"

"I rented a room today in Primm which is just up the road so we could clean up. You guys could share that room," he answered. "I'll get another room for the night."

"You guys are getting a little chummy, sharing a room like that," she teased.

"Tammy! It's not that way," he refuted. "She's from Southern California and I'm from the northern mountains. It may never develop into anything."

"Yeah, yeah, country boy meets city girl. I know all about it," rebuffed Tammy. "You two can't help but get to know each other with as much time as you've been spending together."

"Despite our differing backgrounds we do seem to get along," agreed Josh. "But there is one thing that worries me."

Bryan stayed overnight in Jean, Nevada. He dreamed about walking in the legendary cavern that contained the "River of Gold" that night. He wondered how such a thing could dovetail into the Captain's cryptic note about the "river below."

This part of the Captain's mystery could be more difficult to solve," he thought to himself. What he needed to do was go into more of a stealth mode because now the area of search had been drastically reduced. With that in mind, Bryan decided to drive up to Las Vegas and rent a four-wheel drive Jeep and play the part of a desert tourist. They gave him permission to leave his vehicle in an overflow lot. After transferring his stuff over, the salesman was a bit astonished when he noticed that Bryan slipped a cover over his aged truck.

It took a half hour for Bryan and Tramp to get back on the road. Tramp didn't seem to like the Jeep Grand Cherokee, perhaps because of the scent. Bryan's older truck was full of his scent and had plenty of room on the seat to sit and lie down.

The thought of those eight miles that Earl Dorr mentioned in his affidavit kept coming back to him. Camino's "black bird" was definitely many miles south of Clark Mountain.

Suddenly, Bryan had an epiphany. The "downward sun" must have a special relationship with the "black bird" as denoted by it being held in its beak. Could it be a place where the sun actually does shine into an underground cavern? Nevertheless, the overall question still remained: Where is this "black bird" and what is it?

That could be a good starting point approximately eight miles south of Kokoweef near the south end of the Ivanpah Range, namely around Kessler Peak. Bryan also took note that Mitchell Caverns in the Providence Mountains was directly in line and south of the Ivanpah Mountains. Could the same geological formations run throughout that region? He realized he would have to be careful about building a whole new paradigm surrounding the Earl Dorr story.

Another area of consideration was a place called Hole in the Wall, a couple of miles east of the northern tip of the Providence Range. Somewhere out there was this great black bird, but where?

"Tramp! I need a good bird dog right now," Bryan half-laughed.

A pang of conscience again ran through him reminding him underneath it all he was still hurting. He should have known that separating Tammy from her city ways would be difficult.

Heat waves stirred the desert air as he drove on. Taking the Nipton turnoff it was only a short distance to the Ivanpah Road. After two miles the narrow paved roadway branched off to the right onto the Morning Star Mine Road that ran south paralleling the Ivanpah range and Kokoweef Peak, which was about five miles west. This was his first look at the controversial mountain

175

range which had a grey-white appearance due to the banded limestone tilted on end.

After several miles Bryan approached Kessler Peak at the southern tip of the Range. Dust boiled up behind him as he cut across the flat desert plain. Nearing the mountains the route came around a number of hills to finally run along the base of the range itself. Driving another two and one half miles he stopped at a small promontory to make observations.

Letting out Tramp, he put a hat on and took off his sunglasses. Grabbing his field glasses he stood at the front of the Jeep to view the outstanding landmarks. Bryan took his time in studying sections of the slopes in detail, but nothing seemed remarkable. There were a number of mining sites scattered throughout the adjoining hills, probably dating back to the thirties and forties. Some of the overgrown tailings may even have originated with the time of the Spanish miners.

Kessler peak eight miles south of Kokoweef was a dome-shaped light brown granite formation that showed no characteristics of a bird shape.

Perhaps a key to the whole thing was the word—black, which was only revealed through the cryptic interpretation of the clue built into the land grant document. Another adjective that was no doubt an additional clue was the word—great, which could indicate that the bird was quite large. But black would indicate that the "great black bird" was in fact volcanic in nature. The reality was that nothing in the Ivanpah lent itself to that particular geological formation. There seemed to be no link with the Kokoweef legend.

On the road again Bryan continued south on the Morning Star Mine Road to Cima, which in Spanish meant summit or high point. This was the high point in the desert floor. It was named because of its location on the Union Pacific Railroad that was built many years before. A small rustic post office and a store was the only life in town. The rest of the town was basically a number of tumbled down shacks scattered in the sagebrush.

Beyond Cima, Bryan took the Cedar Canyon Road through what was called the Mid-Hills, over the hump into an area that was more volcanic. The pavement ran out after about a mile, but it was still a well-graded dirt road. He realized he was moving more into the center of the Captain's land grant. To the north was the New York Mountains and to the south was the Providence Mountains where the Mitchell Caverns were located. Bryan still had the cavern thing in his head. He wondered to what depth this cave penetrated. Indications were that the volcanic field stretched all the way to the northeast corner of the cave system.

Black Canyon Road now took him south through the heart of the maze of lava flows and volcanic buttes which included the Hole in the Wall which was an area of geological interest as well. It included a campground and also a small information center which was not manned in the summer. From this point on the roadway turned to pavement, and it did not take long to eventually break out into the downward slope of the vast basin of Clipper Valley.

The rugged Providence Range was now plainly visible five miles to the west. He quickly reached Essex Road which led directly up to the Mitchell Caverns. Making a right turn he followed the paved road toward the mountains. As Bryan drew closer, he could make out the limestone formation that was lying up against the Providence Range. Once into the foothills, the roadway became narrower, but the slope was still moderate.

Two buildings were visible above him. First there was an overflow parking area, then a switchback to the left that brought him up to the main parking area and the visitor's center. The perimeter of the site was well landscaped with native cacti, stonework, and many benches. The building itself was small and lined with stone around the exterior walls. It definitely was not peak season approaching the hottest time of the year. There were only three vehicles parked up near the visitor's center.

It was definitely time to take a break, walk the dog, and eat a little something before going in. He found a picnic table that had

177

some shade provided by a mesquite tree. From his vantage point Bryan could see a trail winding its way along the bluffs south of his location leading up to the cave entrance.

Bryan was a little concerned about his appearance since he had not shaved or bathed in days. But there was little he could do to remedy the situation at this time.

Leaving Tramp on the front deck of the building Bryan went in to look at the exhibits and ask a few questions. There was not much room in the small building for exhibits or visitors. He noticed a main counter toward the back where individuals could talk with one of the rangers. Maps, photographs, minerals, and sections of stalactites were on display. One wall was covered with flyers and pamphlets covering places of interest in the area. A sign disclosed that it was a constant 65° in the cavern, and if you paid four dollars you could sign up for a tour and be cool. That made him smile.

An older ranger sat behind a desk in the corner. He must have been about fifty years old. Behind the counter were two young women in their early twenties. One nudged the other after seeing Bryan. He ignored that as he came up to the counter. A brown-haired young woman dressed in uniform smiled at him. Her name tag indicated that her name was Emily.

"And how can I help you?" she asked in a flirtatious tone.

"You can help me find a black bird," he answered.

"Black bird?" Emily questioned losing her smile.

"It's a landmark or something," muttered Bryan.

"Oh," she replied not knowing what to say.

"I'm curious though on how deep this particular cave system goes?" he asked.

"There are new galleries being found all the time, but in general it is several hundred feet deep," answered Emily.

"Hmm, I was hoping for something much deeper."

Emily's eyes brightened up. "Would that include a relationship?" she whispered.

Bryan bent his head down and looked at her. "How about just a tour of the cave for starters," Bryan replied.

"In five minutes," answered Emily after glancing at the clock. "Tour starts in five minutes," she announced to the whole room.

"I've been out in the desert for days, can you tell?"

She smiled, "Yes, I'm afraid I can."

Three others joined the tour which began with a half mile hike up to the cave entrance. Tramp trotted along with the group as they went.

"So, are you a spelunker? Is that why you're asking about the depth of the cave?" asked Emily as they walked the paved path.

"I have done my share, but my forte is really mountain climbing," he replied. "How long have you been here?" Bryan asked her.

"Just this spring," she answered. "This is my first assignment in working in a State Park."

"I can understand why you crave companionship way out here, but there are those you just can't trust. It might be more prudent to just dwell out here in the desert and not have a relationship with anyone," he commented.

"Wow, sounds like someone has cheated on you or something," she gathered. Bryan gave no further comment.

Arriving at the first cave entrance, Emily unlocked the metal door and switched on the lighting system. Again Tramp had to wait outside and watch for their return. It was definitely cooler in the cavern and dark compared to the hot, bright conditions on the outside. There were three separate areas of the cave; two of them were very large. The lighting back-lit many displays of soda straws, flowstone, and numerous stalactite clusters decorating the ceiling. Emily used a laser pointer to highlight some of the outstanding formations.

In one particular section of the cave, the walls were strangely discolored in places. Their guide explained that in 1990, one sequence from the movie, "The Doors" was filmed here. Indian pictographs were painted on the walls with a vegetable-based dye that was supposed to have washed off when done, but it didn't. In time the chemistry of the Cave would make them disappear.

One chasm they passed over was called the Bottomless Pit, but in actuality it was only a couple hundred feet deep. Passing through all three rooms they were soon back outside by way of a second entrance or exit in this case.

The trail brought them back around the mountain to the first entrance where Tramp was patiently waiting in the shade.

"Nice dog," commented one of the visitors. "How long have you had him?"

"Funny you should ask," replied Bryan. "It's just been a few days. I rescued him up near Death Valley."

"Really? What happened to his owner?" they all began asking.

Bryan took a deep breath. "He was buried in a cave-in at an old abandoned mine."

"Was he your friend?" concernedly was the next question.

"No, I never knew him. It was a number of days after the incident that Tramp actually found me," he explained.

Emily came up behind him and grabbed his arm above the elbow to speak in his ear. "Did you know they are looking for you?"

"Yeah, probably, but I have to finish something important first," answered Bryan.

"They are calling you the mystery man of the desert. You appear and disappear," she added.

"Emily, I want you to forget that I was here. And only if someone by the name of Josh or Jo should appear, tell them I'm fine and I will soon reappear," he quietly requested of her.

Releasing his arm she led the group back down the trail to the visitor's center. As everyone scattered Emily turned to Bryan.

"You asked about a black bird. There is a butte in the Hole in the Wall. I think you should check out," she informed.

"Thank you for that. You are like a refreshing spring in the desert," complemented Bryan.

"I don't know what you are looking for, Bryan, mystery man of the desert, but I hope you will find it," she responded stepping up on the deck.

As Bryan drove away he noticed Emily still standing on the deck in the lengthening shadows watching him go. He waved squinting into the sun.

Along the way Bryan pondered his strategy. Either he had to continue pushing to get to the end of this, or stop and just forget about Captain Camino and pursue another life elsewhere. But he couldn't just walk away. A wrong had to be righted. In a broader sense he did wonder as Emily had alluded to—what was he really looking for?

"Tramp, I guess we better head back to Hole in the Wall where all the desperados are holed up," Bryan announced giving him a pet as they made the turn onto Black Canyon Road and headed north.

Besides location, Emily's tip gave the Hole in the Wall a heightened possibility. There was still enough daylight to do a little recon before dark. There was a campground nearby, but it was too open. He needed to find a secluded spot.

A small information center was also located here, but it was closed for the season. The area was characterized by a reddish-brown rhyolite lava formation perforated with indentations and holes created by massive gas eruptions. It was the Swiss cheese of rock formations so to speak. There were a number of posters mounted inside the glass on the exterior of the information center that explained the mechanics of the different volcanic episodes that created the present landscape.

Bryan could understand why this place was so popular. It would be fun to explore all the nooks and crannies of these unique formations. There were a number of designated trails that led back into this geological wonderland.

He noticed on a map a nameless butte that was up behind the Hole in the Wall formation. To get to it would mean traversing through some of the most rugged passageways. It was too late to go back into these to do a search that evening.

181

Traveling north Bryan noticed there was no one in the campground, but a half mile further he found a side road that dead-ended in the hills. This was an ideal spot to be out of the public spotlight. He was feeling a little self-conscience about his hygiene after visiting Mitchell Caverns that day. Heating a pan of water he attempted a sponge bath.

Settling down for the night he had a moment to pause and reflect. He felt a pang of loneliness. In some ways he realized he still desired human companionship of some kind.

It was very quiet the next morning as Bryan went about taking care of chores. Breaking the silence was a small flock of birds making their way along the bluffs. During the night it had cooled off to about 60° and the humidity was quite low.

Back at the Hole in the Wall, Bryan parked near the trailhead and made preparations for the hike. He decided to pack light except for water. Tramp was noticeably anxious to start. He reminded him of Graffiti, their family dog, and all the adventures they had shared.

The most direct route appeared to be the Rings Trail that wound its way through the maze of rock formations. Entering a rocky narrow canyon the convoluted shapes were extraordinary. Elephant ears, faces, and giant erector sets of bizarre creations were everywhere. The floor of the slot canyon took a sudden drop down a steep slope. There were metal rings anchored into the rock to ease hikers down the slope; thus the name Rings Trail. It was tricky getting Tramp down, but he basically slid and carried him the rest of the way. It was still cool in the shadowy ravines, but coming out into the open he could feel the heat from the sun.

Rising high above him directly south of his position was a tall reddish-brown butte. It reminded him of a conning tower on a submarine. It did have a bird head shape at the top with a jutting rock structure that resembled a beak. In the different layers of its geological makeup was evidence of its volcanic history.

182

There was a moderate slope up to the base of the rugged butte. They soon reached a point almost under the protruding beak that jutted out from the rock tower.

"Well Tramp, let's walk around and take a look," stated Bryan after they had a good drink.

According to what was depicted on Camino's map the 'downward sun' was being held in the bird's beak. So the beak was the key he thought to himself. Directly beneath the beak was a large rock bulge at the base of the butte, but nowhere on its surface were to be found any markings, nor upon the wall of the butte itself. This was disappointing, but Bryan kept checking around the wall of the butte.

He was so busy working along the wall that he did not see the danger that was afoot. Bryan heard the rattle of a snake near his ankle and jumped back. The venomous creature came out of its hiding place on the attack. Bryan stumbled on the retreat, but Tramp came to the rescue barking which gave him time to escape.

"Thanks Tramp, that was close. I was not paying attention," he praised the dog while petting him. "It's a Mojave rattler I do believe. We're the offender in this case; let's give him a wide berth."

It took about thirty minutes to circle the base of the rock tower, but again there was nothing to be found. Bryan used his field glasses to scour the horizon. He realized this site was a major failure. The reddish-brown rhyolite formations were in no way black, and the butte itself did not show itself to be the full body of a bird. The conclusion of the matter: it was time to move on.

On the return trip, Bryan and Tramp followed an alternate trail through another section of ravines and formations. A loud roar above them gradually manifested itself. It was most likely some kind of aircraft, probably a helicopter. Exiting the rocky canyon he glimpsed two helicopters flying away from him. If they were looking for him, it was a good thing he had been hidden in the rocks he thought to himself. Plus the Jeep had no connection to him. That may have saved his skin. Bryan had a feeling that it had to be the Feds, but how did they know where to look?

Climbing back into the Jeep he wondered, what next? Using the process of elimination, he began shading in the areas on his map in which he had visited. It appeared that ranges to the east and to the north were the next likely subjects, namely Woods Mountain and Hackberry Mountain.

16

PLANE DOWN

Next morning, Josh could tell that Tammy and Jo were trying to get along, which was a great relief to him. After a good breakfast they headed south into Ivanpah Valley.

Putting their plan into action, they started out by stationing Tammy's car at Cima near the store. The girls monitored all the traffic that passed between the two mountain ranges. Josh drove around the loop that included the Ivanpah and Cedar Canyon Roads. If Bryan was anywhere in the northern section there was a good chance they would cross paths.

Well stocked with water and snacks, the girls sat there trying to keep themselves alert while the hours ticked by. Josh made the loop twice reversing direction on the second trip.

While Tammy was more focused on the direct approach, Jo was still trying to figure out the mystery of the final symbol, thinking it would be the quickest way to find Bryan.

"While Bryan and I were at the Big Pine Fire Camp, we met a man who was familiar with many of the petroglyphs of the Mojave region," related Jo. Tammy felt uncomfortable about Jo relating anything that transpired between her and Bryan. "He seemed to think that the 'downward sun' related to something that was dark, dangerous, and possibly even subterranean," she continued.

"Subterranean," repeated Tammy thinking about that possibility. "Isn't there a cave or two around here?" she wondered.

"Yes, I think there is," replied Jo rustling through her maps. "Just south of here about twenty miles is the Mitchell Caverns," she pointed.

"Maybe that's why there is no sign of Bryan in this northern section," commented Tammy.

"When Josh gets back, let's talk to him about heading down to the Caverns," suggested Jo.

"That sounds like the thing to do," agreed Tammy.

Thirty minutes later Josh returned clearly frustrated. The girls shared with him what they had discussed and it seemed good to him.

Back on the road, Tammy drove her car while Jo navigated. Josh followed closely in his pickup except when the dust began kicking up. The route was an easy drive on pavement, then onto a well-graded dirt road, and finally back to pavement again near the Hole in the Wall. It must have been about two in the afternoon when they arrived at the Cavern without sighting Bryan anywhere on the way.

Tammy wasted no time in getting out and entering the visitor's center. She took off her sunglasses and let her eyes adjust to the light. Glancing around Tammy took in the whole room and stepped up to the information counter. A young woman smiled and greeted her.

"You may be able to help me. I'm looking for a young man that may have been here recently. His name is Bryan Anderson, he is about five foot eleven, and has black hair," inquired Tammy.

"Possibly, but let me check with the other ranger," she replied. After an interchange of words with the other ranger, the second ranger glanced at Tammy. She approached just as Jo and Josh came in. Tammy noticed she had such searching eyes.

Taking note of her name tag she asked again, "Emily, have you seen a young man by the name of Bryan?

186

"What is your name?" asked Emily.

"Tammy Holden," she replied.

"Who are your two friends?" Emily further asked. This continued questioning was making Tammy impatient for an answer.

"I'm Josh and this is Jo," he introduced.

"I have a message for you two," declared Emily. "But who are you?" she asked of Tammy.

"I'm Bryan's fiancée," answered Tammy getting a little testy.

"Oh, so you're the one who has been insincere with him," replied Emily.

"How is it you know this?" demanded Tammy.

"Because Bryan was here a couple of days ago and he hinted at a few things. He said if Josh and Jo should come by, I was to let them know not to worry, that he is fine, and he will reappear again in a few days," related Emily.

"How did he seem?" questioned Tammy.

"He was okay, even though he hadn't shaved or bathed in a while," she laughed. "But it did seem there was some kind of cloud over him."

Josh observed, "You seem to be very protective of Bryan. It's okay, I understand, he seems to have that affect on women."

Emily smiled. "So Jo, you're not his mistress or something are you?"

"Jo blurted out with a laugh. "Yeah, I'm next in line if something should happen to Tammy, and I guess that puts you in third place. I'm joking! No, we're just concerned for him and plenty worried that he is going to do something foolish."

"Jo, I'm glad you cleared that up," commented Tammy.

"Say," came a woman's voice from the other side of the room, "I couldn't help but overhear your conversation. If this guy is so great where can I sign up?" she asked. Everyone laughed clearing the air.

"Is there anything he said that would indicate where he was going next?" asked Tammy.

"Ah, yes, I think it would be good if you did catch up with him and settle matters," she replied addressing Tammy directly. "He mentioned he was looking for a black bird, a landmark of some kind. I knew of a rock formation at Hole in the Wall and I suggested that he try looking there."

"Oh, one more thing, was there a dog with him?" asked Josh.

"There was, his name is Tramp, a Border collie," confirmed Emily.

"Thank you. You sure helped narrow our search," appreciated Jo.

"I'm curious though, what is it that Bryan is pursuing?" asked Emily.

"It's kind of complicated," stated Tammy. "Sometimes I wonder if he is just exploring the limits of his own ego."

"Emily, it's probably better you don't know anything at this time, because the U.S. Government is involved in this," informed Jo. "We don't want you drawn into the vortex."

"If it doesn't hit mainstream media, we'll fill you in later. Maybe we'll have a big get-together and you're invited," added Tammy.

It was late enough in the day to consider where they would spend the night, but it was too early to just stop there. They decided to head back north to the Hole in the Wall. Logic dictated that since Bryan was no longer at this location that he must not have found the 'black bird' and had moved on. But unsure of where to camp that night the decision was to stay at the adjoining campground.

"I'm wondering how it came about that Bryan is looking for a 'black bird,' " spoke up Josh setting up the camp stove.

"That crossed my mind too," replied Jo sorting her tent poles.

"He must have found additional clues somewhere. Maybe there was something at the owls head or elsewhere along the route," interjected Tammy as she dug into Josh's camp box.

"If it's a 'black bird' we're looking for, then I would think that the landmark may be basaltic in nature," thought Jo.

"Apparently not these reddish-brown formations," agreed Tammy.

After dinner Josh decided he was going to check out the rock formations before it got dark and asked if the girls wanted to go exploring, but they declined. An hour and a half had passed since he left and it was beginning to get dark. They realized that Josh had not taken a flashlight or anything. With only twenty minutes of daylight left the girls found a couple of flashlights and a handful of glow sticks, locked the vehicles, and headed out on the path that led to the exhibit trailhead.

"I sure hope nothing has happened to him," stated Tammy.

"Where would we be, two women alone out on the desert?" replied Jo.

"We need our men don't we?" reflected Tammy.

"Yeah, especially when you have feelings for them," Jo confessed.

"Really?" asked Tammy.

It's been kind of subtle, but I think so. But don't tell Josh," she requested.

"I'm afraid as regards Bryan and myself, he probably hates me right now and I don't know what's going to happen when we catch up with him," expressed Tammy.

"I think he will come around," reassured Jo.

"I'm not so sure," commented Tammy.

Reaching the main trail they proceeded into the canyon of bizarre formations as light dimmed in the passageways.

"Joshua! Can you hear us?" called out Tammy.

Jo raised her voice too, but there was no reply. Walking slowly into the dark recesses shadowy figures leered at them at every turn. Turning on the flashlights didn't seem to help. Light and dark scary figures kept presenting themselves.

"Could be animals hiding in these holes," spoke up Jo as they crept along.

"Don't say that it's creepy enough," warned Tammy.

"Josh, you come out here right now!" demanded Jo. "Before we die of fright," she added under her breath.

There was a faint call somewhere way back in the recesses of the rock formation.

"Did you hear that?" whispered Tammy.

"Yes, let's keep moving straight ahead," replied Jo.

"Josh! Can you hear us?" again called out Tammy as they also flashed their light around hoping that would help him come towards them.

Gradually, Josh's voice became louder and they closed the gap. But then there was no more response from him and everything was silent.

"Where is he," demanded Jo.

"What is that?" asked Tammy noticing some form of illumination along the upper wall of the ravine.

That glow grew larger as they rounded a corner. A low sound resembling something produced by an animal was heard directly ahead. Suddenly, there was a loud yowl that made the girls cringe and scream. At that moment Josh jumped out of the shadows with a limp.

"Just me," he informed.

"Joshua! You tried to scare us," protested Tammy.

"No, I just stubbed my toe on a rock," he explained.

"Josh, what happened to you?" asked Jo in a demanding tone.

"I got turned around in my directions and apparently took a wrong turn and ended up in the back forty," he recounted. "And by the way, thank you for coming to look for me."

"I'm so happy you're okay," responded Jo giving him a quick hug.

Tammy smiled to herself seeing them respond to each other in a touching way.

"What is that strange light up there near the top of the ravine?" pointed Tammy.

"Moonrise I do believe," informed Josh.

"Oh," she laughed.

It didn't take long for them to retrace their steps and re-emerge back in the open where it was a bit lighter.

"Look at that moon!" declared Jo.

"Wow, that's out of this world," commented Tammy.

They stood in awe of a reddish tinged crescent moon rising out of the desert floor. It looked so large that it appeared that the moon was at a near collision point with the earth. Heat waves along the horizon scattered the light creating a layer of transparency giving the moon a sense of aloofness.

"That is one of the most amazing things I have ever seen," reiterated Jo.

"Not exactly a romantic moon," commented Josh.

"But it is a hint of red in the evening," observed Tammy.

The moon continued to rise above the horizon with various stars now gathering around it in the increasing darkness.

Back at camp, Tammy had something on her mind to present to the others. Jo made a comment about the uncertainty of how to proceed the next day. Josh thought they should head back north looking for a more basaltic volcanic area. After hearing their ideas, Tammy thought it was time to reveal her plan.

"Josh, Jo, I have an idea that I have been thinking about to help us cut to the chase," spoke up Tammy.

"What do you have in mind?" asked Josh unrolling his sleeping bag.

"By way of a ground-based search we have not been able to close the two day gap. My idea is to charter a small plane with a pilot of course and cover the whole area in about two hours," she proposed.

"Can you afford to do that?" questioned Josh.

"I can't afford not to," Tammy replied.

"Okay," agreed Josh, "how can we co-ordinate our activities?"

"There is a primitive air strip about ten miles east of here where we could meet if we had to," recalled Jo.

"That would work," thought Josh. "Jo and I could park near the runway. If there is a development you can have the pilot drop you off and we could drive directly to the location of the sighting."

191

"And if there is no sighting, just have the pilot make a couple of circles over us and return to the airport," added Jo.

"He has to be out there somewhere," believed Tammy. "What do you think? Is it worthwhile, or will it just put us back another day?"

"I think it's worth a shot," answered Josh.

"I have to admit, it is a very good idea," thought Jo. "Besides, we could utilize the morning searching the area between here and the airstrip, while you are making the arrangements for your flight."

"Thank you for your vote of confidence. Okay, it's settled. I will leave early in the morning and head for the closest airport," finalized Tammy.

"That's probably going to be in Henderson, Nevada," informed Josh.

"Good, that's not too far," acknowledged Tammy.

Sometime after dark when preparing to turn in for the night they heard the sound of a vehicle and could see headlights on the main road approaching their camp. It was unusual for anyone to be out late on these desert back roads. The vehicle slowed as it approached coming to a stop near Josh's truck. The driver's door swung open with the engine still running.

"Hello!" called out a female voice. "Is there a Tammy Holden here by any chance?" she asked.

"Who is asking?" inquired Josh who had walked part way out toward the visitor.

"Rachel!"

"Rachel?" he questioned.

"Rachel? Is that you?" spoke up Tammy.

"Yes, it's me," she disclosed.

"Park your car next to ours," directed Josh.

"My goodness, Rachel, what are you doing way out here?" asked Tammy rushing over to hug her.

"Who is this Rachel?" inquired Jo quietly to Josh.

"Tammy's best friend, and roommate at the University," he answered.

"What is she doing out here?"

"I don't know, let's find out," stated Josh.

"Tammy, are you okay?" asked Rachel. "That phone call scared the living daylights out of me."

"What phone call?" asked Tammy.

"Ah-h, you didn't call me?"

"No-o. I probably should have called you when I got back, but I didn't," she informed.

"Then who called me and how did they know you were here in the desert?" wondered Rachel. "Oh, no, don't tell me I've been sucked into the old cloak and dagger."

"It would seem so," interjected Josh.

"Hi, Josh," greeted Rachel.

"Rachel, I would like you to meet, Jo, and Jo this is Rachel," he introduced.

"Glad to meet you," they interchanged.

"Rachel, grab your stuff, I'll fill you in," informed Tammy.

"Josh, she is here for a reason, and I'm not for sure why," determined Jo.

"I don't think Rachel would intentionally bring harm to any of us," he defended.

During the night Tammy could hear the wind picking up and the flaps on the tent fluttering. She was still quite surprised by Rachel's sudden appearance. But feeling cozy she soon fell back asleep trying to dream about flying over and seeing Bryan standing by his pickup waving at her beckoning her to join him.

Next morning a consistent breeze was still blowing out of the north. It would prove to be a very eventful day especially for Tammy. Rachel was up and around soon after Tammy helping her to break down the tent.

Josh hadn't seen Rachel in many months and had forgotten how tall she was.

"Tammy has asked me to stay for a couple of days to help find Bryan," commented Rachel.

193

"No offense, but Big Brother may be using you to find what they're looking for, and that would not necessarily be Bryan," frankly explained Jo.

"We talked about that last night," defended Rachel. "If for some reason we are on the verge of such an earth shattering event, I will immediately disappear."

"They may have planted a tracking device in your car or among your belongings," speculated Josh.

"If that is true then search my car, and Jo can check my belongings," she suggested. "Their intelligence on your location was not exact. I was given a number of different places to look."

Rachel gave Josh the keys to her '90 Saab so he could check for electronic bugs. Josh looked carefully through the trunk and the passenger department, but found nothing. Slipping under the edge of the car he looked up along the frame, and spotted a suspicious dirty grey box. It had no wiring or anything connected to it. Could it be magnetically attached he wondered? Using the tip of a tire iron Josh pried it off. It did appear to magnetically mounted. He did not expect this and it proved to be very unsettling to him. His first thought was to destroy it, but no, it actually could prove to an asset later. Taking it over to the girls he showed it to them. Jo was visibly dismayed, and Rachel was shocked that someone would actually do such a thing. Tammy was more concerned about finding Bryan and was not surprised. Josh shared his idea on how to use it as a decoy when the time came. The others thought that was an excellent idea, but in the meantime it would have to be taken to an arbitrary location.

They settled into a quiet moment contemplating their new circumstances while munching on a cold breakfast. Finishing packing, Tammy was about ready to go. Jo gave Tammy a map and acquainted her with many of the visible land marks and the roads that would serve as boundary lines. Josh pointed out the airstrip that was called Conner's located just north of Hackberry Mountain where they would watch for her. Tammy left leaving a trail of dust behind her.

There was no real hurry for them to head out so Josh took the opportunity to make a couple of minor repairs on his camp gear.

Jo hopped up and sat down on the tailgate of the pickup next to where Josh was working facing him.

"What's up, Sunshine?" he asked noticing how she smiled at him.

"Josh, thank you for holding this whole thing together. It was good that Tammy came and joined us. My apprehension was unfounded," she confessed.

"I'm glad it's working out, and hopefully it's all going to end well," commented Josh.

"Okay then, let's go find Bryan, a 'black bird' or something before we're all busted," stated Jo hopping back down.

Tammy had no traffic to contend with until she was on the freeway. Just south of Las Vegas a sign indicated that Henderson Executive Airport was a few miles east of the Interstate. It seemed to be a more logical place to charter a plane than at the International Airport where the major carriers were.

Taking the exit she followed the highway across a vacant stretch of land. A small plane was approaching from a distance. Large buildings and hangers now became visible. Chain-link fence guarded the perimeter of the airport which appeared to be quite modern in all appearances. Entering the main gate two signs caught her eye, Nevada air and Mojave Transportation.

Nevada Air, did charter planes, but were all booked up for the day. At Mojave, they didn't have anyone available at the time. She was told by the flight scheduler that if she could wait an hour or two they could have another pilot available. Tammy looked at her watch and said okay, if they could find someone by eleven that morning.

In the meantime Tammy sat in the waiting room watching various aircraft taking off and landing. A gust of wind sent dust blowing across the runway. She leafed through a gardening magazine. Seeing a picture of a flower garden beside a stylish house caused a pang to run through her. Casting aside the magazine she felt a degree of sorrow and guilt.

After an hour or so an older gentleman walked in asking if she was Tammy.

"Yes, I'm Tammy."

"I'm Ed," he introduced. "I'll be your pilot today."

"I'm very happy you are available," she answered.

"Come into the office, we need to fill out a flight plan and do a little paper work first," he informed.

"Sounds good," Tammy replied gathering her stuff.

Unfolding her map on his desk she pointed out the boundary of the area that she wanted to fly.

"Are we looking for someone?" asked Ed.

"Yes, I'm looking for a young man with a faded blue pickup," she answered.

"Shouldn't you notify the Sheriff's Department?" he asked.

"No, they won't act on this for a number of days yet," responded Tammy.

"Okay, let me gas up and do a pre-flight check and I will come and get you when it's time to board the plane," he finalized.

She could see a small white and gold striped Cessna taxiing up to the fuel pumps. Ed got out and began servicing the plane. At that point she felt nervous about the flight. In a few minutes he came in and declared everything was ready. Stepping up into the plane he helped her get strapped in.

"First time up?" asked Ed as he got in.

"No, I've flown a number of times on the large commercial jets and even a military helicopter, but never in a small plane like this," she answered.

"You were in the military?" he asked.

"No, it was on an actual rescue mission," explained Tammy. "Matter of fact it was involving the same person," she realized.

After communicating with the tower the pilot was given clearance to begin taxiing. Tammy took a deep breath as she was once again getting nervous. At the end of the runway they waited about one minute before they were cleared for takeoff. She held on to a crossbar as they accelerated. Tammy could feel the buoyancy as the plane lifted off. Buildings, fences, and roads were now underfoot as they powered their way higher and higher. The area to the south of the Airport was predominantly open desert with a few buildings scattered about.

"Okay, miss, where would like to start?" asked Ed as he checked his instruments.

"I was thinking of a south to north approach between the two Interstates starting on the west side in line with the Ivanpah Mountains," she answered while unfolding her map.

"Not many people know the names of these mountain ranges," commended her pilot.

"Yeah, it seems I've had to make a quick study of them," reflected Tammy.

"What relationship do you have with this guy, if I may ask?" he inquired.

"He's my fiancé, his name is Bryan," she answered.

"Oh! We better find him then."

"Absolutely," agreed Tammy.

Reaching altitude, a gusty wind began buffeting the small plane making their ride a bit rough.

"Winds are expected to get up to forty miles an hour today," commented Ed. "So hang on!"

"Oh, Ed, one more thing, do you know where Conner's Airstrip is at?" she asked.

"I do, it's out in the middle of Lanfair Valley," he answered.

"If we find Bryan, the plan is for you to drop me off there," informed Tammy.

"That old bulldozer runway is a bit rough as I recall," commented Ed.

Their course was due south passing to the west of McCullough Mountain and to the east of the jagged peaks of the Piute Range. Turning west they passed south of the Providence Mountains to make a sharp turn north through the Ivanpah Valley. Tammy pulled a pair of binoculars out of her bag and began scouring the desert floor and adjacent mountains. Along the way a rare vehicle or two caught her attention. It wasn't long before they were over Cima skirting the Ivanpah Range. Having no success they made a one hundred and eighty degree turn near Clark Mountain to head south paralleling their first course about five miles further east.

The ride was a bit smoother now that they were flying with the wind and not bucking against it. The air currents however did seem to be increasing in velocity. There were a number of mines on the west slope of the Providence Range, but no recent activity or human presence was visible. Cutting across the southern tip of the range Tammy could see Mitchell Caverns below them. She thought of Emily for a moment and the strange meeting they had.

Coming up to I-40 they reversed course once again heading back north repeating their pattern. As they made the turn a strong wind could be felt buffeting the tiny plane.

"We'll have to keep an eye out for sandstorms. If the wind gusts any higher we could be caught in one," warned Ed.

"What do we do if one develops?" asked Tammy.

"Fly out of it as quick as you can and get down on the ground," he answered.

"Woo!" exclaimed Tammy as the plane was suddenly jolted upward.

"Are you sure you want to finish this today?" asked her pilot.

"Yes, I really do," she replied.

"Okay, let's persevere and hope for the best," he responded.

Tammy could see Hole in the Wall just below on their right side. She could also see the campground, and no one was there. The situation brewing behind the mountain range is what they could not see. Their course was to take them over the Mid Hills that filled the gap between the Providence and the New York Mountain Ranges. Just before the crest of the mountain she spotted a green jeep and a dog running toward the rocks. That would not have normally caught her attention, but a sudden realization hit her that he could have switched vehicles. Tammy looked again and could tell that someone was standing at the base of the rocks. A pang ran through her as she realized that could very well be him.

"I don't like the looks of that sky to the north," declared Ed in a concerned voice.

"Looks dirty," commented Tammy.

As they passed over the main ridge the wind became ever more turbulent and a view to the west side of the rugged New York Mountains revealed a frightening sight. A brown cloud of sand and dust loomed only a few miles north.

"Sandstorm!" called out the pilot. "We'll have to dodge it and get back down on the ground. Sorry, that's all we can do today."

"That's okay, I may have just spotted him," she replied.

"I'm going to turn back and get in behind the New York Range and use it as a shield," he strategized.

Coming back over the Mid Hills she could see a glimpse of the Jeep but nothing else. Tammy guessimated the location and marked it on her map. It did not take long for the sandstorm to top the barren mountains and come pouring over like water out of a bathtub. The dust cloud quickly engulfed them, swirling like ocean currents.

"I'm going to drop down a bit," muttered Ed.

Tammy could tell he was nervous making her even more afraid. Visibility was only a thousand feet or less. After a minute the engine began to sputter.

In a move of desperation Ed abruptly turned the plane sharply to the right and tried to fly down and out of the cloud. It was scary not seeing anything. Tammy gripped the seat. Suddenly, the engine stopped. He tried to restart the engine but to no avail.

"Hold onto your seat lass we're going to try to glide her down," he announced. At that Ed radioed a mayday.

She was definitely scared now. It was ominous, only hearing the wind as it buffeted the plane as they continued flying blind.

"The air is starting to clear a little. I think I see the faint outline of something," believed Tammy.

"Could be Castle Peaks," he guessed. "And it looks like we're going in. Prepare yourself for a crash landing. I'll put us down in between the peaks, but we will have to do a belly landing.

He glanced at her, denoting the seriousness of their predicament. A frightening thought occurred to her. If she was to die, she would not be able to reconcile with Bryan.

Visibility improved enough for Ed to guide the plane into a small canyon between the pinnacles. The terrain was extremely rocky. To slow the plane, Ed pulled the nose up putting it into a stall.

"Put your head down, we're going in," he warned.

Complying, she closed her eyes, and ducked down putting her hands on her head. Seconds seemed like hours as she waited. Then Tammy felt the bottom of the plane hit the ground extremely hard with several impacts and then they skidded and collided with some jagged rocks. Violently the wings were sheared off and they were flung sideways smashing into the left canyon wall. Everything went black.

17

CASTLE PEAKS

"Josh you are so quiet this morning," noticed Jo as they drove around the north end of Woods Mountain.

"Oh, I was thinking about my jobs back home that I left unfinished," he commented.

"Yes, this little adventure is consuming a bit of time," she agreed.

"Oh, don't take me wrong," replied Josh. "Bryan is my best friend I'll do whatever it takes."

"You are a loyal friend," she complimented patting him on the shoulder.

Josh smiled. He glanced in the mirror to see Rachel following behind them. The wind was kicking up dust which blew across the dirt road in front of them.

On the north flank of the mountain was a small forest of pinion pine and juniper sharing the same microcosm. Further around the mountain they entered into Woods Wash and stopped to look around. Getting out they walked up a small knoll to get a better view of the area. Taking turns with the binoculars they surveyed the terrain in all directions.

"I'm not seeing a black bird anywhere," stated Josh handing Jo the field glasses.

"Maybe the 'black bird' is a shadow that only appears at a certain time of day," considered Jo.

"That is a stroke of genius," praised Josh. "If that is the case then the downward sun in its beak could mean that it would be at sunset."

"Woo, one genius deserves another," she replied.

"You'll have to explain to me what this 'black bird' is all about," requested Rachel.

"We really don't know," replied Jo leaving it at that.

"Looks like we're being watched," tipped off Josh.

The girls whirled around to see two wild burros watching them from further down the wash.

"Jack and Jenny!" laughed Jo.

"I guess we better locate that runway," reminded Josh.

"It's amazing how burros can survive out here," commented Rachel as they walked down to the vehicles.

Back on the sand and gravel road they came around to the north side of Hackberry Mountain, and almost immediately on their left was a primitive airstrip that came into view.

"It doesn't look like it has been used very much in recent years," observed Josh.

"Not when sage is trying to grow on the runway," agreed Jo.

"All we have to do now is sit and wait," stated Josh feeling a little frustrated.

"You want a drink?" offered Jo.

"No, but an ice cold beer does sound good right now," he replied.

"I noticed, you don't drink that much," she reflected.

"No, I don't need that artificial buzz to get along," Josh replied.

As they waited, Jo sat with Rachel in her car for a while visiting and sharing some of their mutual academic experiences.

The wind again caught their attention as it gusted by them. Jo was first to hear a plane coming from the south near the Providence Range. After a short time a plane could be heard again coming north this time a bit closer. Josh watched with the binoculars and finally spotted it near the direction of the Mid

Hills. He thought it could be Tammy's plane and handed the glasses over to Jo to take a look.

"The dust is sure blowing," complained Jo as she tried to follow the aerial speck. "It's passing over the Range."

"Yeah, and the sky is looking kind of murky over that way," noticed Josh.

"Like a dark haze," agreed Jo.

"Dust storm!" exclaimed Josh.

"That could cause a real problem for the plane," realized Jo.

"Do you see them anymore?" asked Rachel.

"No, the storm is spilling over the mountain range and I'm not seeing anything in that direction," she answered.

Josh took the glasses and closely viewed that stretch of the mountains, but no plane was visible.

"Let's hope they dodged the storm somehow," spoke up Josh.

"What about us? It's headed our way too," observed Rachel.

"So much for the best laid plans," complained Josh. "Landfair Road is not that far," he considered. "If we travel around to the leeward side of Hackberry Mountain, it should provide us with some protection."

"Yes, good, let's go-go-go the storm is already on the flat headed for us," urged Jo.

Bryan spent a day and a night in the Hackberry Range without anything to show for it except the sighting of a small herd of bighorn sheep climbing its rocky slopes. This reminded him of the many petroglyphs that depicted daily life of the natives that centered their existence upon this desert animal.

This prompted him to think about Jo and the friendship they shared. Leaving her and Josh in the lurch was not a pleasant recollection for him.

His next area of investigation was in the Mid Hills and the Table Rock area between the Providence Mountains and the New York Mountains about ten miles northwest of Hackberry Mountain.

On the way he reflected about the beauty of the open desert and the beckoning of faraway places, and that euphoric feeling that beyond the next gleaming mountain range he would find everything that he desired.

Table Rock was on the edge of the volcanic zone, but further west toward the Mid Hills the geology turned to more of a granitic nature.

The thought occurred to him that his search was bringing him closer and closer back to Kokoweef Peak in the Ivanpah Range. Maybe the "River of Gold" and the "river beneath" were all one in the same.

Up in this region there were a number of ranch sites most of which were now abandoned. Many of them still had operating windmills with storage tanks. Circling Table Mountain, Bryan tried to get a fix on the shape of the table-like plateau. After getting most of the way around, he determined its shape was that of a pinto bean, nothing as complex as a bird with wings. He took note of the large number of active springs that were scattered in two different areas around the mountain.

Later in the afternoon he pulled into a vacant campground located in the Mid Hills just west of Table Mountain. The ugly scars of a fire were apparent in one part of the campground and on the hillside beyond. Being in the leeward side of the Hills this was the natural home of a mixed forest of Pinion pine and juniper. This was the nicest campsite he had been to in the last few days. The tangle of juniper made for a private setting and a feeling of coziness.

After settling down for the night as twilight was coming on he tuned in his favorite radio station that he had come to adopt. Bryan could clearly hear Tumbleweed's distinctive voice and his theme music for the show. It was like he was sitting in his own living room listening to the music and the daily news. He awoke to find the radio making a popping noise and the station having gone off the air. Bryan realized he had fallen asleep. Turning the radio off, he and Tramp went right to bed.

Next morning Bryan found it to be annoyingly windy and it proved to be a pain in the neck to get anything done. He decided to sit in the jeep and enjoy his coffee while rummaging through his papers and maps scrutinizing his next move.

Was there anything that he was forgetting to look for? This rectangular shaped land grant was quite large. Where within it was the bird? It's supposed to be on the 'western rise' of a great cage as he recalled. But there was no indication of a "cage" or a "black bird." Bryan was somewhat baffled by his inability to solve this. Was there a higher level of logic that he could not see?

Bryan thought he would hike up into the bluffs to get a good view from the Mid Hills to gain a fresh perspective of the adjoining area. He delayed his departure hoping the wind would settle down, but it didn't. Bryan drove a mile or so to reach a convenient spot close to the bluffs that was somewhat sheltered from the north wind. He stuck a couple extra handkerchiefs in his pocket in case dust became a problem. It took a minute or two to wind his way to the base of the granite formation.

Looking back, Bryan noticed that the wind and dust was getting worse out in the open. At that moment he heard a plane approaching out of the south just as Tramp came running up to him. He couldn't spot the plane until it passed directly overhead. Going a short distance further Bryan could see that the sky was getting murkier. He thought to himself, "Uh oh." Bryan turned around immediately to make a beeline back to the vehicle.

In doing so he noticed that the small plane had again reappeared over his left shoulder and watched it turn northeast behind the New York Mountains to escape what was coming.

And come it did, blowing a dust cloud over the hills and rocks. Visibility was reduced to only several hundred feet. Nevertheless, Bryan recognized the landmarks he just came by and was able to keep a hold on Tramp as they worked their way back to the Jeep.

"Whew! Tramp, it's getting nasty out there," declared Bryan as he closed the door. "I guess all that we can do is go find a hiding a place. Another day lost," he grumbled.

Driving slowly, he crept back down the eroded slope to hunker down behind a large rock outcropping. The storm raged on for another hour and a half before it began to dissipate. A light wind continued to persist for the remainder of the day.

Bryan decided to return to the bluffs and follow through with his plan to recon the area. The sky was still hazy, but he could see Cima and Cima Dome as well as the cinder cones that dotted the horizon in the far west. Looking to the east and southeast it was ever murkier. Woods and Hackberry Mountains were but dark silhouettes in the gloom. There was no cage and no black bird to be seen anywhere. Bryan concluded that he was not approaching this mystery with the right viewpoint. He was missing some key element.

Returning to camp, he had to shake the sand off of everything and sweep out the tent. A lizard poked his head out of the sand to look around wondering if it was safe to come out. After catching up with his housekeeping duties, Bryan organized things for the evening. He decided to stay there one more night and contemplate his next move.

Later as the sun was beginning to set, while he was taking care of a few camp chores something on the radio made him stop in his tracks. There apparently was a plane missing in the Mojave Desert. It was after the sand storm had swept through the area that it turned up missing. He listened closely to what followed.

"Edward Daniels, the pilot and Tammy Holden a passenger were the only occupants," replied the announcer. "They were reportedly searching for a missing person themselves. The San Bernardino County Sheriff's Department is actively searching in an area to the south of Mountain Pass."

"Tammy!" exclaimed Bryan in disbelieve to what he heard. Tramp sat up wondering what was making his master so upset. "Tammy was out here looking for me? How can that be? She could be hurt or something much worse he realized. Tramp, it must have been the plane I seen earlier today that crossed these Hills, and then it veered in behind the New York Mountains." Bryan realized the Sheriff was looking for them in the wrong area, on the opposite side of the Range.

"Wow, what can I do?" Bryan asked frustrated.

The quickest way to find her would be by plane lso he reasoned. He could do that without jeopardizing his anonymity. Bryan noticed how red the sunset was that evening with all the dust in the atmosphere. A pain ran through him as reality set in that she could be dead! Had he somehow contributed to this? Bryan felt bad about this whole thing.

He determined there was no other recourse, but to go look for her himself. Bryan started packing up all his excess stuff. His plan was simple, just get to the airport at sun up and get a plane lined up to make his own search near the north end of the New York Range.

Tramp was slow to get motivated the next morning perceiving that the sun wasn't all the way up yet. It wasn't until Bryan started collapsing the tent that Tramp finally got up.

"You are getting to be one lazy dog, you know that Tramp?" stated Bryan.

After packing and loading all his gear he noted the sun had risen to just above the horizon.

"Okay, Tramp, let's go," called out Bryan holding the door open. "We'll catch something to eat later."

Once on the way it didn't take long to get back to pavement and head north on the Morning Star Road back to civilization. Bryan ended up at the same airport from which Tammy had departed from. He didn't know this or notice her car until later when someone mentioned that the missing plane was from Mojave Transportation.

Bryan was the first one through the door when Nevada Air opened up. It did not take him long to line up a flight, but it was with a novice pilot that just got his license and was eager to fly. The tall lanky young man was named David. There was something about khaki that he must have liked, because he was dressed head to foot in a matching outfit.

Bryan was pleased to get up in the air so quickly. He was quiet about his true intentions and just explained he wanted to fly over an old mining claim. If they did spot the plane there would be nothing they could do, except call in the location. Bryan was hoping for a better outcome.

Their course was due south. David thought if they passed between Castle Mountains and the Piute Range they should be right on target to sweep around and follow the east side of the New York Mountains. Bryan was impressed with Dave's navigational skills.

Before long they had passed between the two mountain ranges and after several miles began their turn toward the New York Range. Lanfair Valley was on their immediate right and was basically a large flat desert expanse with a couple of volcanic hills near the center. Hackberry and Woods Mountains were straight below them with the Mid Hills directly ahead.

Bryan looked down to see Table Mountain and the pattern of the associated mountains and buttes. Then it struck him. They made the shape of a gigantic bird with its wings extended upward. He took a double take. Yes! It was real. It was not his imagination.

"Dave, could I get you to make a 360° turn. I need to take a second look at something," requested Bryan.

"You're the boss," he replied.

Banking the plane to the right they gradually turned in a slow arc. He glimpsed Mitchell Caverns and the Providence Range as they came around. Returning to a west-northwest aspect Bryan could clearly see once again the 'great black bird,' and as he widened his consideration of the adjoining landscape he realized that the whole Lanfair Valley was the "cage." The arched outline of the "cage" was made of the seven separate mountains or mountain ranges that surrounded the whole Valley. And yes, the "black bird" was located on the western side of this vast cage of mountains. He drew a line around Table Mountain and its appendages. This was exciting, but the situation with Tammy cast a grey shadow over this discovery.

"Shall we continue on up along the New York Mountains as you mentioned earlier?" asked Dave.

"Yes, let's continue right on up," confirmed Bryan.

Bryan didn't have time to think about how his great great grandfather had realized the relationship and shape of these mountains. More importantly, he had to focus on trying to find Tammy. The question is how far did they fly in the storm before they went down?

"Do you know the pilot that is missing?" asked Bryan.

"No, not really. I've seen him around, but I've never met him," replied Dave.

"Is he an experienced pilot you think?" further asked Bryan.

"From what I hear he is a very experienced pilot, He answered.

Bryan shook his head in acknowledgement as he took that in. The New York Mountain Range proved to be a very substantial range of mountains. It was not totally barren. There were scattered trees in many of its sheltered hollows. Bryan was getting nervous as they flew on. So far there was nothing.

"Shall we continue all the way to the north end?" questioned Dave.

"Yes, go beyond the point where the Range runs out and I'll direct you after that," directed Bryan looking at his chart.

"Looks like Castle Peaks coming into view," observed his pilot.

Bryan looked closely as they passed to the left of these castle-like peaks. Beyond that point the Mountain Range gradually ended and sloped down into the desert floor.

"Let's go back to the Castle Peak area and make a couple passes through there," spoke up Bryan.

"Ten-four," replied Dave banking the plane to the right once again.

He navigated the plane between the main peaks and then over an area of lesser peaks that were more rugged. The canyons were narrower and deeper the further south they flew. Bryan thought he had seen a glint of something in one of the narrow canyons, but on a subsequent pass nothing caught his attention. He marked this location on his map.

One last resort was to return to Castle Mountains three or four miles further south of their position. A number of mining operations were visible on this small mountain complex. There was no sign of a plane here either, nor on the desert floor south and west of these locations. Bryan thought they could have been forced down to make an emergency landing out in the desert, but there was no sign of them.

On the return trip Bryan had him fly on a continuation of the course that led along the back of the New York Mountains to see if they had ditched on the Nevada side of the mountains, but again there was nothing along that route either.

Bryan wasted no time after getting back to the airport and returning to the Lanfair Valley area, not to look for the "black bird," but for Tammy. He had a suspicion that the glint he had seen was in fact something caused by glass or metal. Taking the Ivanpah Road he crossed the New York Mountains back into Lanfair Valley and followed a major dirt road that got him close to Castle Peaks. Bryan did some four-wheeling to get him near the base of the Peaks. He believed he had the correct canyon picked out. It was going to be a moderate hike up into the hills to access that particular canyon.

What did he need? Extra water, food, a first aid kit, and a trusty walking stick were a must. It was about noon and getting hot, but that wasn't going to delay his departure. Tramp let Bryan know that he didn't want to be left behind this time.

"Okay, Tramp, let's 'hit the dusty trail,' " he finally announced locking up the Jeep.

With map in hand he sighted on one of the pinnacles and struck out in that general direction gradually climbing the moderate slopes that led up to the rocky crags and the deep canyons that were hidden within. Sage and other desert shrubs dotted the hillsides all along the route. There were a number of minor plateaus that they had to ascend on the way up to the rock outcroppings. Bryan kept an eye out for snakes especially wherever there was a rocky recess. The direct sun was cooking them, but there was no other way but to pace themselves, stopping periodically to drink and rest. Bryan kept looking back, using the Jeep as a reference point.

Nearly a half hour into the hike they finally reached the base formation that Castle Peaks sat on. It was a sloping rock shelf about a thousand feet in width. A few scattered boulders sat idly on the rock apron. Larger boulders were heaped near the base of the pinnacles. Bryan and Tramp worked their way to the entrance of two deep canyons. The shade was welcome in this heat.

After a restful pause Bryan decided to search the left canyon first not knowing which of these was the correct one. Rock debris layered the floor having fallen from above. The width varied from fifty to one hundred feet as it meandered around the bases of the grey rock towers. Bryan couldn't see how a plane could land in such a confined space and survive. About a half mile in he could see a long distance and nothing was visible to the furthest extremity of the canyon.

Turning Tramp around Bryan headed back to enter the second canyon. This gorge climbed upward and finally leveled off after passing a mound of large rocks. The distance between the walls was far greater in this section he noticed.

Bryan spotted Tramp up ahead investigating something lying in the rocks on the right side.

"What did you find?" asked Bryan as he approached.

It was a wheel, a small wheel that could have come from a plane, he realized.

"Tramp, go find," ordered Bryan pointing ahead. He called out, "Hello! Can anyone hear me?"

He was afraid of what the next few minutes might reveal. Tramp ran on ahead.

Bryan called out again. "Hello, is anyone there?"

He then heard Tramp bark and then an indistinguishable sound. Hurrying and stumbling over the rocky terrain, Bryan noticed other metallic objects strewn about. Tramp barked twice alerting Bryan that he had found something.

Adrenaline pounding Bryan called out again, "Tammy! Tammy! Is that you?"

"Whose there? Can you help me?" called out a female voice.

"Tammy, is that you?" he asked not seeing from where the voice was coming from.

"Yes, I'm over hear, is that you Bryan?" came the questioning voice once again.

"It's me," Bryan answered finally seeing her up against the canyon wall in the shade. She struggled to get up. "No, don't move. I'm coming to you," he ordered.

Stooping down he could she was weeping, besides being battered and bruised. She immediately grabbed him and held him tight.

"My prayers have been answered," she said.

"You're alive that's what is important," declared Bryan. "How badly are you hurt?" he asked while she clung to him.

"I'll be okay, now that you are here. Will you kiss me even if I don't deserve it?" asked Tammy.

Bryan complied, but she could sense it was reserved.

"I have a first aid kit, water, and some food," he informed taking off his pack. "Oh, what about the pilot?" wondered Bryan looking about.

"He went to get help. He mentioned something about a place called Hart," she answered. "Ed has a broken arm, but I'm worried about him because he had a huge bump and a cut on his head. But since he could walk, he wanted to try. And that is what he decided to do."

"Hart, that's south of here over by the Castle Mountains, if I'm not mistaken," replied Bryan. "Your cheek has taken quite a smack," he noticed.

"I was completely knocked out when we crash landed," she revealed. "My left knee got banged up pretty bad and I was unable to stand for a while."

"It's amazing that the pilot was able to get you down in one piece in these canyons," commented Bryan looking over at the wrecked fuselage.

"So, this is your dog that I've heard about," realized Tammy. "Come here boy," she beckoned. Complying, he readily came to her and licked her wounded cheek. "So, you're Tramp."

"He was a desert tramp when I found him and he seemed to respond to that name," explained Bryan.

"Bryan, I need to tell you," reflected Tammy in a change of mood. "I was wrong in what I did. But I thought it was the right thing to do. They came to me and said if I didn't do what they said, they would take your life. I was scared."

"It is a relief to know that you didn't break my heart just because you loved city life more than me," he replied.

"Absolutely not, I love you more than anything," she confirmed. "It took me a while to come to my senses. Can you forgive me?"

"Of course I can. You know I love you. That's why it hurt so much." At that he then gave her another reassuring hug. "Don't talk now, let me doctor you up. Here, drink some water first," ordered Bryan.

"Usually, I'm the one doing the doctoring," Tammy commented.

Bryan was relieved to find Tammy alive and to realize that all the drama was caused by the Government once again trying to manipulate him to solve what they could not. But here he was thinking he could out run them all and still win. Somewhere out there he was being monitored, but how and by whom? His ability to stay in stealth mode was soon to come to an end.

"There, that's all we can do for now," spoke up Bryan. "I've missed you," he confessed looking into her eyes.

"I felt so empty without you too," she agreed hugging him again.

"Do you think you can walk?" he asked.

"Right now I think I can fly," Tammy answered. "On second thought I'd rather stay on the ground."

He laughed as he reached into his pack and said, "Here, eat the cheese and crackers I brought along, this will give you some energy. While you're doing that I'll write up a note, to let them know you have been rescued."

"Yes, by my knight in shining armor," she replied.

Bryan laughed. "No shining armor here, I haven't had a shower in days."

"No, but it's all good to me," shared Tammy.

Bryan included in the note about Ed's intention to walk to Hart for help. He placed it on the fuselage of the wrecked plane. After packing up, he made an adjustment to his walking stick so that it would serve as a crutch for Tammy.

Bryan extended his hand to raise her up. "Are you with me, woman?"

"Yes, I am," she replied extending her arm. "That is, if you'll still have me?"

Bryan pulled her up and replied, "Absolutely."

He outfitted her with the walking stick under her right arm and put his arm under her left arm to take the weight off.

"I think we're ready to take our first step," decided Bryan.

"Thank you kind sir," she replied optimistic that everything was going to work out between them.

Tammy took a couple steps and declared it felt good as long as she was able to keep the weight off her left side. Tramp trotted ahead to lead the way.

"I appreciate you coming out to look for me, but I was not lost," stated Bryan.

"We were afraid you were going to put yourself in peril," explained Tammy.

"We? Are you talking about Josh and Jo?" questioned Bryan.

"Yes, and Rachel is with them too. We had been following you for several days when I got the bright idea to get in a plane to find you. But now I'm probably just a handicap to you."

"No, actually it was because of you that I have found the 'great black bird,' " he revealed.

"Because of me?"

18

THE GREAT BLACK BIRD

J osh and Rachel were frantic after hearing the news that Tammy's plane had gone down; and Jo did her very best to comfort them while lapsing into tears herself. There was not much sleep that night.

After sheltering in behind Hackberry Mountain they drove back to Cima and made a phone call to the airport. At which time they were informed that Tammy's plane was missing. A bit in shock, the three of them decided to do their own ground search between the two mountain ranges in the perceived direction the plane had gone. Continuing until after dark, no sign of a plane was found.

Next morning, the three of them met two deputy sheriffs in their off-road vehicles at Cima monitoring the communications between the ground and a search plane that had been dispatched out of Victorville. The plane had arrived and was searching in a north to south pattern between the Ivanpah and the New York Mountains.

"I can't believe this is happening," commented Josh standing between the vehicles.

"Don't think bad, they could have set down somewhere and they'll be fine," Jo encouraged. "How is her family handling it?"

"Not well, they're making arrangements to come down," answered Josh.

Later in the afternoon after an unsuccessful search in the morning, it was extended another ten miles in all directions including over the New York Range that laid to the east. Josh knew he had seen or at least he thought he had seen Tammy's plane disappear to the west of the New York's. It did not make any sense why they had not been found.

While this was going on, Jo noticed a strange dark colored vehicle. It was parked at some distance from their location, on one of the back streets that had been part of the old town site. They were situated so that no other vehicle coming and going on the main roads could get a good look at them.

Jo pestered one of the deputy sheriffs to see who they were. And finally he decided to drive over to their location and check them out. But as soon as he headed their way, they drove off and proceeded to head north on Cima Road. The deputy did not pursue and quickly returned.

This bothered Jo. She recalled how someone had been at the ranger station in Bishop, inquiring about their whereabouts. How ironic, they were following Bryan, and perhaps someone was following them.

"Hey you guys!" called out Josh. "The pilot has been found in the desert near a place called Hart and he said Tammy is okay. She can't walk very well, and is still at the crash site. But she is alive!"

"Oh, what a relief!" exclaimed Rachel.

"Where is she?" Jo asked.

"A place called Castle Peaks," he replied.

"That's on the opposite side of this mountain range, about twenty miles north," explained one of the deputies.

"Wow, we were way off," commented Jo.

"You can follow us if you want," announced the same deputy closing the tail gate on his vehicle.

The route they followed took them up and over the New York Mountain Range and onto a series of dirt roads that led north and east toward a range of pinnacle-like peaks. Winding their way through the Joshua trees it was late in the afternoon when they finally reached the end of the existing primitive road. This was as far as Josh and Rachel could take their vehicles. The deputies got out and communicated with the search plane, who gave them coordinates of the crash site.

It was determined that they had to off-road a ways to get in closer to effect the rescue. The three of them were allowed to ride along in the two sheriff's vehicles. They contoured through the sage and mesquite as well as bumping their way across a couple drainage swales. Josh noticed another set of tire prints that seemed to track in the same general direction they were going. After a half mile they found themselves at the base of the pinnacles.

They were asked to stay with the vehicles as the deputies hiked up into the ravines. It was less than an hour before the rescuers returned, but Tammy was not with them.

"It appears that the young lady has already been rescued," they announced.

"By whom?" asked Josh.

"By a friend," was the answer they were given. "Here, read the note yourself."

Jo and Rachel peeked over Josh's shoulder as he read it. Jo immediately recognized the handwriting and squeezed his shoulder. Josh looked at her in acknowledgement of the unimaginable truth.

Bryan who was still trying to stay under the radar took Tammy to a local medical clinic in Primm. Tammy hobbled out of the doctor's office with a crutch still complaining that she really didn't need it.

Not far from the clinic was a quiet out of the way diner and a public telephone from which she was able to make a call to alert her family, leaving a message that everything was okay and that she was with Bryan. Calling the aviation company, they were happy she was fine, but they wanted her to see their doctors for an evaluation. She just hung up on them after they became insistent. Tammy also left a message on Rachel's voice mail to come alone and meet them.

Going inside they ordered a meal and conversed while they waited for Rachel.

Tammy began, "If you recall it wasn't too many years ago that a certain young cowboy told me: 'catch me if you can.' I want to know what's in your heart. I want things the way they were before all these distractions separated us. I want you to love me as you did before."

"To be honest I should love you all the more," he conceded. "Because what you did, you did for all the right reasons."

Bryan took a deep breath and leaned forward. "I've been contemplating just giving up on this whole thing. I know that will make you happy, and Josh too no doubt, but Jo is horribly caught up in this thing."

"Yes, but what do you want to do?" she asked again.

"I don't want anyone to get hurt over this, but I'm afraid what has been set in motion will not go away," he reflected. "I finally have the evidence from the well firmly in hand, but that will put me back to square one in an adversarial position with Big Brother."

"So, you did go back again to the Alamo?" she asked.

"Yes, and we were successful," he replied.

"Who is we?" she wondered.

"Someone I hired," brushed off Bryan.

"Well, this whole thing just continues on without any end in sight," commented Tammy. "But I'm afraid you'll never be able to really let this go until it's done. You're used to running with your hair on fire," she reflected.

"Like I said, it grieves me to put you guys in danger," repeated Bryan. "I'm so relieved you're okay," he added putting his hand on hers.

"Me too, I'm just so happy to be with you again and that you're safe," she paused adding, "except, you could use a shower and a shave."

Rubbing his whiskers he replied, "But I kind of like myself with a beard, don't you?"

"It does give you a certain appeal, but I still say a shower is warranted," she said smiling.

"I agree. But, since this thing has been set in motion and it will not go away. I need to see it through," he concluded.

"So, where is this 'black bird?' " asked Tammy leaning over the table.

Bryan smiled. "Not far from here," he answered under his breath.

"Let's go find it together," she suggested. "Either we're going to live together or we're going to die together."

"Just like the old days?" asked Bryan.

"Yeah."

"Except, we better not have Josh and Jo join us until we have this nailed down," he reflected.

It was near evening when Rachel arrived to join them. She was much relieved to find both of them doing well.

"This is great, Tammy is safe, and you've been found," she declared.

Bryan inquired, "How are Josh and Jo handling all this?"

"They have been pretty stressed, but relieved to find out you both are alright and together," replied Rachel. "So, what's next?"

"Bryan is close to solving the 'great black bird' mystery," whispered Tammy.

"One thing that bothers me, Rachel, is the timing of your arrival down here," explained Bryan.

"I'm sorry everyone is having a cow over this, but I heard the cry for help and I came running," she related.

"You did what a friend should do," he commended. "Yet, it makes me think whatever method they were trying to keep tabs on me failed, so they looked for another way."

"I've inadvertently been drawn into this and I'm sorry. What can I say? Hello! 'The Eagle has landed,' " bellowed out Rachel.

"Rachel, not to worry," laughed Tammy. "As long as we have not made an actual discovery, and your tracking device is kept in an obscure location, they should remain at bay."

"The three of us will disappear for a day or two, and then I would like to bring Josh and Jo back on line once we have a degree of security," planned Bryan.

"Then I should disappear right?"

"Yes," he confirmed, "but only in the sense you'll be driving around Vegas as a decoy."

"Oh, by the way, Tammy, your mother and aunt should be arriving tonight or in the morning some time," informed Rachel.

"Really? They must have left before I got the message off," she realized.

Next morning the three explorers set out in the Jeep for a day of discovery. Taking back roads they skirted around the east side of the Mojave Preserve. Turning toward the west the road cut directly across Lanfair Valley toward Table Mountain.

Bryan glanced back at Tramp lying on the back seat. "I think Tramp is adjusting to the fact that he can't always ride shotgun," he observed.

"Tramp is sure a good dog to have been found out here in this inhospitable environment," commented Rachel petting him.

"The desert actually has a lot of beauty if you just stop and look around," he replied.

"I'm still partial to green and trees and all of that," shared Tammy.

"If you look ahead, the right wing of the great and illustrious 'black bird' is now coming up on our left," announced Bryan

"That whole volcanic range?" pointed Tammy.

"Yes, the 'black bird' is quite large," confirmed Bryan.

"How large?"

"It has about a six mile wingspan and from head to tail I would say it's close to five miles," he informed. "And it was only because of the rescue flight that I was able to see the 'black bird.' It just jumped out at me."

"So in a sense I was instrumental in solving the final part of the mystery," reflected Tammy.

"Yes, but if I had known that your life was to be put at risk, I would've said, no way!" stated Bryan. "Look, the head is now visible. We're there. Notice how the sweeping neck comes up from the main volcanic body," he pointed.

"Basically, it's all a series of volcanic buttes and fissures that were extruded through the earth's crust eons ago," understood Rachel.

"That is correct; but now what we have to do is drive as close as we can to the beak protruding out of the bird's head," replied Bryan.

Turning off the main road onto a more primitive set of tracks they reached a point opposite the volcanic ridge. Bryan shifted into four-wheel drive as they went off-road into the rocks and sage brush.

"As the ridge descends it does form a point like a beak," observed Tammy.

"The entrance is somewhere up there," stated Bryan, "as depicted by the bird symbol with the downward or subterranean sun held in its beak."

"Wow, I'm impressed, but is there a clue on how to find the entrance?" asked Rachel.

"There is, but only one thing that will unseal my lips," he replied.

"And what's that?" wondered Tammy.

"Tell me you love me."

"Oh! Yes! I do love you," responded Tammy.

Rachel exclaimed, "Alright you two love birds lets focus on this other bird."

Bryan laughed. "The clue is similar to others that the Captain has left us before. As I recall it said: 'The shadow of its eye descends into the great abyss.' "

"Sounds interesting, but where did you run across that clue?" Tammy asked. "I don't remember that in any of the initial stuff we had."

"I was sitting at a campfire at Owlshead Mountain reading over the original land grant. When I noticed, between the writing on the front and the back there were new words being formed wherever they crossed over themselves," explained Bryan. "After I translated the words, it was apparent that I had clues to the location of a fortress in the Owlheads, and to our illustrious 'great black bird.' "

"That's right, the first bird was an owl," she recalled. "And you found a fortress?"

"Yes, and probably half a million in black sand," he added.

"You found gold up there?" excitely asked Rachel.

"I believe it's just a taste of what's to come," confirmed Bryan.

"No one else knows about that do they?" questioned Tammy.

"Right, you two are the only other persons who now know," he clarified.

"Ouch!" protested Tammy after they hit another bump bouncing them upward. "You might go a little slower."

"Sorry," he apologized.

The black volcanic ridge that formed the black beak descended right into the floor of the desert just ahead of them. It showed signs of weathering having eroded into pockets of soil dotted with sage and cacti.

"What is it that we are supposed to find here at the 'black bird'?" asked Rachel.

" 'The river beneath,' " he quoted.

"A river?"

"Yes, a 'River of Gold.' 'Find the great black bird that sits on black sands' is the way the clue reads. If my suspicions are correct there is a large cavern that runs under the floor of the desert and within it is an ancient river whose shores are lined with black sands," Bryan explained.

"Oh, no, we're not going into another cave are we?" protested Tammy.

"It's a lot cooler in there," he enticed. "But first we have to figure out where the entrance is," Bryan stated as he brought the Jeep to a stop.

"Maybe a good place to start is to find something that will project a shadow," suggested Rachel.

"Smart girl, let's go have a look before it gets too hot," he coaxed.

"I'll have to go slow," reminded Tammy.

Bryan prepared his pack and made sure the walking stick was going to work for Tammy once again. He also gave her a floppy-brimmed hat and Rachel a baseball cap that would protect them from the sun.

Tramp was at first confused as to where they were going, but once on the way Bryan pointed the way and he took the lead.

It only took a minute or two to reach the tip of the volcanic beak of the "great black bird." Tammy thumped on the rock with her stick.

"Alright, bird, open up," she demanded.

"Tammy, this bird has been asleep probably for forty thousand years or more. I don't think that will help," he chuckled.

The climb was not easy even at a slow pace. Resting numerous times they finally found shade in a small outcropping. Occasionally, a glint from a vehicle could be seen many miles away.

"Tell me about the girl at Mitchell Caverns named Emily," suddenly spoke up Tammy.

"Emily? You met Emily?"

"Yes, you were just two days ahead of us," she answered.

"Well, she was helpful," he answered.

"Now come on, what did you say to her that made her so interested in you?" probed Tammy.

"I guess she felt sorry for me," thought Bryan trying to down play it.

"You didn't go flashing your eyes at her did you?" she wondered.

"Tammy, no. Like I said, she was just helpful."

"Okay, just checking," she smiled.

Hiking further up on the ever widening ridge the terrain became more rugged. A tall rock formation dominated the scene just ahead.

"Are we still on the beak or on the head of the Captain's mythical bird?" wondered Rachel.

"Hard to tell, but looks like we're making the transition," answered Bryan.

"Rachel is probably wondering where the 'eye' of this bird is," reasoned Tammy.

"That's the idea," she confirmed.

"Let's go up and take a look," he suggested.

"I don't know if I can go much further," informed Tammy.

"There's some shade up ahead," coaxed Bryan helping her over the rocks.

Finding a comfortable spot, they left her to rest while continuing their hike up around the rock formation. Tammy sat there a bit paranoid thinking that a snake might appear at any moment. She was hoping that Bryan would hurry and get back. Far below sitting at the bottom of the formation she noticed that the Jeep looked to be about the size of a gnat. After a short time Bryan returned and plunked down beside her. Rachel and Tramp soon followed.

"Did you miss me?" he asked.

Putting her arm around him she leaned against him. "Indeed I did," she answered.

"We walked up and found a basaltic pinnacle that is unique to the surrounding area. It's about a hundred feet in diameter at the base, but quickly tapers to a point about one hundred and fifty feet tall," shared Bryan.

"So that could be the eye that produces the shadow we are to follow," stated Tammy.

"It has to be, it fits," believed Rachel.

"I do not see any other rocks or formations that could produce such a leading shadow. The clue stated that the 'shadow descends into the great abyss' which tells me that the timing on this must be during the mid-afternoon, given the orientation of this ridge," concluded Bryan.

"The sun is almost at its zenith right now," observed Tammy. "So, as the sun swings around to the southwest and descends behind the rock, the shadow should start to creep out and descend the hill as you mentioned," she motioned with her arm.

"We can sit right here in the shade and watch it all develop," concluded Bryan.

As they nibbled on the snacks that Bryan had packed they enjoyed the moment looking out over the far reaching expanse of the desert.

Bryan wondered about the flowers they had planted at their homesite, whether they were still alive or not. Tammy said she watered them with her tears so to speak, but didn't think they would survive.

In the meantime, the shadow from the rock outcropping was growing longer in a northeast direction, but as it grew it also moved to the right, closer to the alignment of the bird's beak. Bryan got up a couple of times to check the location of the tip of the shadow as it began disappearing down out of sight.

About mid-afternoon they moved down the hill to a secondary observation post. The shadow now seemed to lengthen exponentially. It was jumping across gullies and passing over the high ground.

Finally, they had to get up and walk with the shadow to keep up with it. Bryan could tell Tammy was getting tired, but they were steadily getting closer to the vehicle. It must have been about five in the afternoon that the shadow passed over a small ridge on the north side of the volcanic formation and fell into a hollow.

"You girls stay here, I'll go down and check out that spot and see if there is anything worth investigating," recommended Bryan.

"Be careful, looks like a lot of sharp loose rock down there," warned Tammy.

This particular location the way it was situated seemed to have promise. It wouldn't be too much longer when the mountain range to the west would soon cut off all direct sun completely eliminating the lengthening shadows. The primary shadow was moving gradually toward an abrupt slope, and would soon pass beyond this location.

Basalt boulders were quite numerous leading up to the slope that appeared to be a mixture of geological activity. The upper side was a basaltic formation of lava and beneath was a slope covered with basaltic rocks of various sizes. Walking up through the rocks proved difficult. It looked as if a whole landslide of rock was forced over the precipice. A root from a desert plant angled its way down the rock face and disappeared in a small opening just above him. Could this be a clue? Absolutely! Climbing up to the root, he peeked into the hole, but couldn't see anything.

Putting on a pair of work gloves, Bryan moved a couple fifty pound rocks down the slope to widen the opening. Removing a flashlight from his pack he looked again using the light. There was more rock, but wait, this had the look of a stacked rock wall he thought to himself.

"This could be it. I'm going to dig back a bit further," he called out to them.

"Be careful something could fall on you," warned Tammy. Having said that they decided to work their way closer to where Bryan was working.

The only tool that he had with him was a rock hammer. Bryan moved more rocks to enlarge the opening to reveal more of the inner wall. Making sure the overburden was solid, he tried prying apart the rocks that were in the back of the hole. Nothing budged. Bryan wiggled his way back out of the opening feeling a bit frustrated.

"Hey gopher boy, the shadow is long gone," Tammy called out.

"I'm aware of that, but I think there's a stacked rock wall hidden behind here," he replied. "Tammy! You're not supposed to be walking down here," protested Bryan seeing she had worked her way up close.

"I wanted to be close to you," she answered.

"That is a nice thought," he acknowledged, "but, I don't want to have to pack you out. Say, this has the appearance of the wall we encountered at the *Obelisk*, remember?" asked Bryan.

"How could I ever forget that? I was so scared, especially when the wind was making that dreadful moaning sound," recollected Tammy.

"That was pretty intense," he commented. Grabbing up his rock hammer he contemplated his situation. "This is the only tool that I have to work with."

"How about the walking stick?" suggested Tammy.

Bryan looked up into the hole. "Hmm, there is a layer of smaller rocks along the roof," he reported. "Let me see that for a moment. I'll try to be careful and not bust it."

Taking the stick he poked it back up into where it was hard to reach and hit the point against the smaller rocks. They seemed to move a small amount. Finally, two of them backed off, followed by a larger adjacent stone.

"I think I have some movement in here," he yelled out to them. "This is as bad as working underneath an automobile."

Grabbing the rock hammer he swung it up and gave the larger rock a whack. It moved back about three inches. Hitting it again it disappeared, and he thought he heard a thud beyond the wall.

"I think I have a breach started," Bryan declared.

"Good! I'm getting hungry," replied Tammy. She heard Bryan laugh which made her smile.

After a little more effort a few more rocks became dislodged and he was able to push them out of the way. Retrieving the flashlight he stuck it into the hole to take a look. It was just a black void. He could see the ceiling and a side wall for about twelve feet in and that was all. Bryan shimmied back out and tried dusting himself off.

"It appears there is a cave in behind," he declared handing her the walking stick back. "My puny light can't penetrate the darkness; it could be huge back in there."

"Bryan Anderson! Do you know I love you?" she announced laughing at the patchwork of dust that covered him.

"Yes, I believe I do," he replied in a matter of fact tone while dusting himself off.

"Do you think this is it?" asked Rachel.

"Yes, I believe so. It's time to bring in the cavalry."

19

RIVER OF GOLD

Josh was brushing his teeth when the phone rang. He thought it must be Jo or his mother letting him know they were ready to head over for breakfast.

"Josh, is that you? It's Tammy," came the voice over the phone.

"Tammy! It's about time! You jumped ship on us, and I guess Rachel has too, but I'm glad you're okay," he replied.

"We're all on the same side, but the order in which things have developed has been a little complicated," she commented. "Bryan wants you guys to meet up with us, but you must be careful no one follows. You will find an envelope under your door. It contains instructions. See you soon, bye."

Josh put the phone down and took a deep breath. He knew things were about to jump to light speed. Going to the door he found the envelope on the floor. Josh sat on the edge of the bed and read its contents. Finishing getting dressed he walked over to Jo's room and knocked on the door.

"Good morning," she responded with a smile opening the door.

"D-day has arrived," announced Josh.

"D-day?" she questioned.

"Bryan and Tammy want us to meet up with them," he elaborated.

"Finally," responded Jo.

"Here are the directions," added Josh holding up the envelope.

She took it and read it. "Okay, seems simple enough," thought Jo.

"Let's get together with my mom and my aunt and inform them about what's going on. Then we can get a bite to eat and be on our way," he figured.

"They were yakity-yakking till late last night," shared Jo glancing over toward their room.

It did not take them long to get on the road in anticipation of what was to come. The instructions directed them first to Ivanpah, from there they were to travel 12.3 miles south and wait for a signal. Josh noticed that Jo was somewhat nervous; and she would occasionally look back.

The desert had a strangeness that morning. A low haze lay across the Lanfair Valley. Using the odometer as a gauge they went the required distance and pulled off the road in the middle of nowhere.

"I guess all we can do now is wait," stated Josh as he turned off the truck.

The minutes ticked by. A small breeze scurried across the valley floor. Josh looked at his watch. Suddenly there was a flash of light from the mountains on the far side of the Valley. It was a repeating sequence of three flashes that lasted for half a minute. They looked at each other.

"That must have been our signal," concluded Jo.

"Yes, but now what? Do we just drive in that general direction?" wondered Josh.

"It may be just that simple," replied Jo. "We are about here on the map," she pointed. "And the light came from somewhere over here."

"What's this road that cuts across?" he asked.

"Cedar Canyon," Jo answered.

"That has to be the way to go," concluded Josh.

"Let's go!" she agreed.

231

After driving south a couple of miles they turned onto the Cedar Canyon Road and continued west across the desert plain. Jo looked at the map again and scribbled some marks at different locations.

"What's that?" he asked.

"You know what is unique about the place where we stopped?" queried Jo.

"No, I have no idea," answered Josh.

"In all directions there is a twenty mile radius of visibility," she discovered.

"Oh, I get it, Bryan is making sure that no one is following us," he understood.

Five miles later, the flashes again appeared still being a long distance away. The road began meandering gradually to the north. A third set of signals came eight miles later.

This time the flashes were to the southwest and not that far away. Was it coincidence that they were at a junction with a lesser traveled road? Time would tell. Taking the side road they approached a windmill and a large metal water tank situated adjacent to a large cottonwood tree.

No one appeared to be around as they drove up. The road apparently dead-ended at the well. Josh and Jo were a little baffled as what to expect next. They got out and looked around.

Suddenly, a lone figure wearing a hat came out from behind a crumbling concrete rock wall and walked toward them. They were in suspense as to who this was. A familiar female voice called out to them. It was Tammy.

"Tammy! You had us so worried," scolded Josh. "But it's good to see you walking, talking and alive!"

"Good to see you guys too," she smiled hugging them both.

"Tammy? There is something different about you," claimed Jo. "I know what it is. You're happy, because you're back with Bryan," she realized.

"Yes, that is true," confirmed Tammy.

"Where is Rachel?" wondered Jo.

"She's waiting in the Jeep just out of sight. Josh, if you're agreeable the plan is to have Rachel drive your pickup back to town, pick up her car with the tracking device in it and frequent a location north of Vegas."

"Yeah, that sounds okay" acknowledged Josh.

"Smart thinking, setting her up as a decoy far from here," commented Jo.

"Where is Geronimo hiding?" asked Josh.

"Bryan is up on the mountain just a little ways from here," she informed. "I'm to bring you two up in the Jeep. So bring the things you will need for the day and any digging tools you may have."

"I take it that Bryan has solved the mystery of the bird?" questioned Jo.

"Yes, Bryan believes we have," she answered. "The 'great black bird' is this whole system of volcanic buttes and ridges. We'll be going up to where this 'black bird' held the downward sun in its beak."

"Wow, I'm impressed," replied Jo. "Bryan actually figured this out?" she determined.

"Yes, but with a little help from me," answered Tammy. "I'll explain later, let's go up and see Bryan. He needs your help Josh to clear a passage into the cavern."

"Okay," he acknowledged. "This is federally controlled land you know," reminded Josh.

"So? Camino's Spanish land grant, far as we are concerned supersedes all claims including the Federal Government," stated Tammy.

After walking up to meet Rachel it wasn't long before she left on her mission. Getting into the Jeep it didn't take long to drive the rugged trail around to the north side.

"From here on foot it's another five minutes," informed Tammy bringing the vehicle to a halt.

"What is this back here?" asked Josh turning around in his seat.

"A generator," she answered. "Bryan has already carried the light stands up to the site. Bryan wants you to help him carry that up to the cave later."

"Bryan is always trying to put me to work," he laughed.

Tammy led the way up the shady side of the ridge and around a couple of outcroppings to arrive at the 'hollow.' Tramp barked and ran up to greet them. They could hear banging coming from an irregular shaped opening in a wall to their left.

"Bryan! They're here, come on out," called Tammy.

After a moment Bryan worked his way back out and approached them dusting himself off.

"Welcome, Josh and Jo, it's good to see you two again," he greeted. "I hope you're not too mad at me."

"You had us so worried that you might do something crazy," replied Josh giving him a hug.

"And Jo what can I say?" stated Bryan.

"Go ahead, Bryan, give her a hug too," allowed Tammy.

"I'm relieved you're safe," said Jo giving him a hug. "But this is for getting me hooked on this thing," she retorted giving him a swat in the shoulder. Everyone looked at her in surprise.

"I'm sorry, but I'm worried how all of this is going to end," she spoke up giving way to tears.

"Why would you say that?" asked Josh trying to understand her.

"Because I care for you guys," answered Jo.

"It will be okay. We're going to proceed with caution," encouraged Bryan.

"Yes, but sometimes things you don't know about can hurt you," she stated.

"That is true, but if there is anything you're aware of, you would tell us, right?" he asked unsure of where she was coming from.

Pausing she replied, "Of course."

"Well, so much for our reunion," stated Tammy trying to change up the mood.

"Josh, let me show you what I've done so far," said Bryan.

After they left Tammy asked, "Jo, are you okay?"

"There is a lot of danger out here. I think we should just go and deal with this another time," pleaded Jo.

"Bryan and I had a similar discussion, but realized we would always be watched and under scrutiny. So we figured we might as well continue forward unless something becomes a real show stopper," expressed Tammy. "Come on, take a look at what the map has led us to," she coaxed.

Jo followed Tammy up to the opening where the boys were. Josh was squatted down looking at the back wall that was still in place. Bryan had moved more of the rock apron that hid the inner wall.

"Soon as Josh and I disassemble more of the wall, we can go in and look around," Bryan explained to Jo as she stooped down to take a look.

"The way that wall is put together definitely is not natural looking," recognized Jo straightening back up.

Working together it took Bryan and Josh another hour to clear a passageway, giving them access into the black void. Having purchased additional lighting all of them were able to go in for a preliminary look around. Anticipation was running high as they prepared to go in. Bryan had Tramp stay behind and wait for them just inside the cave. He knew the routine.

Just beyond the wall was a landing littered with the remnants from the wall demolition. The actual floor was about four feet below the opening and trended downward. The cave at this point was about sixty feet in width and about forty-five feet in height. Sections of the ceiling and walls had a glassy look, and other sections of the ceiling exhibited hardened drippings and curtains of volcanic rock. The coolness of the cave was instantly felt and appreciated.

Tammy working along the left wall made the first significant discovery. It was a large downward sun symbol, establishing that this was the correct site.

As with most magma caves the floor was relatively smooth. The angle of descent must have been close to fifteen percent, reminding Josh of the descent down into an underground train station. Their voices echoed as they clamored down the passageway. Josh tried some wha-who-o echoes only to get the girls all creeped out. The tunnel weaved and turned, but kept the same general direction until they reached about one thousand feet below the desert floor. Abruptly the passageway turned right and passed into a limestone formation.

"Everyone stop!" ordered Bryan. "Turn off your lights."

"What's going on?" questioned Tammy.

"You see that?" he asked.

"There be light ahead!" exclaimed Josh.

"Dim light," laughed Jo at his attempt of sounding like a pirate.

"Come on, let's take a look," said Bryan.

The tunnel abruptly ended into open space. A dull light filtered down from the surface through an area of fractured rock.

"That's incredible," first spoke up Jo.

"An underground canyon," realized Josh.

" 'The river beneath,' " quoted Tammy.

It was clear that the era of volcanism in this region was superseded by even older formations beneath, limestone laid down by ancient seas. It must have been a good quarter mile across to the other side of the underground canyon. A system of naturally eroded terraces and stalactite type formations made up the mosaic of the far wall which descended into the dark depths below. Above them the ceiling of the cavern vaulted over the canyon showing signs of weakening.

"Be careful, it's quite a step down," cautioned Bryan helping them.

"The magma coming out of this tunnel must have emptied straight down into the canyon," contemplated Jo.

"The 'River of Gold' must be down there too," believed Bryan.

" 'River of Gold'?" questioned Josh and Jo.

"Yes, I believe that black sands that line its shores may run for miles," he informed.

Josh walked ahead and declared he had found the remnants of an old wooden structure out on a protrusion with a portion of it still anchored into the ceiling.

"What do you make of this?" pointed out Jo looking at a worn pathway on the floor.

"They must have had animals walking back and forth," guessed Josh. "This probably had to do with a winch system."

Bryan agreed, speculating this was where they must have hoisted things up from below.

"Looks like someone had constructed an earthen ramp down to the next level," noticed Jo flashing her light around.

"Wait a minute, we need an interpreter," called out Josh highlighting the wall behind the site.

"Where's Tammy?" asked Bryan

"Over here," she answered coming into the circle of light. Tammy muttered to herself as she tried to figure out the Spanish words. "Okay, it appears to be a warning not to use explosives, and there is great danger from rock falls," she translated.

Bryan looked up at the ceiling again. The instability of the cavern worried him.

"Come on, there is more to see," coaxed Jo who was already half way down the ramp.

"Wait up Jo," called out Josh. "You don't want something to grab you out of the darkness."

"Ha ha," she mocked. "Besides, if that was the case you would be down here protecting me."

"I'm on my way," he replied.

Everyone quickly caught up waving their lights all around. Reaching the next level, the terrace ended forcing them back in the opposite direction. The natural pathway descended quickly and passed four to five hundred feet below the protrusion. The narrowing bench jogged outward and came back in following the contours of the canyon wall.

Suddenly, Tammy screamed and the echo reverberated up and down the cavern, unnerving the group.

"Some kind of skeletal remains," remarked Bryan seeing a distorted array of bones directly in their path. A portion of the remains was encased in a calcareous material, seeping out of the limestone formation.

"They are not human, are they?" asked Josh.

"No, I don't believe so," answered Bryan. "Look at the skull."

"The way that the bones are all in a heap might indicate that it fell from above," suggested Jo who seemed to be a little braver about the discovery than Tammy.

"It's okay, honey," reassured Bryan. "It appears to be just a burro or a mule."

"I think it's getting a little too dangerous down here," commented Tammy.

"You're right Tammy, this would be a good time to implement our lighting system before we proceed any further," he stated.

"Must we quit now?" disappointedly asked Jo.

"Thar be gold ahead, matey. Them bones tell thar tale," said Josh in his pirate voice.

Jo replied in kind, "Avast! thar be danger below, thar be danger above, arrr." They both heartily laughed.

"No use in taking chances," Josh continued in a normal voice. "We don't want to end up like our friend here."

It was not long before they had reached the surface again back into the bright noon sun.

"Anyone hungry?" asked Tammy.

"Yes," they all chimed in. While getting their lunches out of the vehicles, Jo paused looking out across the desert as though searching for something. The portable power plant had its own cart which made it easier to transport up the hill. The young explorers stepped back into the cool of the cave with their supplies to eat and rest up a bit.

After lunch the boys carried the generator down the tunnel and set up the light plant out on the protrusion near the wooden structure. After assembling the lights on the poles they plugged them into the generator. The unit was supposed to be whisper quiet, but within the cavern it was still fairly noisy. Switching on the first million candle power lamp followed by the second really lit up the cave in the immediate area.

"Wow, this place is huge," commented Josh taking in the whole scene.

Bryan's attention was once again drawn to the glaring cracks and fissures in the cavern ceiling. They seemed to run on indefinitely. He noticed too that there was a sag in the roof structure.

Aiming the lights downward they were able to estimate the depth of the canyon to be in the neighborhood of a thousand feet below them.

"We have fuel for about two hours," estimated Bryan. "So, bring your individual lights, sample bags, hand tools, and other minor necessities."

"We'll have to hustle down and back up," anticipated Josh.

"Let's do it," prompted Jo anxious to go.

"Jo, I thought you were worried about us being in some kind danger?" questioned Bryan.

"Well, the dangers that I was thinking about were not the ones down here, which I'm sure are real enough. But, what I was referring to was more of the human element. That is, others who may be interested in what we're doing," she explained.

"Okay, stop right here," ordered Bryan. "Is there anyone to your knowledge following us?"

"I believe there might be," she confessed.

"That's right, there was someone watching us the other day over at Cima during the rescue operation," recalled Josh.

"Is that what you're so upset about?" asked Tammy.

"Yes, it really has been worrying me," she answered.

"Hmm," considered Bryan. "I don't believe anyone has followed you today, but we'll have to be extra careful in our coming and going. Let's keep going."

It did not take them long to pass by the skeleton and continue down the descending trail. The original visitors to the cavern did more trail work further down that once again switch-backed the route in the opposite direction. As they approached the bottom of the gorge the light was getting dimmer and dimmer, but their eyes gradually adjusted to the changing conditions. Soon they were standing on the shores of the underground river which looked to be about twenty feet wide flowing slowly in a southerly direction.

The initial investigation showed that indeed black sand did line the stream and it seemed to run on endlessly into the darkness.

"I guess this confirms it," concluded Josh. "It's all true, there is a 'River of Gold.' How does the Captain find places like this?"

"Through the local natives I would guess," replied Bryan.

"Bryan, come down here," came the echoing call from Tammy.

"Be right there," he echoed back.

Everyone gradually made their way down to her location wondering what she had found.

"Across the stream, look!" she pointed with her light. "On the wall, isn't that amazing?"

"It's a wall painting of two ships," recognized Jo.

"Two Spanish galleons in full sail," added Bryan.

"There's also a panel of writing," noticed Josh.

"We have about thirty minutes, to collect our samples and look around before we have to leave. So while Tammy is decoding this message, let's be mindful to be back here in twenty minutes."

"I wish someone else would have learned Spanish," complained Tammy. "The words are smudgy and hard to read," she added.

"Do your best," encouraged Bryan. "The stream might be shallow enough to cross. Let me check it out." Using his small shovel he checked the depth as he went on across. "Two feet seems to be the deepest part," he reported.

"I don't want to get wet," she protested.

"Okay, I'll carry you over," Bryan answered.

240

"Ha! Bryan you're not serious? We're both going to fall in," believed Tammy. "Ah!" she shrieked as he picked her up and carried her across to the other side.

"Hey you two, no fooling around," jokingly spoke up Josh from downstream.

While everyone was busy, Bryan went about gathering information on the orientation of the cavern by taking compass readings, followed by gauging the velocity of the stream based on the time it took for an object to float twenty feet. He thought that would have value later.

Gathering back together, the four young explorers soon made their way to the top level just before the generator ran out of fuel. Leaving the light plant and approaching the entrance they were greeted by Tramp who was anxious to see them.

"It's unbelievable that such a place exists out here in the middle of nowhere," commented Jo setting down to rest.

"What's really hard to imagine is that this used to be at the bottom of an ocean," reflected Bryan.

"We need to pack up and get out of here before something bad happens," Jo reminded.

"Having found billions in gold, it does make me a little nervous," commented Josh.

"Before we leave, there's an even greater issue at hand," replied Bryan,

"I noticed you seemed to be quite concerned about the cracks in the cavern ceiling," recalled Tammy.

"Yes I am, despite the fact that the ceiling has been stable for perhaps a hundred thousand years, it looks like there could be a catastrophic failure any day," he explained.

"Burying the gold," reflected Josh.

"More than that!" answered Bryan raising his voice. "It could create a domino effect."

"What do you mean?" asked Tammy.

"We have no idea how far this cavern system goes and what lies above it. There could be towns, highways, railroads, canals,

241

so forth and so on. Many lives could be at risk; no one knows," he further explained.

"I never thought of that. Oh, by the way, the message on the wall indicated that the mining operation was suspended and moved downstream to what is called the bird's claw," shared Tammy.

"Ha, ha" laughed Jo, "were going to the birds again."

"Well, Bryan I guess we should just seal it up then, right?" asked Josh.

"No, give me one more day," figured Bryan. "If I can get hold of a homing beacon, waterproof it, and send it downstream, I think we may be able to track where this cavern leads," he schemed.

"That might help us find the 'bird's claw' as well," guessed Josh.

"Possibly," replied Bryan. "After the beacon is sent, then we can seal the tunnel and we're out of here."

No one argued with him after he shared what was on his mind. After hiding the entrance they made their way down to the Jeep and drove back to the well site.

"I'll be glad when this is done and we can safely resume our lives," Josh shared with Jo before they left.

"I'm nervous about this too. But I don't think I would ever trade this experience in for anything," Jo replied.

"What will you do after this?" Josh asked.

"I don't know, everything is going to be a let down," she answered. "I guess I'll just fade into the masses never to be heard of again."

"Jo! You'll always have us," encouraged Josh.

"Thank you for that," she smiled giving him a hug.

20

FLAMINGO GIRL

T he next day started out quiet, but it would not end the same way. They had an uneventful trip back to the 'black bird' site. Unloading the gear they purchased the evening before, they prepared to carry them up to the cave site. Bryan and Josh carried most of the items in a small five foot boat up to the cave entrance.

"That's a clever idea using a small plastic boat and a trolling motor?" commented Tammy.

"If it doesn't work, we could offer tunnel of love rides or something," laughed Josh.

"I think the boat is going to be just the ticket to carry the unit safely downstream," explained Bryan. "But, I'm not sure how to secure the homing beacon."

"The beacon must have cost a pretty penny," commented Jo.

"Oh, it did," he answered. "I put down a large deposit. But there is a possibility that we may never be able to retrieve it."

"So, once the unit is on its way, your plan is to follow it from the surface, right?" asked Jo.

"That's correct," he confirmed. "It comes with a directional finder that is made for drilling operations so it should track the beacon quite well. Before we descend down to the river I want to seal the sending unit in these plastic bags to make it as waterproof as possible, even though they claim it's made for it."

With the girls guiding the way with their flashlights, the boys carried the boat down the tunnel. Once again Tramp had to stay behind and guard the entrance.

Stopping at the light plant they refueled the generator and started it up to illuminate the cavern and the ledge trail that led down to the river. Again they were awe struck by the magnificence of the cavern.

Picking up the boat again they were off into the depths of the canyon.

"This is really getting my wrists," spoke up Josh as they neared the stream.

"Mine too, let's set it down here." announced Bryan.

"Phew! I'm glad," replied Josh.

"This should not take long, and then we can be on our way," remarked Bryan.

Getting to work, Jo helped Josh mount the trolling motor on the stern of the boat. At the same time Tammy assisted Bryan in placing the beacon in a small inner tube. They secured it to the boat with a web of duct tape.

"Barring a catastrophic situation this should be able take the bumps pretty well," believed Bryan.

"One more wire and I'll have the battery hooked up," reported Josh.

Suddenly, they could hear Tramp barking way out at the entrance to the tunnel. Everyone froze.

"We may have company," realized Bryan. "Let's finish the boat," he ordered stooping down to switch on the homing beacon and recheck everything to see if it was ready.

Josh made sure that the trolling motor was locked into the forward position. "I think she's ready," stated Josh.

"Okay, the SS Camino is off," announced Bryan setting the motor on slow and letting it go.

It slowly picked up speed and quietly disappeared into the darkness. Their attention was drawn to the movement of shadows being cast on the ceiling far above.

"Bryan, I'm scared," confided Tammy.

Jo did not say anything, but looked worried. The light from the generator suddenly dimmed.

"Don't panic, we'll be fine. Let's go see who our visitors are," stated Bryan.

"Could be Big Brother," thought Josh.

"If it is, I have dealt with them before," he commented.

They gradually made their way back up the ledge trail. Suddenly, there came a hair-raising scream not that far above them, followed by a flurry of talking then silence.

"They're at the skeleton," whispered Tammy.

"Obviously, there's a woman with them," added Josh.

Slowly continuing, they crept up to the distorted skeleton, but no one was there. The intruders most likely had retreated and were waiting for them, since there was only one way out. Coming up to the upper level no one was visible under the subdued light of the generator. Flashing their lights around they glimpsed someone standing in the darkness.

"Bryan! It's so good to see you again," came a female voice from a tall woman stepping out of the darkness. Simultaneously, a young man stepped out with her.

"Priscilla! What are you doing here?" asked Bryan completely taken by surprise.

"You're hard to track down," she stated.

"Who is this," demanded Tammy.

"She is part of the story you're not aware of," he answered.

"Tammy, Josh, and Jo, meet Priscilla Wyatt and her brother, Corey," introduced Bryan. "I hired them to assist me in San Antonio about two or three weeks ago."

"You went back to the Alamo?" asked Josh surprised.

"Yes, I pretty much headed there directly, thinking that no one would suspect where I was or what I was doing," he answered.

"Where did you meet them?" inquired Josh.

"Priscilla popped out of a box in one of those Vegas shows," revealed Bryan.

"You hired a flamingo girl?" rhetorically asked Tammy. "They have the morals of a —"

"You know it sister, 'what happens in Vegas stays in Vegas' or in San Antonio as was the case," she insinuated.

"Bryan! Tell me it's not true," begged Tammy.

"It isn't," he replied. But before Bryan could comment further, Priscilla cut back in.

"Bryan, tell her the truth. You were feeling really down, in need of a friend, and you were drinking a little too much. One thing is bound to lead to another."

"That's not true," stated Bryan. "You're a real troublemaker."

Tammy remembered back to a time before when Bryan did drink too much and ended up doing things he regretted.

"So, you're the one who has been following us," realized Jo.

"You are so correct," Priscilla answered.

"Why are you here?" demanded Bryan.

"Whatever it is you're involved with, we want in on it," she replied.

Jo and Tammy noticed that the young man had a side arm on his hip.

"Frankly, what we have ended up with here is a potential geological catastrophe," stated Bryan.

"Not so fast!" echoed a loud authoritative voice from the direction of the exit tunnel. "What you have found here belongs to the Federal Government and you are all in violation of Article 17 of the Statues of the United States of America," informed a man dressed as a federal agent coming out of the darkness.

Six men with fire arms filtered out of the darkness taking a position all around those that were present. Two National Park Rangers also came in and stood alongside the Commander who was giving the orders.

"We are not with them," argued Priscilla and her brother.

"I'll deal with you later. Take them out," he ordered. "Get that light turned up."

"You can't arrest me!" declared Bryan.

246

"Oh, yes I can," was the reply.

"Not if you don't want the historical truth concerning the Alamo to be in every evening newspaper across the country," challenged Bryan.

"Apparently, you were successful with that bluff in the past, but you do not have such proof," the head agent asserted.

"But I do this time," countered Bryan. "Remember that incident in San Antonio a number of weeks ago? Guess who? I have the proof nearby. Do I need to reveal actual details to everyone who is present here?"

"No! I will look at your so-called evidence presently," he snarled. "Agent Flynn, step forward!"

Everyone looked around wondering who he was talking to. Unexpectedly, Jo stepped forward.

"Jo? You were one of them all along?" questioned Josh. She just looked at him expressionless.

"Why have you failed to report in the last several days?" he asked her.

"I have decided to resign," she announced.

"Oh, so you think you can just resign," he angrily replied. "You are also under a number of charges of insubordination."

"What you are doing is wrong, and I will testify to that," stated Jo.

"You won't be testifying in front of anyone," commented the agent in charge.

At that he gave an order that sent three men equipped with lights down the ledge into the canyon.

"Jo, you were a Federal Agent?" asked Bryan wanting confirmation.

"Yes!" she answered in a subdued emphatic manner.

"My, oh my, there's all kinds of truth coming out," snidely remarked Tammy. "Is there anything more you want to tell me, Bryan?" she asked under her breath.

Bryan gave her a meaningful glance, but did not answer. He had more pressing things on his mind. "Before you go making all kinds of threats that you may be sorry for, I suggest you examine what could become public and see how quickly your house of cards could come tumbling down. Should I call Jonathan Rothchild and see what he thinks?" stated Bryan holding up a business card.

Taking the business card he looked at it and frowned. "I could put you six feet under and no one would be the wiser," he mumbled. "Very well, show me this so-called evidence. Let's go," he motioned directing them to the exit tunnel.

Reaching the entrance they found Tramp tied up and unhurt. Bryan reached down and untied him giving him a pet and a commendation. No one talked as they made their way down to the vehicles.

Finding the packet of photographs and information that detailed what was depicted on the 'Grinstad wall' in the second well at the Alamo, Bryan handed it over for them to examine. It clearly showed that the U.S. Government purposely allowed the Alamo to fall.

After getting on a special two-way radio and speaking with a couple of different individuals, the agent in charge came back. It was hard to read his face as he approached. The answer was that they would agree to a trade of sorts, pending their silence on a couple of matters. Bryan agreed to that; and was asked what he wanted in return. His answer was quick and immediate. That all charges would be dropped for the four of them, including Jo, and they were not to be followed henceforth. Additionally, on a second thought, he requested that somehow, his great great grandfather, Captain Camino, would be restored to his rightful place in history.

In the end it was agreed that the first request could be granted, but not the second. What happened at the Alamo and the Captain's involvement was inseparable. It would also have to remain unknown.

Nearing the end of the negotiations, the men who had gone down into the cavern came back and reported their findings. After which the agent in charge told the Park Rangers that they were taking jurisdiction over this general area and were no longer welcome on this site. They adamantly objected and left to contest this sudden annexation of the National Preserve.

Almost immediately, trucks, and helicopters began roaring in.

"You need to be careful about causing a disturbance in or over the cavern, it's a geological nightmare ready to happen," warned Bryan.

"We'll make that determination," was the response.

Bryan could tell the National Park Rangers were squirming in their boots and were having a cow over this, but once again the military being the mighty arm of the Executive Branch had the upper hand.

"Let's go," urged Josh grabbing him by the arm.

"Yeah, it's time," he agreed. "We're done here."

Motioning everyone to get in the Jeep, Bryan drove them down to the well site. He glanced at Jo, but said nothing.

"Tammy, I want you to know that nothing went on between me and Priscilla," spoke up Bryan breaking the silence. "At the time my judgment may have been a little impaired when I hired them; and no doubt I should have sought someone else out, but that's the way it happened."

"She was quite convincing," Tammy said raising her voice.

"It did not happen that way," he firmly responded.

"Josh, take me to my car," she requested getting out.

"I think Flamingo Girl was just plain jealous that she couldn't get her hooks into Bryan," commented Jo.

"Tammy, it seems so strange, you risked our relationship to save my life, and now you're just going to walk away, again, not knowing the facts," argued Bryan.

"You, yourself, may not even know the facts," she contended closing the door.

"Josh, are you going to leave too?" asked Bryan.

"Yes, but I'll be back. We still have things to resolve," acknowledged Josh.

"Very well, I'll meet you at Hole in the Wall in about three hours," figured Bryan looking at his watch. About the same time he noticed that Tammy had gone over and was talking with one of the agents at a makeshift command post.

"Okay, I will see you soon," agreed Josh. Glancing at Jo he wondered what she was going to do now.

This was all too much. Bryan leaned his head forward resting it on the steering wheel and closed his eyes.

After a few moments, Jo came around to the driver's door. "I'm sorry Bryan, this is not the way I wanted this to turn out," she spoke up. "I hope somehow we can still be friends."

"It's not entirely your fault," he answered. "You were an innocent party in all of this. So, what will you do now?"

"This is kind of awkward. I have nowhere to go; my professional career is over," Jo answered.

"You want to see this thing through?" Bryan offered.

"Jo, do you want to ride with us?" asked Josh coming back over.

"No, I'm going to stay," she responded glancing at Bryan.

Josh was a little surprised, but made no comment. Bryan and Josh were informed they would be escorted out of the area and that roadblocks would be set up right behind them.

"Go ahead and get in Jo. This might not be over yet," invited Bryan.

Josh and Tammy immediately left with Bryan and Jo following just behind them. At the main road they split ways with Bryan and Jo heading west towards Black Canyon Road. Military vehicles accompanied them as promised. Once past the intersection a roadblock was set up behind them. One vehicle continued to closely shadow their movement.

Bryan's first thought was to get to higher ground south of the 'great black bird' where he could see a considerable distance to get a fix on the direction of the cavern. He wondered how far the boat had traveled in the intervening time. His rough calculations showed that the stream's flow at the 'bird' was about 2.72 miles per hour. The addition of the trolling motor could almost double that he thought. Bryan worried that the homing beacon would end up busted to pieces in some underground water fall or caught in something.

More helicopters passed overhead carrying cargo and equipment.

"This is unbelievable," commented Bryan. "This must have been all prepared well in advance."

"Looks like it," agreed Jo. "You were the catalyst, the missing link."

"So, I take it you were a plant right from the beginning," he surmised, "and a very good one at that."

"Yes, that was my job, to stay close to you and monitor your movements," she acknowledged. "With my climbing experience they thought it would be a natural fit.

"So, where did you get your knowledge of archeology?" wondered Bryan.

"I had studied it in college, but then decided to make a career change, obviously not the best choice. To be honest, at first it was just another assignment. But eventually as I got to know you, that all changed. Plus I came to like Josh and Tammy too. Matter of fact, I struggled with trading sides, especially if you were to say the right words. I became attached to you guys and this search for the mysterious Captain Camino. And so a few days ago I decided to stop reporting in and turned off my tracking device."

"Thinking back," recollected Bryan, "After I got to know you it seemed you were someone that could be trusted."

"I didn't know when they would come. But I was hoping we would be long gone from the cavern before they realized where we were," she revealed.

Changing the subject Bryan said, "Josh seems to like you a lot."

"I don't know if that's the case anymore," stated Jo. "You know I have feelings for him too, but it's probably too late for that now. And I'm sorry about Tammy; I thought everything was going to work out for you two."

251

"Tammy is dealing with what I had to deal with in the not too distant past — the issue of trust, and I haven't made it any easier," replied Bryan.

"That was sure some negotiating you did back there," praised Jo changing the subject.

"I could have asked for more, I guess, but I didn't want to have anything more to do with them," he commented.

"So, Bryan what's up your sleeve?" she wondered.

"Game on!" We're going to the 'bird's claw.' And if it's on BLM land we have a chance to file a mining claim and still get a piece of the pie. They will no doubt be sending surveyors and geologists downstream. But there's one scary thing that bothers me."

"What's that?" Jo wondered.

"The possible collapse of the entire cavern system," he answered. We need to track where it goes and what it would affect, and give warning to those in potential danger."

"That's right," she recalled.

"First, let's catch up with the SS Camino," stated Bryan. "Grab the map out of the glove box."

"All my maps and stuff are in Josh's pickup," commented Jo pulling out Bryan's ragtag map. "Looks like the only place we can actually drive close to it would be just south of Woods Mountain. There does appear to be a couple of dirt roads that run out that way."

Driving another four miles they passed Woods Mountain on their left. Soon a corrugated road presented itself that led out into Black Canyon Wash. The vehicle that was shadowing them continued to observe their movement from the main road.

"We must be getting close," thought Jo.

"Okay, let's try the directional finder, and do a compass check," he replied pulling over into a wide area.

Everyone jumped out including Tramp. Jo brought the map around to where Bryan was standing. He turned on the directional finder, but there was no detectable signal. Taking out the compass he used the leveling bubble to get the needle to swing free.

"The bearing runs roughly just east of Hole in the Wall and apparently right down into Clipper Valley," he eyeballed. "The question is where is the true alignment? Jo, set the map down and put a pencil dot just east of the Hole in the Wall."

"Okay, what's next?"

"All we have to do is take the compass and pivot it ten degrees left of north and draw a line from the pencil point," he explained. Placing the compass on the map he did just that.

"I see what you are doing," she realized.

"So then, what's your conclusion?" he asked.

"We're about a half mile west of the "black bird" formation," Jo estimated.

"Then that's what we have to do, travel another half mile," concluded Bryan.

Climbing back into the vehicle they continued on the road until they approached a series of hills on the far side of the Wash. Once again he tried the finder and this time discovered a faint signal coming from the south.

"The boat has already passed this location," reported Bryan.

"That's great it's working," excitedly replied Jo.

"Put a line on the map. This is where it came through," he believed.

"Look at the hills south of here, they have the appearance of tipping inward toward the underground cavern," observed Jo.

"That's a keen observation," he commended.

21

THE DREAM ENDS HERE

"Josh, am I being stupid about this?" asked Tammy.

"Yes, you are," he said frankly.

"What's wrong with me?" she rhetorically asked. "Maybe I hit my head harder than I thought in that plane wreck."

"You two just need to get married and stop all this foolishness," added Josh.

"Yeah, but he's off running around the desert with Jo," complained Tammy.

"And whose fault is that?" asked Josh.

"Bryan's! Well, I don't know, maybe not," she confessed. "I want to grill that flamingo woman and get to the bottom of this. The two of them were apparently taken to the sheriff's substation in Baker. I'm going to confront her."

"You go do that if you think you need to," replied Josh.

"Oh, we can't forget Rachel," recalled Tammy. "I better just send her back home."

"That's probably best, considering the way things are," he agreed.

Tammy dug through her purse and found a business card. "Leave a message at this number and let me know where you are," she requested. "I'll check messages this evening.

Back on the main road, Bryan and Jo continued south toward the Hole in the Wall. Stopping just north of the campground they checked the signal strength and found it to be much stronger and moving ahead of them.

"The stream gradient must be fairly steep through this section of the cavern," commented Bryan standing in the middle of the road. "It's really on the move."

"I'll put another mark on the map," informed Jo.

"We can park in the shade down by the information center and wait for Josh," he suggested.

"Our shadow is still with us," noticed Jo. "I thought they agreed not to follow us anymore."

"Yeah, they better stop soon or I'll have to confront them," figured Bryan.

"Before long we'll have to think about food," she anticipated.

"They may have something at Mitchell Caverns or down on the Interstate," speculated Bryan.

"That's right we could go up and see your girlfriend, Emily, at the Visitor's Center," teased Jo.

"What! You girls are merciless," he responded.

"Well, we get competitive when we see something good," she explained.

"Please explain what is 'good' to Tammy would you," commented Bryan.

"She'll come around," optimistically said Jo.

"What things south of the Interstate could be affected if the cavern continues on this course?" he asked changing the subject.

"Well, there is an area called Cadiz that could be right in the crosshairs," observed Jo.

"You're from Southern Cal, what's down in that area," wondered Bryan.

"Not much, it's an old railroad siding. I think they have a few salt evaporation ponds in the area too," she recollected. "Oh wait, there's a huge project underway in that vicinity. I read about it a few months ago. They're drilling water wells into the aquifer that's under a number of dry lake beds."

"Dry lake beds, hmm. My concern would be the drilling. Let's check it out before we quit for the day," concluded Bryan looking at his watch. "Where is Josh?"

"They could be drilling day and night, and there may not even be a superintendent on site after hours," she guessed.

Josh finally arrived about forty-five minutes later and was quickly updated.

"Wow, I'm impressed that the beacon is actually working," expressed Josh. "Maybe we're not done yet."

"Let's get going," urged Bryan.

"The next spot we can check for a signal is on Essex Road near the Mitchell Cavern turnoff," informed Jo.

"Very good, why don't you ride with Josh, and lead us to our next spot. Besides Tramp would like his co-pilot seat back," encouraged Bryan.

"Alright, if Josh will let me," she said getting out of the truck, adding, "Don't give up hope I think Tammy will be back."

"I really don't know," he replied looking off into the distance.

Jo walked over to the pickup and told Josh that Bryan had suggested she ride with him now. Looking a little unsure Josh finally motioned for her to get in.

Jo climbed in asking, "Josh, I hope you will forgive me."

"Can you tell me why I should? I had my suspicions something more was going on. But we trusted you and I even thought there might be something between us."

"I came into this not knowing you Josh. Can't you see I'm on your side now? Remember, I quit my job because I believed they were in the wrong."

"Yes, you did give your career up for us," he acknowledged. I do believe you're being earnest with me."

"It's the absolute truth, Josh, and you're right I do have feelings for you," she said with conviction.

"I'm glad to hear that, and I do forgive you Jo."

"Thank you, I appreciate that very much," she responded teary eyed.

Josh reached over and gave her a comforting hug. Starting the engine he signaled to Bryan they were ready to go.

The two vehicles continued south getting back onto pavement. Making good speed they arrived at the next checkpoint about a half hour later. The beacon signal was exceptionally strong just west of the intersection of the two roads. At this point it was noticed that the surveillance vehicle was no longer following them.

They suspected the next point where they could intersect the signal would be on Interstate 40, at the southern boundary of the Mojave National Preserve. The Essex Road took them south and east. By the time they got to the Interstate they had to travel west ten miles to get back on alignment. This time they were about twenty-five minutes ahead of the beacon, which gave them time to adjust location to fine tune the actual point of crossing.

After munching on nuts and crackers, the caravan was off again continuing west to the Amboy turnoff. Amboy with its famous crater was a little off their route, but there was a gas station and a café where they could get food, and Josh could leave a message for Tammy. Leaving Amboy their course took them along historic Route 66 eastward toward Cadiz.

It was getting late in the day and sunset was imminent. Closing in on Cadiz they could see tall well drilling derricks clustered in scattered locations miles and miles apart. Bright lights were coming on as dusk fell. Near Cadiz was a major well site that Jo thought would not be far from the projected path of the limestone cavern. The area was fenced, but lacked any kind of real security. Through an open gate they could see a trailer that was plainly the site office.

Mounting the portable steps, Bryan opened the door and they all stepped inside the brightly illuminated room.

At first no one appeared to be there as they approached a main counter. Josh pressed a buzzer, and a dark-haired man about thirty years of age suddenly appeared out of a doorway on the left side.

"What can I do for you?" he asked.

"We would like to talk with a superintendent or someone who has knowledge about the drilling operations," answered Bryan.

"This doesn't have to do with that environmental lawsuit that's pending, does it?" questioned the office worker.

"No, we just have some questions about the drilling operations themselves," he clarified.

"Okay, let me see if I can scare up Jack, he's on the site somewhere," was the response. "Take a seat, it might take a few minutes." Picking up a two-way radio he communicated the need for him to return to the office.

While waiting they viewed all the illustrations, maps, and diagrams that were on the side wall that dealt with the project. All the cities and water districts that were hopeful recipients of the water were all shown on a map that showed the greater Los Angeles Basin. Adjacent was a diagram showing all the contributing watersheds including the Fenner, Bristol, Cadiz, and Orange Blossom Wash watersheds.

"This is interesting," noticed Jo. "Look at this geological crossection. It shows two aquifers at different levels beneath the desert floor."

"This drawing over here shows a sliding scale of the chemical compositon of the soils from west to east across the Cadiz Valley," Josh also reported.

"A composition gradient," read off Bryan. "Calcium bicarbonate gradually changing to sodium bicarbonate. Makes sense, right?"

"Yes, if limestone is the parent rock on the west side of the Valley," agreed Jo.

"Where the cavern probably runs through," realized Josh.

"Sounds like we have some young geologists here this evening," came a booming voice from the other end of the room.

"No, just amateurs" answered Bryan. "We have a few questions though."

"Fire away," he replied coming up to the counter and setting his hardhat aside.

"Since you have been drilling out here have you run into anything that you would consider odd?" asked Bryan.

"Define odd," he requested.

"Have you bored into a void in any of your wells?"

A cloud came over his face and he hesitated to answer at first. "Why do you ask?" inquired the superintendant.

"There is a ninety percent chance that you could be drilling into a large cavern at one or more of your sites," explained Bryan.

"We have been following a cavern that appears to pass very close to your well sites. And we're worried that your operations could cause a major collapse," added Jo.

"Well, I would say you are crazy," he started out, "except for the fact that in the last couple of months we have lost three drill shafts into an unknown void. Our geologists are still trying to access the situation."

"Where are these wells located?" inquired Josh.

"They are in Pod No. 9, which is over here in what we call the Northwest Quadrant," pointed out the supervisor stepping around to the schematic on the wall.

"You may have just caught the edge of the cavern," thought Bryan.

"Where were you six months ago when I needed to know that?" he asked.

"At home having a normal life," sarcastically answered Josh bumping Bryan in the arm.

"We are concerned that if there's a weakening of the cavern roof it could mean a catastrophic collapse," reiterated Bryan.

"This is sobering," he reflected.

"We may be able to give you a more exact location later," contributed Jo.

"Thank you, I'll have this looked into," concluded the supervisor.

"Very good, we have to go. We have a boat to catch," replied Bryan on the way out the door.

"Boat?"

"Explain later!" Bryan yelled back.

"It's a shame we have both vehicles that we have to drive around," considered Josh as they made their way back to where they were parked.

"Check with Jack, the superintendent, and see if he would let you park your truck inside the fence for a couple of days," suggeseted Jo.

"Good idea, I'll be right back," he replied.

"Better get your stuff together," anticipated Bryan.

Soon Josh was back with the news that they would allow him to do so if he left his keys in the office on the keyboard in case they needed to move it.

"You guys realize we're going to be pulling an all nighter don't you?" asked Bryan.

"Yeah, we had talked about it on the way down," replied Jo getting into the back seat with Tramp.

"Back to Route 66," declared Bryan.

" 'Get your kicks on Route 66,' " sang Josh.

"You sound good," commented Jo.

"Can you sing all the words to the song?" asked Bryan. "Including all the town names, St. Louie, Barstow, Kingman, so-forth and so on?"

"I used to be able to," replied Josh.

"Let's hear it," she encouraged.

While Josh struggled to remember the words they made their way back to the narrow highway that was Route 66 to check for the beacon's signal. Finally, moving further to the east they found the signal, but it was still north of their position.

"It must have slowed down," realized Bryan.

"The troller motor battery may have become depleted," suggested Josh.

"It appears to me our underground river is turning," observed Jo after she plotted the latest location. "Taking into account the location of their Pod No. 9 it looks like it's on the way to align with Cadiz Valley, which is running south, twenty degrees to the east."

That's a thirty-five degree turn," calculated Bryan.

"Where to now?" asked Josh.

"Looks like we can make an attempt at an intercept twenty miles south on the Kilbeck Hills Road. There are sand dunes and a couple of salt extraction facilities out on the dry Cadiz Lake bed," she reported.

"Good thing we have a woman navigator," commented Josh.

"Why?" asked Bryan. "Is it because they like to hit all the yard sales?"

Did you say, yard sales?" excitedly piped up Jo causing everyone to laugh.

"No," Josh laughed. "It is because guys notoriously won't stop and ask directions."

"I don't think there's anyone out here to ask," replied Bryan. "Who would have dreamed of such a thing for someone to be up all night chasing a subterranean boat across the desert," reflected Bryan.

It must have been about one in the morning when they parked at the edge of the dry lake bed and waited for the beacon to arrive.

"Say, anyone know the words to: 'Do you know the way to San Jose?'" piped up Josh after a long silent spell.

"'Parking lots and parked cars,'" muttered Jo half asleep.

"Just sleep," Bryan recommended. "I'm going to take Tramp with me and walk out on the flat. I'll set this lamp on low and leave it on the hood so I can find my way back."

"Okay, keep an eye out," warned Josh.

Air temperature was mild as they walked out onto the flat. The starry canopy was amazingly clear and bright. Switching on the locator he was surprised to find that the beacon was close by moving at a reasonable clip. It made him wonder how far did this underground system could go? It took a few minutes for the transmitter to pass near him.

Returning to the Jeep, Bryan asked Josh to take over the driving so that Jo could have an opportunity to sleep. Back on Cadiz Road they continued south to the next intercept point, at the edge of another dry lake bed, Danby Lake.

Arriving a couple hours ahead of schedule they took a catnap.

About four in the morning the SS Camino floated by. Its position had moved to within a hundred yards of the main road.

The next checkpoint was near the intersection of Cadiz Road and Highway 62, which ran east and west. Bryan noticed on the map that the Colorado River Aqueduct crossed just east of the same intersection.

"Where are we?" asked Jo waking up.

"We are near Highway 62," informed Josh.

"Wow, I'm sorry for conking off. My body just shut down," she apologized.

"Actually, it was a good thing," replied Bryan. "We need to switch drivers. The sun will be coming up in about an hour. Perhaps you can drive and give Josh a turn to take a nap," he recommended.

Pulling off the road about an hour later just north of the intersection they waited. Grey dawn was now beginning to establish itself in the east.

At about six in the the morning, Bryan stepped out to check for a signal and found it to be red-hot on the left side of the vehicle. Excitedly, he called out that it was beneath them, and he was going to follow it on foot. Entering the intersection, Bryan turned east on Highway 62. He motioned to them that it was turning. They followed him in the vehicle with the four-way flashers on.

Getting back in the Jeep Bryan said, "It's slowly moving north of the highway. But guess what's a little further on?"

"Don't have a clue," answered Josh.

"The Colorado River Aqueduct," he answered.

"You mean the cavern goes right under the aqueduct?" questioned Jo.

"Yes, for quite a stretch it looks like," Bryan confirmed.

"Wow, what a mess that could be," she considered.

Seeing the first rays of sun break over the horizon, Bryan recommended they switch places again. Jo seconded that as Bryan crawled into the backseat with Tramp. He must have slept for nearly three hours when a sudden bump awakened him.

"What did I miss?" he groggily asked.

"Not that much," filled in Josh. "We paralleled the beacon for a long distance until the highway began swinging north and the underground channel continued east. We decided to cut across on a graveled road that takes us to a place called Vidal on the railroad right-of-way."

"From there we can take a dirt road out towards the Riverside Mountains to our next intercept," added Jo.

"We must be getting awful close to the Colorado River," guessed Bryan.

"Just around the corner so to speak," she confirmed.

"What happens when the cavern meets the mighty Colorado?" wondered Josh.

"Good question?" acknowledged Bryan.

"The signal from the beacon has been getting stronger," mentioned Josh.

"I have an idea that our underground river may not be as deep as it was," he replied.

About ten in the morning they traveled about two miles down the Blythe-Vidal Road and detected a signal to the southeast.

"Looks like our last stand on this side of the Colorado River will be on State Route 95," announced Jo.

Returning to Vidal, which consisted of just a handfull of abandoned buildings clustered around a railroad crossing, they turned onto Route 95 and headed south. At this point they could see the blue ribbon that was the Colorado River on their left and large tracts of green farm land on the Arizona side of the river. Further down the two-laned highway, the Colorado River Indian Reservation was clearly designated bordering the river.

"The cavern must pass right under the tip of the Riverside Mountains," eyeballed Josh.

"There's a couple of actual towns nearby that have stores and restaurants," hinted Jo.

"That does sound good," seconded Josh.

Stopping along the road Bryan stepped out of the vehicle along the sand and gravel shoulder to take a reading. Signal strength was at thirty percent coming from the west. As it got closer he figured they would inch down the road to match its path. But after ten minutes the strength or the direction of the signal had not changed. Bryan alerted them that the boat may have stopped. Waiting another several minutes he checked it again, but found no change.

"The beacon has definitely stopped," reckoned Bryan. "Let's back track and find it."

"It better not be under that mountain," commented Josh.

"If we go south to Wilson Road and turn right there is a dirt road that leads up to a quarry," directed Jo. "Off of that could be a way back toward this mountain," she thought.

Following her directions they turned onto the quarry road and went a short distance where they spotted a rough jeep trail that led back north. Bumping their way up the makeshift trail they came to a point where the signal was once again due west of their location. Two tire tracks took off up a slope covered with dirt and basalt rock. Following the tracks, the signal got stronger and maxed out at the upper end of a series of rock ridges.

"The beacon has stopped somewhere beneath our feet," declared Bryan turning off the detector.

Jumping out they began looking around to see what was in the vicinity.

"These radiating ridges of volcanic rock is about all there is," commented Josh.

"That's it," realized Bryan.

"You're right," recalled Jo, her eyes lighting up. "It's the 'bird's claw!' "

"Wow, it's like a giant bird footprint," agreed Josh.

"Mission accomplished!" declared Bryan. "Now we can go eat and rest up a bit. We're off the clock."

There was no disaggrement as they piled back into the Jeep, setting their sights on the nearst town, Parker, Arizona. Jo directed them back to Wilson Road that crossed the Colorado River by a narrow bridge.

"The area just south of the road here is called Lost Lake," noticed Jo looking at the map.

"Looks dry now," observed Josh. "But I guess when the river was higher it could have been a lake."

"Nice convenient spot out of the main current to load a large boat," suggested Bryan.

"How true," contimplated Jo.

It wasn't long before they arrived in Parker to clean up and eat. Bryan decided to leave a message for Tammy this time himself. Asking her to just believe him, adding that he missed her and wished she would soon join them. There was no hurry to return to the 'bird's claw.' It wasn't going anywhere.

"What's next boss?" asked Josh as they finished eating.

"I would like to find the entrance to the 'bird's claw' operation, retrieve the homing beacon, and see what's down there," he answered.

"Good, I don't want this to end; there has to be more to this mystery. It's like adrenaline. I need more!" exclaimed Jo .

"There may be more, but we have other responsibilities to keep in balance," replied Josh.

"My old life is gone," she declared.

"But at the same time your new life has begun," countered Bryan. "You're like family to us."

"That's kind of you. And speaking of family, we need to get Tammy back," she responded.

"I gave her the name of the motel across the street," informed Bryan. "Hopefully, she will come."

"Shall we go back and turn over a few rocks?" suggested Josh.

"Absolutely," agreed Jo.

"The afternoon shade should be spreading over that area pretty soon," stated Bryan.

On the way over to the site, Bryan thought about where Tammy might be. Josh had said she wanted to confront Priscilla and Bryan wondered if she really did.

Arriving at the 'bird's claw' they found that the shade was close by. Parking above the natural feature the three of them along with Tramp began walking down the 'claw.' Coming to the ends of the claws and finding nothing of significance they turned around and rewalked back to the heel of the 'claw.' The height of the extruded rock was highest at the heal.

"Just ridges of rock," Josh reinterated. "Nothing new."

Tramp gave a muffled bark. Everyone turned to see him with his nose sniffing between some rocks.

"Tramp has the ability to smell water," believed Bryan. "He did at Owlshead, and he may be doing it again here."

Tramp backed off and barked again. There was one big heap of loose rock in that particular section.

"Weren't the Spanish known for burying a prospect when they left it?" recalled Josh.

"Yes, quite often," confirmed Bryan.

"Well, just don't stand there, lets toss some of this rock!" exclaimed Jo.

So work began, tossing, rolling, and pushing the odd-shaped rocks out of the way. Finally, the heap was lowered down to ground level. The shade was welcome as it enveloped them.

"There's a definite hole here," observed Bryan. "These rocks seem to be a little smaller, but it's going to take work to lift them out."

Again the work began with Bryan and Josh lifting and moving the rocks up to the edge so they could be rolled away. At about four and a half feet down a hole opened up in one corner of the excavation. Clearing more rock the boys could tell there was a passageway leading down at a significant angle.

"Jo, we've found it," declared Josh.

"Let's take a break, and get prepared to go down," suggested Bryan crawling up out of the hole.

But no one seemed to be interested in resting. Jo started digging out all the lights. Bryan placed the locator and a length of rope in his pack. While Josh grabbed some sample bags and miscellaneous hand tools.

"This tunnel is a lot smaller than the one we found at the 'black bird,' " commented Josh.

"Watch your head as you go in," warned Bryan as he slid back into the hole.

Josh followed and he helped Jo down. Tramp once again had to wait on the surface, but it seemed he was getting frustrated about being left behind again.

Adjusting their packs and making sure everything was secure the three explorers ducked down and proceeded into the dark cave. Once inside they could stand up and visually inspect its interior. The passageway was horribly distorted, bulging outward in places and restrictive in others. It was evident that great pressure must have vented through this particular fissure in the ancient past. Several hundred feet down, the whole left side opened up into into a black void.

"This must be the cavern," thought Josh.

"Let's keep going down on this ledge and I'll use the locator to find the homing beacon," replied Bryan.

Descending another three hundred feet they came down to the waterline of what appeared to be a lake. This particular chamber looked like a great oval basin that allowed a lake to form.

"The cavern must have collapsed where the Colorado River crossed it," figured Jo.

Turning on the locator, Bryan scanned from right to left, and found the strongest signal coming from their left. Walking around on the shore they could see further evidence of the cavern's collapse.

"This whole lake bottom has collected tons of black sand over the centuries," reported Josh shining the light into the water just off shore.

"Here it is!" yelled Bryan. "Right at the edge of the lake."

"Oh wow, look how scuffed up it is, and there's water in it as well," noticed Jo.

"It must have rubbed the walls of the channel on its way down," replied Josh.

While the boys freed the beacon from its webbing Jo walked a bit further to look around.

"There's another wall mural over here," called out Jo. "Three Spanish ships this time, as well as a written message."

"Hang on, we'll be right there," responded Bryan.

Finally, getting over to where Jo was waiting they could see the three large Spanish galleons at full sail stationed on either side and above the writing.

"It's almost like the Captain is saying: 'I'm done here, and with my small fleet I have moved on,' " thought Jo.

"We need Tammy to translate, but she's not here," spoke up Josh.

"I'll write it out," replied Bryan. "It so happens that I have a pocket translation book in the Jeep."

"Look, at the hull of the ships. Could those be the names of the ships written on their side?" wondered Jo.

"I think you might be right about that," agreed Josh taking a closer look.

"The top ship appears to be named, Estrada," stated Bryan struggling to read it.

"The left one is called, Ascensión," made out Josh.

"And the last is, La Rosa," added Jo. "I've got to take some pictures of this," she resolved.

"After you finish that let's get some of this black sand bagged up," suggested Josh.

Ten minutes later after copying down the words Bryan walked over to check on them. "Are we done?" he asked.

"I think so," answered Josh.

"I'm anxious to find out what the message says," expressed Jo.

Back on the surface, they hid the opening with sage and other natural vegetation. Walking back to the Jeep the three weary explorers unloaded their gear and heavy packs.

"Let's have a look," said Bryan finding his little book. "First word is el queno, which is to dream. Second is concluir, having to do with something that ends. And the last word is aqui, which means something that is here at this location."

"So putting it together, it reads: dream, ends, here," vocalized Jo.

"The dream ends here," repeated Bryan contemplating its meaning.

22

THE GREAT RIFT

That phrase bothered Bryan. What did it import? Could there be an inherent trigger point here for disaster? Or was it simply a message that the Captain had moved on and he should do the same?

Tammy called Bryan that night while they were at the motel in Parker to let him know that eveything was fine. She first apologized and asked for forgiveness for not trusting him as well as making a fool of herself.

"That does seem to be an issue for both of us," reflected Bryan. He asked how her confrontation with Priscilla went.

"She said I don't deserve you," shared Tammy. "Priscilla finally confessed there was nothing to it. I think she was just plain jealous and vengeful." Tammy next related how her car was experiencing some mechanical problems and she would be stuck in Baker until the next morning.

Bryan filled her in on their finding of the 'bird's claw.' He thought they could meet her at Cadiz the next morning where Josh had left his truck. Tammy made the comment it would be nice when they would not have to be apart.

Jo was moody the next morning as they drove back to Cadiz to rendezvous with Tammy and get Josh's truck. It was the general feeling that things had reached their end and they would soon be going their own way.

Being concerned Josh asked, "Jo, what are your plans?"

"I don't know. I guess I'll just go back home. But, this is not right, we can't be breaking up like this." she answered.

"What more would you want to do?" interjected Bryan.

"I want to know where Captain Camino went and what he did. Don't you?" she replied.

"Yes, but it would take a lot of time and effort to pursue that," Bryan answered.

"We know he had three ships in the Sea of Cortez. The places where he could have went are somewhat limited," considered Jo.

"Perhaps someday we could look into it, but like I said before—life must go on," Bryan reflected.

"Don't forget we need to move quickly on getting a claim on the 'bird's claw' " reminded Josh. "That is if it's even possible."

"Josh, am I going to lose you too?" asked Jo.

"Lose? No, we can always stay close," he answered.

"Josh, I am going to miss you," she stated in a matter of fact tone.

"Jo, you're making this sound so final," replied Josh. "I do have to get back to my business. But let me tell you this—after all the days we've spent together chasing Bryan across the desert, I've grown close to you."

"How close?" she asked.

"Well," paused Josh not knowing exactly how he should answer, "very close."

Jo sat back in her seat a little disappointed that she didn't get the answer she was looking for.

It did not take long to retrace the route passing the dry lake beds to Cadiz. They found Josh's truck covered in dust parked in the exact location he had left it. Josh went in to retrieve his keys from the office and noticed there were a lot of people working inside.

Tammy soon drove up, and seeing them knew she was in the right place. Getting out of the car, Tammy said hello to them and made a beeline right for Bryan. Putting her arms around him, he gave her a big kiss.

"Where can I get a kiss like that?" questioned Jo.

Josh smiled and turned to face her, quickly placing an arm around her he drew her in and kissed her.

"Josh! What was that!" exclaimed Jo. "This is how it's done," she informed kissing him again.

Bryan and Tammy laughed, as they gave each other an acknowledging squeeze.

"Wow! The earth is shaking under my feet," declared Josh thinking it was her kiss.

A low rumble became apparent from somewhere north of them. It became louder and a quivering of the ground under their feet could be felt. They now saw dust and debris being ejected upward perhaps a couple of miles away.

"It's happening!" realized Josh.

Bryan exclaimed! "The cavern is collapsing."

"We should be okay here. Remember it's path is near the far side of this drilling site," recalled Jo.

"Maybe not, there could be explosions, and fires, from the fuel and equipment," speculated Bryan.

"We better get out of here then," recommended Tammy.

"You girls jump into Tammy's car and head down the road a ways. Josh you take the lead and stay close to each other. I'll warn the workers and follow in the Jeep with Tramp," ordered Bryan as he turned to run toward the building.

Tammy objected, but he made her go. Three helicopters now were visible descending on the Project site.

Jack and the other office workers came rushing out of the office trailer before Bryan could reach them. The shaking continued as Jack pulled the emergency evacuation alarm. Seeing Bryan, he froze in a moment of recollection and then shouting orders for all to get in the crew vans and leave.

Turning around, Bryan could hear the terrifying sound as the cavern collapse approached. A quarter mile wide section of desert floor was continually caving in ejecting great plumes of dust and rock vertically hundreds of feet high. As it entered the Project site, loud metallic screeching, straining, and buckling could be heard. A number of the drilling towers began to fall into the trench and some to one side. Buildings and fueling stations exploded in fire as the rampage continued.

Bryan rushed back to his vehicle with Tramp close on his heels. Grabbing him up he jumped into the Jeep. He could see Josh and Tammy's vehicles not that far ahead.

One of the choppers hovered over the carnage while the other two continued south along the path of the developing rift.

Suddenly, a jet roared in from the west turning north into Cadiz Valley flying low aligning with the developing rift. The helicopters split off as the jet neared. Bryan could see him drop something and climb speedily veering off to the west. A bright flash ensued, followed by a ground shaking blast and a large ascending cloud.

Bryan noticed that Tammy's car was nowhere to be seen. Could they have been too close to the blast? A pang ran through him as he realized they may have been lost.

A quarter mile south of the well drilling site, Bryan saw something that was additionally frightening. The ground was rising up ahead of him. It had the appearance of ocean waves. He stomped on the brakes as the first wave threw him upward two or three feet. Bryan ducked as the second wave was to hit, but instead he found himself falling into a void, then everything went black.

Sometime later, he became conscious that someone was carrying him on a stretcher. Bryan overheard talk about multiple fatalities nearby. He instantly thought the worst.

This was not acceptable, after all the things they had been through. This had to be a dream.

How could he put up with the loss of Tammy, the only girl that he ever let into his heart? She was instrumental in his rescue in the High Sierra. More recently, how she had sacrificed herself to protect him. He knew despite her minor faults, Tammy would have made a wonderful wife and mother. It pained his heart.

Bryan recalled his lifelong friendship with Josh and all the days of their youth they spent together along the Stanislaus River fishing and hiking. This also hurt.

What did the loss of Jo mean to him? Those dark hungry eyes and that smile of hers. Remembering her climbing with him, the rescue on Black Mountain and at the fire camp. How empty the feeling was.

"How do I stop this?" Bryan wondered in his thoughts. "How do I stop this?" He slowly drifted off again into unconsciousness.

In a dream-like state he thought he could go back and change things. He imagined going back to the beginning when all this started some five years in the past. Bryan even looked at the calendar on his bedroom wall. It showed it to be June 1993. Looking out the window everything looked the way it would have been. But there were troubling events that were welling up within him. The experiences he had in the 'Canyon of Gold,' running from the police in Washington D.C., crawling underground beneath the Alamo, and finally losing the ones he cared for in a great rift. All of this weighed heavy on him. It was like a frightening dream, but he felt that there were reasons for optimism.

Within moments he recognized the distinct sound of Josh driving up. Beside him was a female passenger. He recollected that Josh's cousin was coming up from the city to visit.

"I want you to meet my cousin, Tammy," introduced Josh.

"Tammy!" exclaimed Bryan. "Are you the girl of my dreams?" he asked.

"Well, I don't know," she kind of laughed.

"In the not too distant future our marriage is going to be threatened," he revealed. "There is going to be a great rift that will change everything."

Tammy's expression was one of shock, hearing these words of endearment coming from a stranger. Slowly, her demeanor changed. Making eye contact, she smiled and shook his hand.

"Hello, I'm Tammy; and I guess I will try my best to avoid this great rift if we are to be married," she answered.

He felt relieved, perhaps there was hope for the future after all.

"Bryan, Bryan," called out a vaguely familiar voice. "Bryan, you're going to be okay."

Trying to open his eyes everything seemed blurry. As his focus improved he became aware of a man standing over him.

"He must have taken quite a bump on the head," he heard someone else say.

"We recognize that you are under no obligation to help us, but we are desperate for any help we can get. We have several men trapped in part of the cavern."

Seeing more clearly, he recognized the man as Jonathan Rothchild, the one he met at the Marine Base. The one who had told him to 'give me a call if you're ever in a pinch.' Bryan had already used his business card as a 'get out of jail card.'

"I have friends too," began Bryan. "I need to find them first."

"Your fiancée, and your two other friends are perfectly fine. Even your dog is here," he was informed. "Miss Holden is quite anxious to see you."

"Really?"

"Yes, it's true," he replied.

"What a relief," sighed Bryan. "I want to see them."

"Yes, but first we need to talk with you," stated Jonathan.

"Where are these men trapped?" he inquired reaching up to feel his head.

"The crew put in north of Highway 62 near Danby Lake to assess the possibility of the Colorado River Aqueduct collapsing," explained another man standing in the group.

"You halted the cave-in?" questioned Bryan.

"Yes, the explosive device we dropped halted the advance, but it did not last very long," answered Assisant Director Rothchild. "The geology team traveled downstream to the Riverside Range when it started up again. The collapse

277

continued, taking out four miles of aqueduct and continuing down to the Riverside Range where it appears to have stopped. Limited communication seems to indicate they are under or past that location. So, what we need to know, is there any place where we can access the cavern in that section," he asked very concernedly.

Bryan sighed. "Because there are lives involved, I will help you. There is a place the Captain calls the 'bird's claw.' If nothing has been disturbed we should be able to access the underground river at that location."

"You will need the doctor's release first. Send in the doctor," he ordered. "We have to move on this before the next section goes."

Bryan shook his head in agreement realizing that a few hours had elapsed. The doctor entered the medical tent to examine him, and after doing so said Bryan was released with instructions to follow up with his primary physician. Standing up he found himself stiff and sore.

"I would like to ask if the others can be transported down with me," requested Bryan. "I want to keep us all together."

"We can do that," he was graciously informed.

The four were able to briefly meet. Seeing them alive and being able to hold Tammy again felt so good. Filling him in she shared how they had driven out to a spot east of the highway that proved to be safe from the blast and the fissures. From their vantage point they could see the Jeep rise up and disappear. They were all thankful that he was now safe.

Bryan explained what was happening and why. No one objected about attempting a rescue at the 'bird's claw' even though it meant giving up the secret of its location.

They were soon directed to a waiting chinook helicopter. A second helicopter with men and equipment was also being dispatched from a nearby military base. Once they were strapped in, it took about a minute before they were given the all clear signal.

Throttling up, the helicopter lifted off with surprising ease affording them their first view of the cavern collapse. It ran further than their eyes could see. Smoke was still rising from the Cadiz drill site. Derricks laid crumbled in the gorge that had opened up. Bryan looked down to see the lateral fissures that had formed due to the bomb blast. One of which he himself had been caught in. Their course took them south following the highway. A large crater soon appeared below them, which no doubt was the location where the explosive device had been dropped.

A few minutes later Tammy was the first to notice all the flashing lights coming into view. "Oh my, look at that," she observed looking out the window.

Everyone looked out to see flashing lights, barricades, and emergency vehicles on either side of the gaping trench that bisected Highway 62. A crane was poised on the west side being made ready to effect a rescue.

"The Colorado River Aqueduct is gone," realized Jo.

"Water is flowing right into the gorge," observed Josh.

"A lot of areas are dependent on that water," commented Tammy.

"The Imperial Valley will definitely be hurting," thought Jo.

Veering left they flew east across the Vidal Valley following the serpentine course of the geological phenomenon. It took a couple of minutes to close the gap to the Riverside Range. Shadows spread across the desert plain as the afternoon waned. Reaching the base of the mountains they could see vehicles and men setting up lighting near the point where the cavern collapse had halted. How long it would remain static was anyone's guess.

"Bryan, this is where we need your help," called out Mr. Rothchild from the front of the helicopter.

Getting up, he worked his way forward into the cockpit and took a moment to take in the view.

"We need to follow State Route 95 south," directed Bryan.

Turning north they began a wide swing that took them around the tip of the Riverside Mountains.

"What happened with Interstate 40 and the Sante Fe Railroad were they also damaged?" he asked.

"I'm afraid so. We even lost a major power transmission line coming from Hoover Dam," he was informed.

"How far north did the collapse occur?" Bryan further asked.

"It's going to be public information anyway," replied Jonathan. "Somewhere up by the New York or the Ivanpah Mountains."

Bryan reflected on the story about Earl Dorr and how he may have brought down a section of the cave at Kokoweef himself many years before.

"What about the people at Mitchell Caverns?" he wondered also.

"It's a State run facility. I believe they had the California Division of Forestry use their fire choppers to fly everyone out."

Bryan overheard a comment from Josh in the back about making sure that the harem was safe. He heard a couple ows following that.

The helicopter banked to the right as they came around the mountain range. Bryan could now see the ribbon of blue that was the Colorado River and the highway that came down from Vidal Junction.

"Follow the road until you see a bridge crossing the River," instructed Bryan.

After a few minutes the pilot reported he could see a bridge. Bryan asked him to slow.

"To the right you will see what appears to be a bird's claw," informed Bryan.

"Affirmative," was the answer.

"The cavern access is in the heal of the claw," was the final instruction.

Jonathan smiled at him. "You know, off the record, maybe somehow we can find a way to give your great great grandfather his rightful place in history after all. Bryan, would you be open to working for an undercover watchdog group?" he asked.

"You certaintly need someone in that department, but no, I have a marriage to get off on the right foot," answered Bryan glancing back at Tammy.

Speaking into the radio Rothchild gave instructions for the second helicopter to find them. They circled once to select a good landing spot.

After the helicopter landed and powered down they all got out. Bryan and Josh walked over and showed them the brush-covered hole that led down into the lake room. It took another fifteen minutes for the second helicopter to arrive.

The rescue crew quickly cleared the brush and removed the rocks that hid the entrance. Bryan and Josh volunteered to lead the squad down to the shore of the lake. With lights in hand they ducked down and began the descent into the lake room where supposedly the 'dream' was to end.

Reaching the shore the missing assessment crew was found in good condition. They were a bit shaken by there experience.

Jonathan Rothchild spotted the small boat at the end of the lake, but made no comment. "Can anyone read Spanish?" he asked the crew, with his light illuminating the ships and the written phrase on the cavern wall.

Finally, one of the rescuers said he was bilingual and came over to their location. After muttering to himself, he translated it as: "This dream ends here," which was very similar to what Bryan and the others had come up with earlier.

"Well, Bryan, this dream may end here, but who says you can't dream again," commented Jonathan.

The echoing sounds of falling rock clamored from the dark depths of the cavern.

"Everyone out!" came the call. "The roof is coming down! Hurrying, everyone quickly made their way to the escape route. The rumbling grew louder as the cavern collapse was again in progress.

"Get the birds in the air," ordered Jonathan as they emerged from the cave. Everybody run!"

The pilots quickly got the engines started and the rotors in motion. There was no time to load anyone. Everyone ran a substantial distance north of the cave entrance. Both helicopters lifted off and circled back to the north holding their position. Every person on the ground could hear the squawk of the radio as the pilot reported that the ground collapse was nearing the bird's foot formation. They could see dust and debris being ejected upward and hear the roar of thousands of tons of rock falling in. But something just as startling began to occur. Millions of bats evacuating out of the cavern formed a black cloud that filled the sky. Soon the rift consumed the 'bird's claw' and continued down slope toward the highway.

"It can't go much further," believed Josh.

"You better get somebody down on the highway, it's on its way out," reported one of the pilots.

"Position yourself to block traffic until we get down there," ordered Rothchild.

"I thought the cavern was already plugged off at that end and couldn't go any further," stated Tammy somewhat surprised.

"I thought so," replied Bryan. "But do you realize if this continues too close to the River what could happen?"

"No way!" she exclaimed. "The entire Colorado River could dump into the rift? That would be catastrophic!"

Everyone hurried down the sandy slope through the scattered sage to the roadway. The good news was that no traffic was visible from either direction. It was apparent that there was no one to control traffic on the south side of the gorge. The helicopter on that side would have to remain on duty until personnel could be ferried over.

Though not as violent the ground continued to fracture cutting off Wilson Road. The helicopter on the south side went airbourne again now that traffic control was in place.

"It appears to be slowing down," reported the pilot. "The ground is buckling and heaving in an area of swampland adjacent to the River."

"That must be Lost Lake," thought Jo.

"Keep us posted," replied Assistant Director Rothchild.

The communications officer reported that the Highway Patrol would be there in thirty minutes from Blythe and forty minutes from Needles on the north side. Caltrans would arrive in an hour or so.

"This better stop right here, or I'll be testifing in front of Congress," commented Jonthan.

A call was put into Hoover Dam to cut its releases to the very minimum. The realization that if the Colorado River was compromised it would dry up all the way down to the Sea of Cortez in Mexico. All the cities and agricultural interests on the way surely would be in a world of hurt.

The communications officer came over again and informed Bryan that his Jeep had been hoisted out of the fissure and they wanted to know what to do with it.

"Just leave it there. I'll get it later," answered Bryan.

"Oh, by the way, they mentioned something about two or three inches of black sand covering the floor boards," remembered the officer.

"Just tell them, I will clean it myself," he smiled.

The green helicopter made another pass across the river and came back around. The radio crackled again. "There appears to be some settling in the marsh," reported the pilot. "Wait! The ground is falling away. The depression is expanding back toward the end of the cavern collapse," he added.

"Oh no!" responded Jonathan thinking that the worst was about to happen.

After an agonizing minute the pilot reported that there was no further ground movement and the area along the river remained stable. There was a sense of relief for the moment.

Again the radio crackled to life. "Something unusual has shown up out in the swamp area where the ground has fallen away. It looks like the hull of an old ship has been exposed."

Everyone was caught by surprise of this new discovery. Tammy glanced at Bryan knowing this could be potentially

283

upsetting to him. He looked troubled as Josh and Jo came over to join them.

"It could have nothing to do with Captain Camino," encouraged Tammy.

The rescued geologists were dispatched to the River's edge to assess stability of the remaining section of ground that held the river back.

"I'm going over to take a look," determined Bryan.

"Only if you stay up on the bank away from the edge of Lost Lake," warned his fiancée.

Borrowing a pair of binoculars Bryan led the way around the edge of the once upon a time lake. As they drew closer, the area that had caved-in came into view. The distance from there to the River was in the neighborhood of 1,500 feet.

"It does look like a ship on its side, but there is so much debris tangled around it," first commented Josh.

"It's definitely an old wooden hulled ship," observed Jo.

"Two masts, at least," Bryan first reported using the binoculars. "The rest is buried in the sediment," he added handing the glasses to Tammy.

"I see signs of burned wood," she believed.

"Let me see," asked Josh. "There are some dark patches," he seconded.

Jo took a turn and agreed with that assessment. Turning to Josh she said, "Lets go further over I want to get a closer angle on the ship."

"I'm sorry Bryan, maybe Camino's fleet didn't sail off into the sunset after all," concluded Tammy.

"As much as I didn't want the Legend ever to end, I think we have found its final resting place," Bryan agreed.

"One way or the other, the Captain is gone. But I want you to know I love you and I'm here to stay," she affirmed.

Bryan hugged her and thanked her for those meaningful words. "I was afraid I had lost you and the others when the blast went off at Cadiz. I don't know if I was unconscience or what, but I felt that the loss of you, Josh, and Jo was too much. This whole thing, from beginning to end, was all part of a dream, and I had to end it. I even imagined we were back at the beginning when we first met and I warned you that there would be things that would threaten our marriage. You kind of looked at me—like: 'Say what?' But—"

"I know," she smiled with stars in her eyes. "Hello, I'm Tammy. I'm glad to meet you too; and if we are to be married then I must try to avoid this rift."

"That's unreal, how would you have known how I imagined it?" he asked.

"It's because you imagined it correctly. Because you truly know me and the love I have for you," she understood. "Furthermore, as I have already confessed to you, when we first met, I was very much attracted to you."

Suddenly, there was shouts of warning coming from the opposite side of Lost Lake ordering everyone to higher ground. Josh and Jo came running back and the four of them hurried back to the highway to see what was up. Apparently, the geologists found a weakness in the riverbank just south of Lost Lake, and it was showing signs of breaking through. Josh took the field glasses and looked in that direction.

"There appears to be a small stream making its way around the edge of the swamp," he reported.

They could hear calls being made to the Army Corps of Engineers and the Office of Emergency Services.

Soon the stream had grown into a small river and was spilling into the present end of the cavern collapse.

"We are witnessing history in the making," realized Jo. "And it's not good."

The flow escalated into a rampaging torrent cascading into the great rift.

"In a way, this is all my fault," stated Bryan.

"No, this event could have happened at anytime," countered Josh.

"I was hounded to solve this thing. But I really did want to solve it," he confessed.

285

They looked over at the Colorado River roaring into the gorge. Tammy noticed Josh and Jo standing near each other and wondered about their future.

"Tammy," stated Bryan turning toward her, "I'm thinking that the great rift in our lives is not so much this earth shattering event, but over the issue of trust," he reasoned.

Tammy extended her hand to grasp his. "Hello, I'm Tammy," she smiled. "I'm glad to meet you. I will honor, obey, and—trust you, if you will please make me your wife."

"Absolutely!" he agreed. "This dream, may end here, but like Mr. Rothchild said we 'can dream again'—perhaps even greater this time."

They both laughed and hugged each other. Tramp barked and jumped up wanting to be included.

"What's the hold up?" demanded Bryan suddenly releasing Tammy and turning his attention to those in charge. "There's a rock quarry right up the road. Someone should go and check it out. We need a thousand tons of rock pushed into the breach. To facilitate that we need truck drivers, someone to operate loaders, and bulldozers to push it in."

"I can operate a loader," volunteered Josh.

"Bryan! We are supposed to be going home," reminded Tammy. "You are not part of this."

"Yes, but we just can't go and leave things like this, can we?" he responded.

Tammy threw up her arms in frustration. Jo walked over seeing how upset she was getting.

"It looks like Mr. Rothchild is authorizing him to organize that operation," observed Jo. "Perhaps more than one rift will be mended here."

"I'm not waiting!" protested Tammy. "No more disasters, no more Captain Camino, no more trust issues, I just just want to get married!"

Four months had passed since the 'great rift.' Bryan and Tammy decided not to let anything else interfere with their lives and were soon married. Summer had quickly passed and the leaves of autumn were now beginnng to fall. Their dream house with the view was almost complete prompting thoughts of a house warming party. This was to include the promise that was made to Emily concerning a future get-together.

Bryan's mom and dad as well as Tammy's mother arrived early to help get things set up. Tammy was getting a little frazzled running around setting the tables and making sure everything was just so.

The other guests soon began arriving. In the first car load was Josh and Jo along with Josh's mother, Mrs. Knight, and Heather who came in all smiles.

"I like all the knotty pine," declared Jo giving Tammy a hug and looking around.

"Oh, let me see your engagement ring Jo," requested Tammy. "Wow, that's beautiful, congratulations."

"Thank you. You look so homey wearing an apron," she commented.

"Well, I'm a house wife and I'm loving it," Tammy replied.

Jo smiled. "I'm glad. Oh, Bryan, I have someone here who wants to meet you," continued Jo noticing Bryan coming in.

"Hi Jo," he greeted giving her a hug.

"Heather, this is Bryan Anderson, and Bryan this is Heather. She was a great help when we were out on the desert trying to find you."

"Finally, I get to meet you," stated Heather.

"Glad to meet you too," returned Bryan. "But I'm not the super hero that you have been led to believe," he commented discerning her enthusiasm.

"Well, I don't know. That's not the way I heard it," she affirmed.

A hello at the door diverted everyone's attention. It was Rachel and a friend just arriving from the city. After another round of greetings it became quite noisy in the living and dining rooms with all the different conversations in progress.

Mealtime was approaching when Tammy received a phone call. Bryan noticed she talked with Josh and he abruptly left the house, which made him wonder what was up. After fifteen minutes Josh returned with two familiar faces. Bryan was sitting on a chair in the dining room when he just about fell over.

"Emily! Katie! Oh, my. This is a surprise," he stammered not knowing what to say.

"It's good to see that you're safe," spoke up Katie. "For a while there, we were unsure."

"Yes, everything has turned out well," replied Bryan.

"Glad to hear that. However, we have missed your daily visits," Katie commented.

"It was kind of home away from home for a while," he agreed. "And thank you for putting up with me."

"Well mystery man of the desert, you sure cleaned up nicely," stated Emily stepping forward.

"Don't make me laugh," he replied. "How are you? Where are you now?"

"I'm doing great. They sent me down to a small park near San Diego for now. Mitchell Caverns as you probably already know has been closed indefinitely.

"I heard that," he confirmed.

"It's good to see you again," she continued. "I wondered for quite a while what happened to you. How do I put this? You were like a dashing character out of a novel."

"Emily, please don't flatter me," begged Bryan.

During dinner Josh talked about how his construction business was really taking off. He even had to hire extra help.

Jo shared for those who were not aware that she was given a stint working on the Colorado River Archeological Site. Thanks to a certain Mr. Rothchild, who was familiar to some of them. Work on the buried ships was progressing well. She added that the Army Corps had begun construction on a dam of sorts that would reinforce the River and provide the ability to regulate irrigation water that could be channeled north to Cadiz. A whole new agricultural district was now being formed.

Rachel repeated her offer to help with getting the story documented, detailing Captain Camino's history. Bryan thanked her, and thought in the near future that was a possibilty. He further commented that maybe the only way to get the Captain's story out there was to present it as fiction. Emily and Katie began asking a ton of questions about Bryan's great great grandfather and the adventure that ensued.

Later in the evening they gathered in the living room in casual conversation as things began to wind down.

"Oh, I don't know if I should say anything at this time, but eventually this is going to come out," spoke up Jo.

"What are you talking about?" everyone asked.

"The Estrada is missing."

"Really?" asked Bryan, his eyes lighting up.

"What's the Estrada?" questioned Emily.

"A Spanish ship," informed Josh.

"Bryan-n! Don't even think about it!" warned Tammy.

www.ingramcontent.com/pod-product-compliance
Lightning Source LLC
Chambersburg PA
CBHW031254170626
46807CB00001B/144